PRESS THE LINE

VOID WRAITH BOOK 6

CHRIS FOX

CHRIS FOX WRITES LLC

To you. I make my living writing, because you read. Thank you.

CAST OF CHARACTERS

Aluki- Whalorian mechanic / pilot with a fondness for rocket launchers.

Annie- Former space miner turned mech pilot. Annie has a southern drawl, a foul mouth, and loves chewing tobacco. Totally not based on Annie Oakley.

Bruth- A powerful and respected Nyar leader.

Major Burke- The commander of Alpha Company, and all around pain in Nolan's ass. If this were a buddy cop movie, Burke and Nolan would be the cops.

Dryker- President of the Coalition, hero of the Eight-Year War, and the Void Wraith invasion. Totally not based on Riker from Star Trek.

Fizgig- Mighty Fizgig, a feared Tigris commander who rose to prominence during the Eight-Year War. She now serves as Admiral of the First Fleet. #dontmesswithfizgig

Grak- Kokar's father and the leader of the Nyar clan.

Hannan- A grenade-loving hard-ass who hates authority. Lieutenant Hannan is fiercely loyal to Captain Nolan, having been with him through the entire Void Wraith war.

Hruk- Kokar's mentor. He's pretty forgettable. If this were a movie, he'd be a paid extra with, like, three lines of dialogue.

Jehanna- T'kon's wife, and a very skilled Adept.

Kokar- A young leadership caste in the Nyar Clan. Kokar has a scar on his right cheek, given to him by Khar.

Nolan- The protagonist. Basically, a super handsome version of the author.

Nuchik- Nuchik is a stoic sniper, who chose to leave Alpha Company to join Nolan's squad. Her name originated from the placeholder I used—New Chick. Yeah, I went there.

T'kon- T'kon is the displaced ruler of the Azi Clan, now a masterless hunter who's pledged himself to help the Coalition destroy the Nameless Ones.

Takkar- Takkar is the Clan Leader of the Vkash, and is the most accomplished fleet leader of his generation. He's lost twice to Fizgig, but who's counting? Pretty much everyone is counting.

Utfa- Utfa is the emissary of the Nameless Ones, which he's starting to realize may not have been his best plan ever.

Yulo- Master Yulo is a Master Adept from the Yog clan. He's advised the empress for her entire life, and has personally tutored her in the arts of metabiology.

Zakanna- Empress of the Ganog imperium, until Utfa booted her off the throne.

PREVIOUSLY ON VOID WRAITH

Whenever I pick up a later book in a series, I'm torn. Should I go back and re-read the first few? Or just dive right in?

When I became an author I decided to offer readers a solution. At the beginning of every book I recap the previous book(s), just like you'd see on a television show. I try to make it as funny as possible.

Announcer voice: Last time, on Void Wraith...

Behind the Lines

The prologue opens with a prisoner interrogation. Takkar, Clan Leader of the Vkash, seeks to learn more about this mysterious Coalition of United Races, or CUR for short. Since CUR is a stupid acronym, I chose to go with Coalition instead.

Anyway, Takkar gets all villainy, complete with the *muhahaha, I'm going to invade the Coalition.* He sets a trap, and we already know our heroes are going to walk into it, because... it's on the freaking cover. Like we can literally see them getting their asses handed to them. Plus, the title is Behind the Lines. Spoilers, right?

The Coalition sends a fleet led by Admiral Fizgig, an angry Tigris based entirely on my house cat, to investigate. Fizgig sends in a ground team, while her cloaked fleet waits in orbit. This ground team is commanded by Major Reval, who doesn't much like our protagonist, Nolan.

Nolan is the non-emo version of most Anime heroes, a dude in his 20s who's a total badass in a mech. Reval makes Nolan wait on the ships while he walks into a *gasp* ambush. We're totally shocked, since we just read the prologue...where we were told this was going to happen.

Reval is attacked by large ape-like aliens called the Ganog. Nolan decides to disobey orders, and leads his squad to bail Reval out of trouble. Then Things Go Badly (TM).

Up in space, Fizgig's fleet engages the Ganog. The Ganog start kicking her ass in a way the Void Wraith never achieved. She cleverly uses the enemy's own ships as cover, but knows that she's going to need to retreat...quickly.

Back on the ground things are going south. Early in the book we're told that there are three mounds erected around the city, and we have no idea what they're used for. We find out when 3,000-meter-tall planetstriders step out (see the cover of this book, or download Planetstrider).

The planetstrider blows up their cruisers, catching Annie in the explosion. Nolan, Edwards, Lena, and Hannan are forced to flee into a rust storm. They take shelter, and realize they have no way off world.

Nolan leads a scouting party into an alien market, where they're approached by a Ganog named T'kon. T'kon says he knows where one of their people is, and will lead them there. Nolan reluctantly agrees, and is brought back to Aluki's shop.

Aluki is a whalorian—adorable little whale people...with rocket launchers. It turns out Annie survived, which is a good thing for me personally. I killed a fan favorite character in my

Void Wraith trilogy, and have been informed that if I go the George R.R. Martin route, snipers will be dispatched to deal with me. I'm constantly looking over my shoulder.

Meanwhile, Fizgig is trying to find a way to deal with the Ganog's superior technology. She returns to the Birthplace, a mysterious (terribly mysterious) system run by the Ancient Primo. Time passes at an accelerated rate there, speeding the Coalition's manufacturing.

The Coalition has created the Theta Cannon, which fires a micro-singularity. Fizgig's ships are armed with these cannons, but it will take time to outfit them all. Time Nolan and Alpha Company may not have.

We flip back to Nolan, who picks up a Coalition signal. He and T'kon lead the squad to the location, racing to beat the Saurian kill squads. There's a skirmish, and Nolan leads a pair of Coalition survivors to safety. Those survivors turn out to be Burke and Nuchik, both of whom hate Nolan and his squad.

Burke is kind of a dick about, well, pretty much everything. Nuchik doesn't talk much, but when she does it's usually to say something dickish. Hannan gets tired of this, and smashes Burke in his smug face with a pot of soup. Things come to a head, but Nolan breaks it up.

He gives a rousing speech about teamwork, then we get a Team America style montage. Nolan's squad starts working together, assembling the parts to build a small warp device so they can send word back to the fleet.

Along the way, Nolan keeps looking for something called Gorthians. If you've been reading the Void Wraith series, you're like...okay, I get it. If not, you're probably wondering WTF a Gorthian is. Every twenty-six millennia, the Gorthians return to our part of the milky way to harvest it, and when I say harvest, I mean eat. The only Gorthian we meet in that trilogy is a moon-sized giant floating eye. Of doom.

They tried that harvesting shit on earth, but Fizgig, Dryker, and Nolan were all like...yeah, no. I won't say more in case you haven't read those books.

Anyway, I bring up the Gorthians because Nolan keeps hearing the Ganog talk about 'Nameless Ones'. The more he hears, the more he thinks they sound an awful lot like the Gorthians. We don't find out if he's right in this book, but anyone who's read this far is pretty damned sure of the answer.

Nolan is pondering this very question when Krekon, the Ganog melter, pops onto the scene. He rolls into Nolan's camp with a whole lot of angry Ganog elites. Fortunately, Sissus is secretly working against Krekon. He manages to warn Nolan, and Nolan is ready when Krekon arrives.

There's a brutal fight where Edwards is crushed under a collapsing roof. All sorts of pew, pew, BOOM. Then Nolan has a duel with Krekon, the toughest, baddest, gorilla alien you've ever seen. Nolan pulls it out at the last second and wins. We're shocked.

Beating Krekon gives Nolan the last missing piece of the puzzle. Now they have access to a ship, the one Krekon arrived in. So Nolan launches a desperate plan to get his people off world. He is going to assault one of the planetstriders, while everyone else captures Krekon's cruiser.

This last part should be easy, since Sissus works for Krekon. Sissus tricks the Ganog into opening the ship, and Burke leads a squad in to seize it. Aluki finally uses a rocket launcher. Annie drawls.

The second part is a little harder. How the hell do you do deal with a 3,000-meter, Godzilla-mutant-mech thing? Nolan, T'kon, Lena, and Hannan scale the planetstrider like it's a mountain. They're only halfway up when the planetstrider punches out of the mound.

It fires into orbit, where Fizgig has led her newly outfitted fleet back into battle. They deploy their theta cannons, and actually have some success against the enemy. They're still getting pounded, though (huh, huh).

Nolan battles his way inside the planetstrider's control room, where we receive a startling revelation. The technology is definitely Primo. That gives them an idea though. Instead of blowing up the control unit, they remove the core and plug in Edwards. Edwards gets to pilot a 3,000-meter planetstrider. Pretty much his dream job.

Fizgig has severely damaged the enemy fleet, but is also taking heavy losses. Her flagship is hit, and things are looking grim.

Lena figures out how to use the planetstrider's warp, so Nolan orders Edwards to warp them into space. They appear near Fizgig's flagship, and just start wrecking shop. Ganog ships are blown to shit, and Clan Leader Takkar is forced to warp away.

It's almost a total victory, except for two problems. Fizgig's fleet has been savaged, and a lot of her booster mechs were inside Takkar's flagship when it warped away. Our very last chapter shows Khar realizing this, and trying to figure out what the heck he's going to do.

That leads us into the book two, which we'll get to on the next page.

HOLD THE LINE

Hold the Line kicked off with Takkar being received by the Empress of the Ganog Imperium. We're introduced to the concept of a Ganog Adept for the first time, and we learn that warriors and Adepts (Ganog monks) don't play nicely.

The Empress makes it clear that she could kill Takkar, but decides not to once he shows her a Coalition core. She agrees to re-outfit his fleet, and to lend her own to augment his forces. Together, they'll crush the Coalition, *muahaha*.

Meanwhile, the real baddy is quietly introduced in the background. His name is Utfa, and he's part of the seeker caste. The seekers are religious zealots dedicated to attracting the gaze of the Nameless Ones, which even Takkar thinks is crazy. More on Utfa later.

Khar manages to escape into the underbelly of Takkar's dreadnought, where he joins forces with a spunky little Whalorian, named Halut. Astute readers caught the subtext that Aluki is looking for her missing husband, and correctly realized that's Halut.

Halut helps Khar board a Saurian transport, and he escapes

into the Imperial City. Khar learns that he needs money to afford a warp home, but that if he can get the money, he can go back to Ganog 7. To get that money, Khar starts fighting in the arena.

Scenes like these are why I write, and 10-year-old Chris would be ridiculously excited about how awesome Khar fighting in the arena is. Hell, 40-year-old Chris is excited about it. Khar, as expected, kicks the crap out of his first opponent.

A weasily Ganog in the crowd tells Khar that he can arrange a fight in the Royal Spire, which will give Khar enough money to warp. Khar agrees, only to find he's been sold out. He and many other Ganog and Saurians have been forced into very lethal games.

Those games culminate with a grand melee where the survivors brawl with a full Ganog elite in their great form. Khar does pretty well, almost blinding the Ganog. The Empress stops the fight, and we learn that Kokar (the Ganog) is the heir to the Nyar Clan. He's embarrassed, and pretty pissed at Khar.

Meanwhile, Nolan and T'kon have landed on the Azi home world. Their fake goal: bring the Azi into the war on their side. The Azi hate the Vkash, because Takkar and his clan broke their only planetstrider and peed on their lawn. Cats were shaved. Dogs got spray painted. It was terrible.

Since T'kon can re-activate the Azi planetstrider, he figures maybe they'll work with him. Instead, they're assholes. It turns out the clan is now led by his former friend, Ro'kan. Good old Ro-Ro also stole T'kon's wife. Ro'kan is in bed with the seekers (not literally), led by a former warrior named Oako.

T'kon is alarmed, for damned good reason. Nolan quickly pieces together that these seekers directly serve the Nameless Ones, and he's also pretty damned sure that those are the Gorthians. It can't be coincidence that the seekers are growing in strength, after being a fringe caste for so long.

So where's Fizgig in all this? She's setting a big-ass trap for Takkar. She knows he's coming, and has given Nolan a super-sneaky secret mission. Make sure that Takkar learns the location of the planet Atreas. Make sure he thinks that planet is the location of the Coalition naval shipyards.

Burke has rebuilt Alpha Company, and has a Team America-style training montage against Edwards in the planetstrider. We see them getting ready to brawl, and we know they're ready. The Coalition fleets start arriving, all outfitted with Theta cannons.

Khar is summoned before the Empress, and is worried that she'll have him interrogated. Instead, she claims not to care about some random, lone enemy warrior. She adopts Khar as a sort of pet, and allows him to observe her court. Khar gets to learn about the Ganog Imperium, and the Empress asks nothing in return.

Sounds like bullshit, huh? What's her plan? Is she trying to secretly turn him? Not really. See, the Empress has much bigger problems. Utfa, the scary seeker guy, is growing in power. Zakanna knows that her days on the throne are numbered. She knows that Utfa is going to make a move.

Unsurprisingly, Utfa makes a move. Several moves, in fact. First, he ends repairs early on Takkar's fleet. The dreadnoughts are still damaged, which both Takkar and Zakanna realize is a serious problem. It's almost like Utfa wants Takkar to lose. But the Empress isn't strong enough to stop Utfa, so she goes along with it. Her only concession is allowing a single one of her dreadnoughts to stay behind as a sort of honor guard.

Zakanna plans to use it to flee, if it comes to it. Spoilers—it will come to it.

Nolan and T'kon go to a party run by Ro'kan. Ro'kan ambushes them, and Nolan narrowly escapes. He's forced to leave T'kon behind, but the squad gets away.

It's okay, though, because that's part of the plan. T'kon gets captured, they interrogate him for the location of Atreas, and then Nolan and the squad bust T'kon out. They deliver the payload, then escape. Beautiful, right?

Yeah, no. Sissus steals the ship, which is not part of the plan. Suddenly, Nolan has no way to rescue T'kon. He fights off the Azi, then reestablishes communication with Aluki and Lena, who are hiding inside one of the mechs. The Saurians haven't found them yet.

Nolan and the squad track the ship, which has set down a few kilometers away thanks to a storm I cleverly (look out Brandon Sanderson) planted earlier in the book. Nolan wants to capture Sissus, but Nuchik disobeys orders and pops his head like a grape. They retake the ship, but tensions are high.

Flash to T'kon, who's being interrogated. Through the interrogation, the reader learns more about the seekers and how evil they are (like super evil). They bring in T'kon's wife, and he finally, tearfully, reveals the secret he was there to plant.

Ro'kan agrees to allow T'kon to die with pride. The next day they'll perform a ritual that looks suspiciously like Japanese Seppuku. At the last minute, Ro'kan says that, instead, they're consigning T'kon's soul to the Nameless Ones.

Nolan busts through the top of the spire in the cruiser, gunning down seekers. They extract T'kon and bug out. Nolan goes to Imperalis, in search of Khar. Earlier in the book, they're watching a broadcast of a spire fight and see Khar on Imperalis (convenient, huh?).

A group of assassins attack the Empress, and Khar saves her life. Utfa is highly annoyed, but he's finally contacted by a Nameless One, and that Nameless One (let's call her Karen), offers him a solution. Karen explains that an army of super powerful guardians has been left in stasis on Imperalis, and that if Utfa can seize control of the beacon, he can control them.

What beacon, you ask? The beacon is a giant, glowing McGuffin, a Primo Core. It's on top of a little island at the very top of the Royal Spire, and it is Zakanna's family legacy. She puts her advisor, the super-badass Master Yulo, to watch over it.

Utfa rolls up to the beacon with a small army of seekers and warriors, and there's a bunch of kung-fu fighting. Utfa's side wins, and Yulo flees. He goes down to warn the Empress. It looks like they're totally screwed, with no hope of survival.

Except, Nolan and his squad have been hanging out planning a rescue. They use their improved cloaking to sneak outside the spire, then punch a hole through the wall with a Theta cannon. I mean, it worked when they pulled out T'kon, so why not use it again?

It works, they rescue Khar, Zakanna, and Yulo, and they flee to Zakanna's dreadnought. The dreadnought warps away, and they appear in the Atreas system.

Edwards and Alpha company are messing up the enemy planetstriders on the ground, while Fizgig is embarrassing Takkar's fleet in space. She pops out of hiding, nukes a couple enemy ships, then re-cloaks. There isn't much Takkar can do, except rage.

When the Empress appears, they call a sudden cease fire, and they compare notes.

Shit, says Fizgig.

Shit, says Takkar.

Shit, says Dryker.

I &*^%ing told you so, says Nolan. The god-damned Gorthians are back.

And we're into the final book of the trilogy...

I really hope you enjoy it. If you do, please consider leaving a review. Those are incredibly valuable to indie authors like me.

Thank you so much for reading. =D

-Chris

Planetstrider

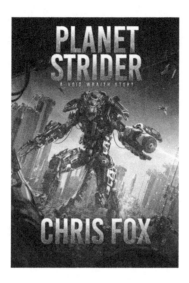

Sign up for the Mailing List and receive a complimentary copy of the prequel story **Planetstrider.**

PROLOGUE

U tfa hated this remote world. Not because of the slightly increased gravity. Not because of the time it took to navigate through the asteroid field. And not even because it took him away from Imperalis.

He hated this world because of what it inspired in him: Absolute, unadulterated terror. The kind of fear children labored under when they crept to the bio unit in the darkest hours. Utfa had never been particularly brave, but he had been bold. Here, that boldness was stripped away.

He continued the last several paces, stopping before the altar. The stains were fresh, made by his own hand and those of his most trusted advisors. Many had been called here— hundreds over the last few weeks. Utfa might be first among the servants, but he was also one of many. Inconsequential, in all likelihood.

Utfa sliced his palm, allowing his blood to run into the ceremonial bowl. He wondered absently why blood was necessary.

A towering voice echoed in his mind. *My physical body lies an incalculable distance away, so vast that your mind would crack to learn the number. Your blood allows me to connect to your location, to resonate with your genetic material.*

Part of Utfa rejoiced at the voice, but the rest recoiled in teeth-chattering terror. The Nameless Ones could hear his thoughts—even this one.

He continued the ritual, smearing runes on the altar.

The voice boomed again. *That is sufficient.*

He didn't look at the yawning mouth in the rock face to his right. Perhaps the Nameless One dwelled inside; he certainly detected a presence. Yet its words seemed to contradict that.

You question. That is good, so long as you obey, the voice said. *I will offer no answers, as these seem to be idle thoughts. I have brought you here for a purpose, vassal. Today I entrust you with a vital task, the most vital that has been given to your kind since they first discovered the stars. My young brethren are coming, and they hunger.*

"This day is spoken of in the whispers, Great One," Utfa ventured. When nothing struck him down, he continued. "What will your brethren require?"

They require sustenance. You must find worlds teeming with life, to sate their hunger. The first of my brethren will arrive soon. When it does, you must prepare a world for it to feast upon. I do not care which world you choose, but that world must be utterly pacified and safe for them to devour.

Utfa wondered at that. Why must the world be pacified, unless Ganog weaponry were a threat to the Nameless Ones themselves? He chastised himself for the heretical thought.

No, the thought is valid. Important. You must understand, if you are to enact our will. We are not indestructible, though we are immortal as you measure such things. This cycle is already turbulent. The Great Eye of Spitha has been slain, a possibility so remote that we had not planned for that contingency.

My brethren are newly spawned. They are young and weak.

Once they have feasted, they will grow strong enough that none can threaten them. Until then, they are vulnerable. You must ensure that they are not threatened during the feeding.

"Of course, Great One," Utfa said, bowing to the altar. "I have just such a world in mind. The Nyar have always opposed your will. I will take the guardians you have given me, and I will scorch their world."

NO. The voice thundered. *Wipe out the defenders, but leave the biological entities. Keep them there, unharmed.*

"Of course," Utfa said, bowing again. "We will ensure that there is sufficient food. Using the guardians you have provided me, I believe I can secure this world well before the first of your brethren arrive."

Be certain. If you fail me in this, the consequences will be...dire.

"Great One, what of the empress and her fleets?" Utfa asked, not wanting to contemplate what a Nameless One would consider *dire*. "What of Imperalis?"

Many now serve me, in every clan. The empress believes herself safe, but she is not. I will provide you the tools to defeat her. As for Imperalis, that world is of no consequence. Focus on securing food for my brethren. Leave one of your underlings in charge.

"Of course, Great One," Utfa said, giving a final bow. He sensed that the presence was gone, but wondered if it could still hear his thoughts. It was best to assume that it could.

Utfa was left with many questions, more than he'd arrived with. Why didn't the Nameless One care about Imperalis? And who should Utfa leave in charge? It would need to be someone both strong and decisive, someone that all clans feared.

Utfa smiled. "Azatok will do nicely." The butcher was widely known—and feared—due to his multiple conquests in the Royal Arena. He was also a confident fleet leader, though his boldness often caused him to overlook traps. Still, as long as he wasn't expected to lead any significant battles he should suffice. The terror he inspired would be worth as much as the man himself.

In the meantime, Utfa had the privilege of ending his most hated enemies. If he could secure Nyar, over forty percent of their clan would be devoured in a single day. That act would seal the fate of the octant, ensuring that the Kthul and their masters triumphed. No one would dare fight back after he made an example of the Nyar.

1

NYAR PRIME

Nolan took a deep breath, then strode into the cargo bay of the battleship *Demetrius*. Soft light filtered down from the ceiling, illuminating fifteen mech stalls. Techs swarmed around the ten-meter death machines, manually checking hydraulics and coolant levels.

The pilots stood in a loose cluster around a tall man with a shock of red hair. He sported a manicured beard now, and there was a weight to his gaze that hadn't been there the last time Nolan had spoken with him. He wore it well.

"Nolan, over here," Burke called, his clear voice echoing through the hangar. The soldiers of Alpha Company turned hostile gazes in Nolan's direction.

Nolan started over, reconsidering his decision not to bring the rest of his squad. He squared his shoulders, walking proudly.

"Get a haircut," someone catcalled from the back ranks.

"Stow that shit," Burke snapped. He glared hard, his eyes spearing pilot after pilot. Then he hopped up on an ammo crate, staring down at his men. "Listen up! I know what you've heard. It's true that Captain Nolan is from the 14th. It is also true that he's been placed in charge of this operation, despite me outranking him."

There were dark grumbles at that, and the hostile gazes became murderous.

"Be that as it may," Burke continued. "We're going to extend him every courtesy. You are going to treat him like a goddamned admiral. The reason you're standing here, the reason we even fought at Atreas, is this man. He won us Ganog 7. So whatever your personal feelings, you toe the goddamned line. Am I making myself clear?"

"Yes, *sir*," Alpha Company chorused.

"Now get your asses back to work," Burke ordered. "I want these mechs parade-ready for our arrival."

The pilots moved back to their respective stalls for final rechecks.

Nolan blinked up at Burke as the major hopped down from the crate. "That was impressive. Looks like you've really settled into the rank, sir."

"I learned from the best. Reval taught me a lot," Burke said, in a low tone. "Listen, I'm sorry, but I've got to be honest. This mission is bullshit, and the men know it. We deserve our own command—and besides, this ship should be protecting our border, not helping the Ganog get their house in order. These people attacked us, Nolan. Repeatedly. A lot of good men died."

"I know, trust me. I don't like it any more than you do, but I promise you it's necessary. The Ganog aren't the real threat, and you know it. The Void Wraith being present on Imperalis changes everything. We both know who they work for, and we're going to need the Ganog if we want to survive the war that's coming. Permission to address the men, sir?" Nolan glanced at Alpha Company, unsurprised by the disdain and anger. A few men were apathetic. None seemed sympathetic.

"Granted." Burke waved at the crate. "The floor is yours."

Nolan hopped nimbly onto the crate, turning to face them. Every eye was on him, every look darker than the next. Yeah, this was going swimmingly. "Listen up, Alpha. I know your reputation. You fought on the line at Atreas, and took down three planetstriders. Your casualties were lower than any other unit. You're the best of the best. And you're wondering why the brass on Earth felt the need to put some captain from the gutter fleet in command over a decorated major."

He paused, watching as curiosity crept into a few faces. "Earth needs to bring the Nyar Clan into the war on our side. The Nyar are prickly, and they don't like other races. They're also even more obsessed with honor than the Tigris. Earth put me in charge because the Nyar know who I am, and will see me being there as a mark of respect. That's why I'm 'in charge.'" He curled his fingers to provide the air quotes.

"We all know I'm not in charge. Major Burke is in charge. You're here to babysit me while I liaison with the Nyar leadership. We shake some hands, I convince them to join the war, and then we get you back into action guarding the Coalition border." Nolan paused again. Most of their faces had softened, though anger still slumbered in a few. "If I need something done, I'll go to Burke. Take your orders from him. Dismissed."

Nolan hopped down, turning to face Burke. That put his back to the men, which let them react however they chose with no fear of reprisal. He knew he was still fighting an uphill battle, but maybe he'd won a small victory.

"You shouldn't have done that." Burke shook his head. "I really like you, Nolan—much to my surprise—but you just don't get command structure. You *are* in charge. The president was very clear on that point."

"It's not that I don't understand command structure," Nolan countered, keeping his voice low so the men wouldn't hear. "It's that I understand morale. It sucks having some asshole put in charge, and now they feel a little better about it. Rigid *do as you're told* thinking is what put us in such a bad position during the war with the Void Wraith. Give these men some agency. Let them invest in the unit, and in their commander. Salvaging their pride at the cost of mine is a small price."

Burke pursed his lips, eyeing Nolan with a great deal of consideration. "I doubt we'll ever agree on most things, especially how I choose to run my unit. What we do agree on is the need to get the job done, no matter what it costs. I'll overlook your...unorthodox methods, if you keep me in the loop. Give it to me straight. What are we walking into on Nyar Prime?"

"It's ugly. We don't know how they're going to react to our presence, or if they'll even let us dock," Nolan admitted. He finally turned back to Alpha Company, which had fully dispersed across the cargo bay. No one seemed interested in him anymore, thankfully.

"Why didn't we bring T'kon?" Burke asked, wearing his skepticism openly. "Or the empress? Seems like the Nyar would have reacted better to one of their own."

"They consider T'kon an enemy, and the Nyar have very little respect for the empress." Nolan shook his head. "Ganog politics are even worse than ours. I did bring an ally though, one the Nyar respect—Master Yulo, the empress's tutor. I'm hoping he can arrange a meeting with their leadership. If not, we're in serious trouble. The Kthul have the Void Wraith backing them now, and I'm positive their next offensive will come soon."

"Well, let's hope these guys play nice," Burke replied, shaking his head. "I just want to get this mission over with, and get back on the line where we can make a real difference."

"You and me both," Nolan said, though only part of him

meant it. The Nameless Ones were out there, getting closer. They might already be here. And someone needed to stop them.

2

WARP ANCHOR

"Will you look at that?" Annie drawled, gaping up at the view screen. Nolan set down his spanner, wiping sweat from his forehead as he rose from the exposed panel on his mech's leg.

Hannan lounged against the wall of the cargo bay. "These Nyar don't mess around, do they? I don't think there's any way to safely reach that world."

The view screen showed a mass of floating rocks of all different sizes. The largest rivaled a small moon, tapering down to rocks no larger than his fist. They moved and rotated around the world in an endless dance.

"That field is denser than I've ever seen," Nolan mused, "and the asteroids are clustered too close together—at least compared to a standard asteroid field. That shouldn't be possible, not unless they're generating some sort of gravity field." He wiped his wrist across his cheek to remove a trickle of sweat, then stretched. "I'd love to know how they do it."

"It is called a warp anchor," Yulo explained, rising from a resting position against the bulkhead. His fur was a pristine, snowy white. He strode gracefully toward Nolan, walking with the same deadly grace Nolan was used to seeing from Fizgig. "It generates a gravitational field that draws in surrounding asteroids. It also intercepts warp fields, allowing it to sync with any ship attempting to warp inside the field. If an unauthorized vessel attempts to do so, the field shunts them into the asteroids. Even dreadnoughts do not survive."

"Sounds nasty," Nolan said, already considering how he might penetrate such a defense. There was always a way. "So how do we get inside? I don't really see a door to knock on."

"We will need to broadcast a challenge." Yulo clasped his hands behind his back, moving to stand next to Nolan. "That challenge should rightfully be issued by you—"

"A challenge? We need to fight to get in-system?" Nolan rubbed his temples. "It's too early for this crap."

"I said it should rightfully be you, but you didn't let me finish. I will stand in your stead. Lieutenant Hannan, open a communication channel with the warp anchor."

Nolan raised an eyebrow, bracing himself for Hannan's response.

"Yeah, so not your bitch," Hannan said, glaring at Yulo. "You want to open a communication, how about you use the comm unit attached to your wrist?"

Yulo's fur remained snowy, but he was silent for a long time before answering. "I apologize if I have offended you. Our ways are...different. I meant no disrespect. I do not understand how to use the comm unit." Yulo's shoulder's slumped.

"It's all right," Annie said. "I know plenty of grunts who aren't good with tech." She sidled over with her comm unit, and aimed the camera at Yulo. "There. I've requested a channel."

Yulo moved to stand near the center of the room, hands still clasped loosely behind him. He waited patiently, staring at Annie's comm.

A moment later, a hologram flared to life above it, showing a Ganog command disk. A single Ganog stood on the disk, scowling at the screen. His fur was a suspicious green-brown, and he wore his confusion openly. "Master Yulo, I did not expect to see you aboard an alien vessel. Apologies." He gave a perfunctory bow.

"Accepted, warrior. I issue challenge. I seek business with your leaders." Yulo shifted his stance with casual grace, but the threat was clear.

"Challenge met and lost." The Ganog gave a respectful bow. "I'd not test your skill, Master. You may warp inside the field. Proceed to the third docking ring, and do not attempt to exit the craft."

Yulo gave a perfunctory nod. "Done."

The screen went dark.

Nolan spoke into his comm. "Major Burke, this is Nolan."

"This is Burke. Go ahead."

"We've just gotten the green light from Nyar command to warp to these coordinates," Nolan explained, transmitting the nadir coordinates to Burke.

"All personnel, secure yourselves," Burke said, his voice echoing from the speakers in the cargo hold's wall. "Initiating warp."

Nolan secured himself against his mech's leg, eyes fixed on the view screen. That was an awful lot of rocks, but glittering between them he could see a rich green-and-white world. It looked like Earth from orbit, save that the waters were a deep emerald instead of blue.

The world tilted, and Nolan's body twisted and folded in on itself. The warp completed with a pop, and the perspective shifted. The view screen now showed an unblocked view of the world—very much like Earth, but with more cloud cover.

An enormous multi-limbed station floated nearby, every bit as large as a Ganog dreadnought. Its spindly arms were pointed in their direction, and the purple reactor flares at the station's center painted it into a vengeful spider.

"We may proceed to the planet, Captain," Yulo said, walking back to his corner. He settled into a lotus position against the wall. "My part in this is done. I will not be able to use further influence to get you an audience with the Nyar clan leader. That, you will have to accomplish on your own."

"One thing at a time," Nolan said, giving a half-smile. This wasn't a big victory, but he'd learned to savor even the little ones. "We're over the first hurdle. We'll get past the others. Nothing is going to stop us from getting this done."

The battleship descended toward the world below, quickly approaching the upper atmosphere. There was a faint shudder from the friction, but nothing compared to what Nolan was used to in Aluki's Ganog cruiser, or even the *Peregrine*. This ship was a titan, a warship of a whole other caliber than anything Nolan had ever served aboard.

There was one more small lurch, then they dropped smoothly through the atmosphere. Below them stretched a seemingly endless blue-and-green forest, the trees butting up against a dark ocean. Here and there, mountains poked from the trees, but most hills were swallowed by a mass of arboreal growth.

A single city was visible, a perfect circle cut into the forest a few kilometers from the ocean. Dozens of black spires stabbed into the sky, the tallest reaching far higher than the towering trees. They were different than the spires on Imperalis—more austere, and forbidding.

The clusters of ships around them were painted in dark tones, more somber than the jeweled cluster of ships around the empress's spire.

These Ganog were warriors, first and foremost. Dealing with them wouldn't be like dealing with the Yog or the Vkash.

3

EXPLAIN

Fizgig paced back and forth before the portable holo, waiting for the call to connect. A two-meter-tall hologram of Dryker finally appeared, its resolution showing every wrinkle in his rumpled uniform. His hair had been combed, but his shaggy face-mane was badly in need of grooming.

"Explain," Fizgig snapped. "I want to hear it from you."

"Hello, Fizgig." Dryker gave a slow smile. The wretched human was immune to her anger. "It's good to see you. You want to hear it from me? Okay, that's fair. You're not getting anything. The *Demetrius* is it. No further vessels will be allocated to any action in Ganog space. Period."

"Dryker, you are no fool. You are a warrior. You know—"

"No," Dryker snapped. For the first time in years, she saw in his eyes the fire that had made her fear this man during the Eight-Year War. "I'm a politician, Fizgig. Not a soldier. I can't just issue orders and expect them to be followed. I have to answer to the goddamned media, and the congressional oversight committee."

Fizgig blinked slowly. "Are you telling me that...politics prevents you from doing what is necessary to win the war for our species' survival?"

"That's exactly what I'm saying. You have no idea how much political capital I burned getting Nolan and the *Demetrius* for you." Dryker's hologram walked to a mahogany desk. He poured himself a drink and turned back to the screen. "Consider it from their perspective. The Ganog invaded our space, forcing us to evacuate worlds. They destroyed multiple fleets. They crippled us. And now you want me to try to sell an alliance? It's everything I can do to keep Congress from declaring war on the entire Imperium. The only thing that let me do that was explaining that while the Ganog tear them-selves apart, *we* could use the time to rearm."

"Dryker, the Gorthians are *here*. I feel it in my bones," Fizgig reasoned, as calmly as she was able. She sat slowly, settling into the cushions she'd had brought when she arrived on Takkar's dreadnought. "Nolan was right about these Name-less Ones. If we do not stop them, they will devour the Ganog, and then they will devour us."

Dryker gave a bitter laugh. "You think I don't realize that? Where's the proof, Fizgig? Where's the footage I can show on Quantum? I can't make unilateral decisions based on your gut, even if I agree with them. I was infected, remember? I have a bigger stake in this than anyone, because I know exactly what the Gorthians can do. I'm telling you the political reality. I can't get you even one more vessel." Dryker paused, leaning against his desk. "I'm staking my career on having you there as an advisor. I've told Congress that's how to ensure that the war is as costly as possible, so the Ganog are too weak to resist us when it's over. Make no mistake, Fizgig, the Coalition will come for the Imperium—probably sooner than either of us is ready for."

"Who's leading this foolish call for war?" Fizgig snapped, digging her claws into the cushion.

"Carnifex." Dryker sighed. "I actually like Carnifex, and you know what? I get where he's coming from. We've been invaded, and we have every right to fight back. Carnifex doesn't care about an unprovable threat we may have to face in the future. He cares about victory over an immediate threat, and a guarantee he won't ever have to flee his world again. What the hell am I supposed to say to that?"

Fizgig's tail lashed. "I see your dilemma. There is no answer his Pride will find acceptable. There is no way to show them the danger, not until we have concrete proof—and the damnable Gorthians make that proof nearly impossible to find."

"Proof Nolan had better get," Dryker snapped. He swirled the liquid in his glass, closing his eyes for a moment. "I'm sorry, Fizgig. It's just this job. It's so much worse than being a captain. It saps the life from you."

"And yet you persevere. Why, Dryker?" Fizgig asked, in a rare moment of introspection. "You and I can speak frankly, warrior to warrior. Why do you still struggle? Why not set the burden down? No one would fault you for it." She had shared so much with this man, both as an enemy and as a friend. No one else understood the burdens of command as well as he did, and the toll they took as the decades passed.

"You know why." Dryker sipped his drink. "We do it because no one else can. I will say this, though, old friend. No matter what happens, this is my last war. I won't be running for re-election." He set the drink down.

He looked so old, so tired. So different from the stalwart warrior she'd first met.

But was she any different? Tired and old, the pair of them.

"I can say the same, Dryker. Whatever happens, this is the

end for me. I look forward to that day, when we can set the burdens down and rest." Fizgig gritted her teeth, rising from her cushions. "But that day is not today. I will report the outcome of the summit. Be well, Dryker."

"Be well, old friend," Dryker said, raising his glass to her. The holo went dark.

4

THE SUMMIT

The transport disk zoomed toward a large island near the center of Takkar's dreadnought. It brought back memories of fleeing for his life, and Khar found it more than a little odd to be returning as an ally.

He hopped from the transport disk, landing next to Zakanna. The empress—if that title was accurate any longer—wore her usual simple gi, the white fabric contrasting nicely with her purple fur. She walked purposefully toward the three-story spire, and Khar kept pace.

"Why did you choose to hold the summit here?" Khar rumbled. "You could have made everyone come to you." His scanners detected nothing out of the ordinary, but he kept alert regardless. There'd been too many nasty surprises recently, and his trust was gone.

"That's precisely why I came," Zakanna explained. "As Empress, I would have summoned them. But I am Empress no longer. At best, I am Clan Leader, the same as T'kon or Takkar. We are equals, and I want to show them that." The words were imbued with her usual passion and fervor. She took ruling seriously—something Khar admired about her.

"A wise course. Takkar, at least, is a proud man. Perhaps this will make him more likely to work with us." Khar disliked Takkar. Takkar was a fine tactical commander, but too sure of himself—much as Khar had been before meeting Fizgig. That was probably exactly what Takkar needed: a tutor like her to teach him humility.

They entered the spire. Khar noted that they seemed to be the last to arrive. Takkar stood on one side of the command dais, with a single Saurian techsmith behind him. T'kon stood on the opposite side, as far from Takkar as he could get. He had also brought a techsmith, and a grey-furred Ganog that Khar thought must be his wife.

Khar moved to stand next to the last person. "Mighty Fizgig." He snapped his hand over his heart and gave a respectful bow.

Zakanna followed a moment later, also bowing to Fizgig.

Fizgig eyed him critically. "Khar. Your fur is a disgrace. Do not think you may stop bathing merely because your body is synthetic." Fizgig turned toward the empress, giving the suggestion of a bow. "Welcome, Zakanna."

Khar found himself licking his wrist, then grooming the fur on the back of his neck very self-consciously. It was out of character for Fizgig to point out something like that publicly, but she always had a reason for the actions she took. Khar glanced at Zakanna, then back at Fizgig.

He was being tested. Fizgig wanted to see if she could make him uncomfortable in front of Zakanna, and she'd succeeded. He'd just betrayed his affection for the displaced monarch.

At least he was conscious of the game now, even if he wasn't yet at her level. He gave Fizgig an affectionate smile. "I've missed you, venerable one."

"Venerable?" Fizgig's tail slashed behind her.

Khar laughed. Fizgig's tail settled into a languid swish. "I've heard impressive tales of the battle at Atreas."

Across the dais, Takkar scowled, his fur darkening. "Before you share any 'tales', I'd remind you that I'm standing right here." He snorted, eyes flaring as his lower nostrils opened. "We may be allies—briefly—but if you make a mockery of me or my clan, I will—"

"You'll do *nothing*," Zakanna snapped, leaping atop the dais. She stabbed a finger down at Takkar. "Your pride is a burden we cannot afford—not now. Not with the survival of our race at stake. There will be no posturing. Today, we come together. Yesterday is debris in the void. Let it go, Takkar."

"You are no longer my ruler, Zakanna," Takkar growled, but his fur softened back to brown. "Yet even I can admit the sense in what you're saying." He looked back to Khar. "Forgive my blustering. My pride stings after the twin defeats at Ganog 7 and Atreas. You must understand—I have never lost, and in my time as Clan Leader have delivered more worlds to the Vkash clan than anyone in living memory."

Zakanna walked quietly back to Khar and Fizgig, hopping down from the dais. She turned back to Takkar. "I lost Imperalis, a world that has belonged to my family for six millennia."

Fizgig made an amused sound, drawing a baleful stare from Zakanna.

"Neither of you understands the scale of the loss we are about to face," Fizgig said. "Three species were savaged by the Void Wraith—seven in ten are dead. My people lost nearly everything." She blinked at Takkar. "The road here is salted with the blood of the fallen. Our people have all suffered. That suffering was not without purpose. It taught me—taught the Coalition—that working with former enemies can sometimes be the only route to survival. Yet such a route isn't easy to walk.

You attacked my people without provocation, Takkar. Every instinct urges me to tear out your throat."

"Tear out my throat?" Takkar threw his head back and laughed. "You are an old woman—a tiny old woman. I do not fear tiny old women, not even in my lesser form."

Khar took three steps back, away from Fizgig. He waited for her to kill Takkar, but her only reaction was the same languid tail swishing. Takkar continued to laugh.

Fury boiled inside Khar. "If you do not cease that braying, I will tear out your tongue, Ganog." Khar ignited the plasma blade on his wrist. "I do not know why Fizgig allows you to continue to draw breath—but if she will not defend her honor, I will."

"Khar!" Fizgig snapped. The word cracked into him like a physical blow. "This is not the way."

Khar stared hard at Takkar, ready to end him—but Fizgig was right.

Khar extinguished his blade, though he offered no apology. He folded his arms, staring a challenge at Takkar. Let the brute come. Khar didn't need a mech to deal with him.

"I am the person with the least standing at this table." T'kon's rumbled words drew everyone's attention. His fur was orange-brown, and his mouth turned down in a frown. His wife wore a matching expression. "We spoke of mistakes. I cost my clan everything—something I have yet to atone for. We speak of working with enemies. No one hates Takkar more than I do. No one has greater cause to claim his life." His eyes met Khar's. "If *I* can ignore the needs of my honor, then you can certainly do the same. Takkar will seek to bait you. Do not let him. We all share the same goal, and if working with people we detest is the most difficult trial we face, we are fortunate indeed."

There were nods of approval all around.

Khar grudgingly added his. "Your words have merit. We do

not need to like each other. We merely need to come together toward a common cause."

"If we are to proceed with that cause," Zakanna said, "we need a fleet leader."

Khar looked to Fizgig, but she said nothing. Nor did Zakanna, despite either being a viable choice.

"I possess the strongest fleet, and have the most experience," Takkar pointed out, breaking the silence.

Khar couldn't let the latter statement stand. "If anyone is placed in charge, it should be Mighty Fizgig. She's embarrassed you twice, Takkar. Surely you recognize that she is the superior commander." He pointed it out not to embarrass Takkar— though if that happened, he could live with it—but to defend Fizgig.

"I could not accept the role, even if it were offered," Fizgig said. She folded her arms, her tail swishing its agitation. "I spoke with President Dryker just before this meeting. I am here in an advisory capacity only."

"That makes Takkar the logical choice," T'kon said. His fur rippled red-brown, and his wife gawked as if she were meeting him for the first time. "I know, my words surprise you all. I do not wish to entrust my people's fate to a brute, but I see little choice. We need a leader, one who has led entire fleets into battle. Takkar is that, if nothing else. The Azi will follow Takkar, if Takkar is willing to accept Fizgig as an advisor—an advisor he will actually listen to."

"Takkar, are you willing to agree to that condition?" Zakanna asked.

"Very well, she may stay aboard my vessel and advise me on my deployments. I give my word that I will listen to her counsel, and implement anything that will give us a better chance of survival. In the end, though, *I* am in charge. I will do what I see fit. Before you make me fleet leader, be certain you can live with that." Takkar folded his arms and stared defiantly in Khar's direction.

"I can." Zakanna folded her arms. "We've already heard from T'kon. Fizgig, will you serve Takkar in an advisory capacity?"

5

FLEET LEADER

Takkar hated dealing with these fools, but one did not always get to choose ones allies. He studied Fizgig as she considered Zakanna's question. Such strange aliens, these Tigris. They possessed fur, at least, but the tail was an oddity.

Yet in that strange body lurked the cunning and intelligence that had so successfully overcome him. Twice.

Zakanna folded her arms. "We've already heard from T'kon. Fizgig, will you serve Takkar in an advisory capacity?"

"As you wish." Fizgig's tail had stopped moving entirely, and her gaze was fixed on Takkar. "It's just as well. President Dryker only procured a single ship, and even that was difficult. The *Demetrius* went with Nolan on his mission to Nyar, leaving me without a vessel. I am happy to serve Takkar in an advisory capacity."

"You possess no fleet to contribute to this war?" Takkar demanded, feeling his fur darken.

"That's correct."

"And also irrelevant," Zakanna said, addressing the group. "We work with what we have. Fizgig has agreed to serve Takkar, and Takkar has agreed to our terms. We have a fleet leader. Now, we can take the next step."

Takkar found himself increasingly impressed with the young empress. She wasn't nearly the flighty Adept she projected herself to be. There were undiscovered depths there —meaning she was probably a good deal more dangerous than he'd originally assumed.

"Very well," Takkar said, "then let us begin by assessing the situation and coming up with a plan." He stared around the table, meeting every pair of eyes. "We all know how dire our predicament, but only one part of it matters: Imperalis. No other battle is of consequence. Without Imperalis, we cannot repair or adequately resupply. If we are to have any hope of victory, we must wrest back the capital regardless of the cost. That world is held by the Kthul, backed by these Void Wraith. I understand the former, but not the latter. How can we over-come the Void Wraith? We must bypass them to reach the beacon. And, if I understand correctly, it is with that beacon that they are controlled."

"You understand correctly," Fizgig said. "The Void Wraith are cybernetic lifeforms. The nervous system and brain of a living entity are inserted into an artificial body, not unlike Khar's. All Void Wraith are designed with a central kill switch and a universal override. The Gorthians—what you call the Nameless Ones—designed the Void Wraith well. Yet in this instance that weakness greatly benefits us. Retake this beacon, and we can unleash the Void Wraith upon the Kthul."

"Utfa will have many defenses in place," Zakanna cautioned. She shook her head slowly. "At the very least, he has the orbital cannon used to cripple the Nyar fleet. Our fleet cannot survive that kind of firepower."

"The Omega Judicators are truly devastating in their own right," Khar added. "Their firepower added to the cannon will destroy any fleet in orbit long before they can ground enough troops to take the spire."

"How do your people know so much about these... Omegas?" It seemed awfully convenient that they had shown up with all the answers just as the answers were needed.

"Our people captured many harvesters during the war with the Void Wraith," Khar explained. The impudence in that one's gaze nearly drove Takkar to violence, allies or no. "They contained cores, some dating back to the original Primo empire. One of those cores contained the schematics for the Void Wraith that were used in the original Eradication, over fifty thousand years ago. Those included the plans for Omegas, though at that time none had been built."

"So why not build one now?" T'kon asked.

Fizgig shook her head sadly. "We have the schematics used to create them, but the manufacturing facilities needed to create an Omega would require a generation to build. The Omega itself would take even longer. The ones they are using must have taken a century or more to construct."

"Which brings us back to where we started," Zakanna added, seizing control of the conversation once more. "We must find a way to destroy the beacon, but orbital bombardment will fail. The Omegas will see to that. If orbital bombardment isn't possible, what do we do?"

"So, *Mighty Fizgig*, how would you solve this problem? Advise me." Takkar did not bother to hide his scorn. She'd won twice, but in both cases there were extenuating circumstances. Had the empress allowed him to fully repair his fleet, Atreas would have been an altogether different battle.

"For now, we can do little." Fizgig folded her arms and watched him with those slitted, green eyes. "We need more information on the beacon, and knowledge of the defenders guarding Imperalis."

T'kon spoke up. "We cannot afford to delay our assault. We have no way to repair, and our opponent does. The Kthul are no doubt already searching for us. There's every likelihood that a techsmith on one of our vessels has already transmitted our location." He shook his head. "I do not wish to rush into combat, but time works against us."

"The Kthul do not perceive us as the gravest threat," Fizgig countered. "When the Gorthians were finally ready to reveal themselves, they attacked the greatest threat swiftly and without mercy. That threat is the Nyar Clan. The Gorthians know it. They will come for the Nyar home world, and they will eradicate it. This is why I have dispatched Nolan—to prepare the Nyar. We have at least a little while before the Kthul can turn their attention to us, and we should spend that time wisely. I have never been to your capital, and so cannot comment on breaching its defenses. So I turn to your expertise, Takkar. How would you suggest we defeat them?"

Takkar's fur became a wan yellow, his frustration at his own incompetence showing. "I do not know."

6

REBUFFED

The disk zoomed to a halt, depositing Nolan and Yulo at one of the highest rings in the spire. Nolan tensed as he and the Adept approached the black-armored Ganog with the long spear over his shoulder. He rose to attention as they approached, and Nolan forced himself to relax.

"I am Nolan of the Coalition, slayer of Krekon," he intoned, as Yulo had instructed him. "I petition for entry to the spire."

"Your petition is refused," the Ganog warrior snarled, without hesitation. He loomed over Nolan, but Nolan refused to back down. The Ganog seemed amused. "Now scurry away, before you make me angry enough to squash you. Rodent."

Nolan ignited his plasma blade, and shifted into a combat stance. "You're welcome to try." He was fairly certain that he could kill the Ganog before he shifted into his great form. The time it took to do that would make his opponent vulnerable. Right now, they were on more or less equal terms.

"Please, reconsider," Yulo said, stepping smoothly in front of Nolan. "All we wish is a brief audience, and you have my word that the matter is of the gravest importance."

"I will not reconsider—not even for you, old man." The

warrior glared down at Nolan contemptuously. "You are fortunate the master is with you, or I'd crush you to jelly. Now begone from my sight."

Nolan looked to Yulo, raising an eyebrow. Yulo shook his head. Nolan reluctantly extinguished his plasma blade, then turned on his heel and stalked back toward the transport disk they'd arrived on.

Yulo joined him a moment later.

"Why didn't you let me challenge him?" Nolan asked, staring at the defiant guard as the disk whizzed into the air. It dropped quickly, moving toward the depths of the spire.

"Because it wouldn't have resolved anything." Yulo eyed Nolan sidelong. "If you had bested him he would have taken us to his superior, whom you'd also need to challenge. How many challenges are you prepared for?"

"Point taken." Nolan steadied himself as the disk zoomed past another island. They were nearing the level where they'd boarded. "There has to be a better way."

"And there is." Yulo hopped from the disk, landing in a crouch on the spire's deck.

Nolan leapt off, landing next to him.

"If you wish to gain audience," Yulo said, "you must find someone who can grant it. Someone who will take you directly to the clan leader."

"I don't know any Nyar." Nolan stalked back through the golden sigils, into the too-bright sunlight. His sunglasses automatically darkened, affording a better view of the spectacular array of ships docked around the spire. None were as impressive as the *Demetrius*. The battleship was still docked, its Theta cannons bristling on all sides, in between the smaller particle cannons. A truly massive Theta cannon was slung under the ship's belly, where the gauss cannon had been aboard the UFC *Johnston*.

Three fighter ports lined each side, sheltered under stubby wings that were nothing but masses of dense tritanium. She was a true warship, able to go toe-to-toe with a Primo carrier—and maybe even a Ganog dreadnought.

"You may not know any Nyar, but I can think of one who knows you. Or of you, at the very least." Yulo ambled toward the battleship, and Nolan matched his pace. "Kokar is the son of the clan leader. He was on Imperalis the day Utfa attacked us. That battle cost his family greatly, and the blame will be placed on Kokar."

"So you're suggesting we get the help of a disgraced noble?" Nolan asked, more than a little skeptical. "Will his father even listen to him?"

"It doesn't matter if the father will listen," Yulo pointed out, "so long as the son can secure us an audience."

"That shouldn't be too hard," Nolan mused. "I saw how desperate Takkar was after losing face, and we might be able to offer Kokar a way back into his father's good graces."

"Yes, I'd considered the same ploy. I believe we can attract Kokar's notice."

"How do you suggest we do that?" Nolan asked, ducking through the outer hatch of the *Demetrius*.

"If I am correct, we already have. Word will spread quickly that an emissary from a foreign battleship was turned away. I recommend patience. Wait, and Kokar will come to us."

7

KOKAR

Kokar squeezed his bulk up the corridor of the strange ship. The ceiling was a bit too low, the corridor a bit too narrow. It was confining, completely unlike the interior of a Ganog vessel. Even the Saurians allowed enough room to move.

He ducked under another narrow bulkhead and passed into a sizable cargo bay. It gleamed under the bright lights above—no sign of dirt, debris, or even rust. This place was immaculately kept, as were the mighty war machines in each of the stalls.

"Their *ka'tok* do an impressive job," Hruk muttered, walking the customary three steps behind Kokar. The old man's hand never left the hilt of his chopping sword. "Their machines are in excellent repair."

"It is impressive, and I'm sure it was no accident that our hosts chose this place to welcome us," Kokar countered. He already disliked these aliens, and likely always would. He raised two fingers to touch the scar on his right cheek. At least the Tigris known as Khar was not among them.

"Kokar," a clear voice rang out, from the far side of the

hangar. It came from a human wearing a standard set of their environmental armor. That armor didn't gleam. It bore scratches and dents. It was the first proof that any of these people had seen battle. "My name is Captain Nolan. Welcome to the *Demetrius*. What can I do for you?"

Kokar narrowed his eyes, and made no move to keep the red from his fur. "I do not play games, Captain. Nor should you. You know why I am here."

"Fair enough." The human shrugged. He seemed unconcerned by Kokar, confident he could deal with the threat. Kokar found that curious. Very few aliens dismissed a Ganog elite. "I'm never really sure. T'kon did tell me you'd be blunt."

"You're an ally of T'kon? You keep strange company, Captain." Kokar spat on the deck. "You sought entry to the royal island. Why?"

"I wanted to speak to your father about the possibility of an alliance. You know why." The human took a step closer, staring defiantly up at Kokar. "You saw what happened on Imperalis. You know what's coming."

"I do, but my voice is drowned out by the wind of war." Kokar shook his head, his fur darkening. "They will not listen. You must understand—to my father, this is the final war. The Nameless Ones are returning, and he stands ready to meet them in glorious battle. It's what we were bred for, what the Nyar have always stood for. We oppose the Nameless Ones, shouting defiantly with our final breath."

"And making an alliance with the Coalition threatens that somehow? We're not trying to take away your war. We're trying to make sure a few of us survive it." He leaned against the wall, relaxing slightly. "You need to make them see that, before they wipe this world off the map. I've dealt with the Gorthians. Right now the Nyar are the biggest threat to their plans, and they react very predictably to threats. They're going to come at this world fast and hard. If we don't stand together, everyone is going to die."

"Human, I do not appreciate your tone, though I admire your fire," Kokar murmured. He raised a hand to stay Hruk's advance, aware of the old man sliding his blade from its scabbard. "It is not me that you need to convince. I understand the threat we face. I saw the Void Wraith, saw their strange, blue planetstriders. I have heard rumors that your people have encountered these Void Wraith. Is there any truth to this?"

"We've not only encountered them—we've beaten them. Those victories were costly until we learned their weaknesses. I'm happy to share those weaknesses with you. We can have full schematics for all known Void Wraith units transmitted before you leave the *Demetrius*." The human appeared relaxed, but mention of the war brought the fire back to his eyes. His war had become personal, Kokar was sure of it. "All I'm asking in return is an audience with your father."

"I will arrange that audience, human," Kokar said. "I will even lend my weight to your arguments. Yet I must be clear—that weight is not great. I am blamed for the death of my people on Imperalis, for the loss of two full dreadnoughts. My father will not listen. The best you can hope for is that he will review the data you've brought. He will never ally with this Coalition. He wouldn't even ally with the other Ganog clans, and only pays lip service to the Yog. My father is a proud man, and quick to anger."

"Yet he is also honorable," Yulo called, rising to his feet and moving to join them. His fur was snowy white, the hallmark of a Master Adept. Kokar eyed him suspiciously. Yog couldn't be trusted—especially their Adepts. "Your father may listen, though he will not much like what we have to say. Let us allow him to judge the worth of our words."

"Very well. Prepare yourselves. I will arrange an audience

after dinner, when my father is at his ease. Be warned, human. Do not bristle at my father as you did at me, or he will tear your spine from your back and keep your skull as a warning to others."

Kokar hoped he wasn't understating the matter, and that the human didn't assume he was speaking in hyperbole. He strongly desired the same things this Coalition did. If his people were to survive, they'd need the help—though he strongly doubted his father would see it that way.

8

GRAK

The stealth belt gave a satisfying clunk as it magnetically sealed to Nolan's armor. The sound was duplicated all around him as the rest of the squad secured their own belts. Nolan picked up his rifle from its perch against the bulkhead.

"All right, people, here's the deal. We're walking into what could be an enemy stronghold. Our mission is to befriend them, but if they get hostile, we bug out. Be ready for anything." Nolan keyed the exit sequence on the airlock, and waited as the mechanism whirred. The door slid away, revealing the spire's outer ring.

Nolan walked boldly toward the arched doorway with the sigils, and the rest of the squad fanned out behind him. Burke had offered to accompany him, too, but Nolan thought bringing that much firepower might be taken as a threat.

Besides, he wanted Burke to be able to bail them out with mechs, if it came to that.

"So we're here as scarecrows, basically?" Annie drawled. She drew herself up to her full height, then snapped her helmet into place, obscuring her face.

"That's the plan," Hannan said, and caught Nolan's eye. "We're an honor guard for Yulo and the captain. We don't say or do a damned thing, unless they get hostile. Then it's stealth and bug out while we wait for the cavalry."

"Can you tell me anything else about how to approach this?" Nolan asked, stepping through the archway into the inner spire. Annie and Hannan trailed behind him and Yulo, cradling their particle rifles.

"I'm afraid not," Yulo admitted, walking gracefully next to Nolan. "I have no idea what the Nyar are expecting of us. They were rarely at court, and keep largely to themselves. Frankly, they look down on not only my clan but all other clans."

"Lovely," Nolan muttered. He made immediately for one of the transport disks. Flying through the air with no handrails was still a little terrifying, and he wondered idly how many people tumbled to their deaths each year.

The rest of the squad stepped atop the same disk, which left only a foot between him and the edge. He bent his knees as the disk zoomed into the air, making its way up into the blackness. This place was much less well lit than the Imperial spire had been.

His stomach lurched as the disk accelerated, the ring on which they'd entered receding below them. The disk carried them high into the spire, finally slowing as it neared a wide, foreboding island. Most of the island was covered by a squat, ugly, stone building.

Nolan spotted guards at most of the narrow windows, each wielding a Ganog pulse rifle. These people were ready for war as a matter of daily course.

The disk stopped at the island's edge, and Nolan hopped off. Yulo landed nimbly beside him, while Hannan and Annie stood a few meters away.

"I guess we just go inside." Nolan started toward the building, walking through a wide doorway.

Inside, a pair of guards eyed him balefully. They wore
midnight-black armor, broken only by painted sigils on their
right shoulders. Each held a long spear with a wicked barb at
the end that gleamed with something wet. Poison, maybe.

Neither guard said anything, nor did they move to bar
Nolan's way. He shrugged and proceeded up the short hallway.
It emptied into a large auditorium with ringed seats like the
classrooms back at the academy.

Inside, dozens of Ganog sat in small groups. Most cradled
horns of a sweet-smelling drink, but all were alert enough to
turn in his direction as he entered.

"Man," he said. "I thought Alpha Company was hostile.
These guys look like they want to tear me apart on the spot."

"Stand proud, Captain," Yulo said, straightening next to
him. "Lead us down to the dais, where Grak awaits us."

Nolan started down a set of wide stairs, threading past rows
of Ganog as he approached the central dais. Standing atop it
was a weathered Ganog in scored armor. The hilt of a massive
axe jutted over one shoulder, and a scar ran from his forehead
to his chin. His fur was soft brown with whorls of black.

Nolan spotted Kokar in the last row, closest to the dais.
Kokar nodded his encouragement at Nolan, and Nolan nodded
back. Then he turned his attention to the Nyar clan leader.

Grak stared impassively at Nolan, watching with disinterest
as Nolan stopped next to the edge of the dais. Yulo stood a
meter or two back, leaving Nolan to weather the full storm of
Grak's displeasure.

"My son claims that you hold the key to our salvation,"
Grak began. "My son is a fool, who preens too much and listens
too little." His fur darkened to a thick, ruddy brown. "I am *not* a
fool, nor do I suffer them. I have no idea what you said or did to

turn my son's ear, but it doesn't take much. So tell me why you've come—and know that if your words or your demeanor displease me, I will crack your bones and eat the marrow."

Nolan considered his answer carefully. He could be diplomatic, but that wouldn't work. Brutal honesty was what Grak would respect most.

"You're no fool?" Nolan asked, folding his arms. He stared hard at the clan leader. "Have you ever fought the Void Wraith, Clan Leader?"

Grak's lip curled upward. "I warned you to mind your tone, little human."

"No. The answer is *no*, you haven't fought the Void Wraith. You have no idea what they're capable of, who made them, or how to stop them. The Kthul—your sworn enemies, as I understand it—now control Imperalis and an armada of Void Wraith." Nolan kept his tone respectful, but didn't mince words. "When those forces come for you, they will crack this world like a nut. They'll tear through your defenses, and they'll ravage this place."

Grak threw his head back and laughed. It went on for long moments, echoing through the room, and when it finally faded Grak speared Nolan with his gaze.

"You have fought these Void Wraith," Grak said, "and bested them. If your pitiful race can do it, then I'm not overly concerned. As for the Kthul, we await them eagerly. Let them come, and let them bring their dark masters with them. We are the shield, and we will not break. They will hurl their forces against us like waves crashing on rock. When that wave recedes, we will stand as we always have."

Nolan changed tactics. "At the very least, let us offer you the technical schematics for the Void Wraith. We can give you their vulnerabilities and their tactics. Everything from battle footage to detailed tactical reports. We don't ask anything in return."

Grak waved dismissively at Nolan. "Cease your prattle, human. The Nyar need not resort to dishonorable tactics to find victory. We are not the Vkash, or the pitiful Yog." He shifted his gaze to Yulo.

If the insult stung, Yulo didn't show it. He remained impassive, arms clasped behind him and fur still snowy white.

Nolan looked to Kokar, but the youth avoided his gaze. Nolan was on his own, and he already knew that no amount of arguing was going to sway Grak. "All right, have it your way. But remember this day when the Void Wraith darken your skies. Remember that there could have been help, if you'd been wise enough to accept it."

"I could kill you, and your companions. I could destroy that little battleship you arrived in," Grak mused, walking to stand at the edge of the dais, towering over Nolan. "I will not. Instead, I invite you to stay on our world. In fact, I insist. I will have your warp engines disabled, to ensure that you remain. When the Kthul arrive, you will be here to witness the battle. You will see for yourself the might of the Nyar. Now get out of my sight, before I overcome the revulsion of your smell and devour your weak, little body."

Nolan turned sharply on his heel, walking slowly from the chamber. He kept his head high, and his pace measured. T'kon hadn't understated the arrogance of the Nyar, and Nolan had no idea how he was going to fulfill his mission.

9

WORKABLE

Nolan's shoulders didn't unclench until he was safely back aboard the *Demetrius*. He made for the command deck, where he knew Burke would be. The rank of major didn't exactly correspond to its use in the old UFC. Burke was part major, part ship's captain. It was a change Nolan himself had lobbied for, made possible through core technology. Since a core handled almost all basic ship functions, a bridge crew wasn't really necessary.

The lift slowed to a stop, and the doors slid open to show the command deck. It was tiny, even when compared to the *Johnston* or the *Peregrine*. A holosphere dominated the center of the room, currently displaying the Nyar system.

Burke's serious face was illuminated by the glow of the hologram, his eyes locked on the warp anchor. He looked up as Nolan entered, giving a neutral nod. "It didn't go well, I take it?"

"About as expected." Nolan shook his head, moving to join Burke at the hologram. "Not only did the Nyar not listen, but they've insisted we remain here to watch the battle."

"Wait, how is that even going to be possible?" Burke asked

skeptically. "I've been wracking my brain about the warp anchor, and I can't think of any way past it."

"I can," Nolan countered. "I wrestled with it too, for a long time. After meeting Grak, I have a pretty good idea of how the Kthul are going to get inside."

"Are you going to share, or are you enjoying that smug ten-steps-ahead thing you do?"

"I'm going to enjoy it for a bit, I think." Nolan smiled at the hologram. "If I'm right, the Kthul should appear any time, in exactly the same spot we did."

Burke stroked his beard with two fingers, then stopped. His eyes widened. "Wait, are you saying what I think you're saying? Those arrogant shit-talkers are going to let them in, aren't they?"

"That's my guess." Nolan wasn't surprised Burke had figured it out so quickly. "If you're the Kthul, you show up and taunt Grak. Grak gets mad and lowers the gate so you can come in and fight. Grak is convinced he'll win this fight."

As if on queue, the holosphere flickered. New vessels began appearing, one after another. The dreadnoughts appeared first, their spidery limbs extending toward the world below. Nolan counted seven. A flurry of cruisers and destroyers appeared next, baby spiders next to their dark mothers.

"How many ships do the Nyar have?" Burke asked, moving to peer at the newly arrived enemy fleet.

"Not enough. I counted five dreadnoughts, but two of them looked like they'd been through a meat grinder. I suspect those were the survivors of the attack on Imperalis." He sized up the enemy ships. "I don't see any Void Wraith with them, but that doesn't mean much. They could be cloaked."

"Did the Nyar accept the intel you offered?" Burke asked. "They'll be able to detect any cloaked Void Wraith."

"Of course not. That would have made way too much sense.

No, Grak and his people are all about the heroic last stand. I don't think he even cares if they all die, as long as they do it spitting in the face of the Nameless Ones." Part of Nolan couldn't blame them for the obsessive hatred. It was a hatred he shared. He would do anything to find and destroy every surviving Gorthian, and if that meant dying...well, he was comfortable with the cost.

"So they refused the intel that would let them fight a brand new enemy they've never encountered," Burke said, clearly dumbfounded, "and they're going to open the door and just let that enemy walk in? How do we think this is going to turn out?"

"Badly," Nolan said. "And I know where you're going with this. Even if I thought we should flee—and I don't—we can't. They've locked us down with the warp anchor. We're stuck on this world."

"So you want to stay here and get slaughtered?" Burke snapped, glaring at Nolan. "Come on, we need a real plan."

"The best I've got is cloaking and hiding. Our improved drive will keep us undetectable to all parties. We watch events play out, and hope like hell we find the right opportunity to help. I have a feeling that the Nyar are going to need us."

"It's workable," Burke allowed. "Let's get the ship battened down and ready to fly. We're going to need to find a safe place in that forest—someplace deep enough to avoid scans."

"I imagine Kokar probably has some ideas about where that might be," Nolan said. "I'll see if I can get hold of him before we leave."

He turned back to the spire with a sigh. The Nyar were about to get the same treatment humanity and the Tigris had gotten when they'd first encountered the Void Wraith.

10

NOWHERE IS SAFE

Zakanna listened quietly as the others debated possible courses of action. It was a tactic her mother had taught her, and one she'd grown up perfecting: Listen to everyone give their counsel, and only when you understood all possible options did you lend your voice to the discussion.

"The only way to win this battle is to secure the beacon— we agree on that," Khar said, resting both hands on the edge of the dais. He stared a challenge at the others, as fierce as ever— perhaps more so.

Zakanna had seen the way Khar looked to Fizgig. It was the same way she looked to Yulo, and part of why she now felt lost without his presence.

"But we do not agree on how," Takkar countered, shaking his head. "Sending in a small strike team is foolish. It would mean entrusting the fate of the fleet to the work of a single squad. If the squad fails, the fleet is wiped out. It's madness."

"It is not madness," Fizgig said, her calm enviable. "Send in a small strike team comprised of our most able warriors. Seize the beacon, and turn the Void Wraith on their masters. Only then do we warp in the fleet."

"If the team fails, you leave them to die," T'kon said, nodding in understanding. "I agree; this is the best plan. Ultimately, we risk nothing but the strike team. We need to move the fleet anyway, so why not jump it closer to Imperalis? We can take up a hidden position within a single jump, then warp in if the team succeeds. If not, we either try another team or warp away and devise a new plan."

Fizgig cocked her head, eyes distant. She licked her chops, then spoke to the group. "I've just received word from Nolan. The Kthul fleet arrived at Nyar. This fool, Grak, has lowered their defenses and allowed the Kthul inside."

"I'm not surprised," Zakanna said, sourly. She kept the emotion from her fur, but only just. "Grak is as hidebound as they come and will not accept change. He honors the old ways, and that means battling your enemy on an open plain. It is the worst kind of pride."

"Clan Leader," came a timid voice from behind Takkar. A Saurian strode forward, bobbing a curtsy next to Takkar. "A thousand apologies, but an enemy fleet has just warped in-system. We are under attack."

Zakanna looked up through the observatory dome. A sizable enemy fleet had arrived—half a dozen dreadnoughts supported by three times their number in heavy cruisers. They were already launching fighters, their main cannons charging.

Six fully functional dreadnoughts unleashed a volley, all aimed unerringly at the *Vkash's Fist*. The vessel shuddered under each impact, the shield rippling to blue, then red. By the third shot, it had faded entirely, leaving the ship naked to the other three shots.

The first punched through the dome almost directly above them, and air rushed out into space. A second hole appeared a few hundred meters away. Debris exploding outward even as the islands under the hole followed. The third hit made something grind deep in the ship, from the engines.

Long moments later, membranes appeared over the holes, stopping the loss of atmosphere.

"I don't understand," Zakanna said, staring up in horror. "What are they hoping to accomplish? We can merely warp away."

"Do it!" Takkar roared at the techsmith. "Order all vessels to warp to point alpha."

"Of course, Clan Leader." The Saurian bobbed another curtsy, frantic pulses of data flowing from her arcanotome. After several moments her face fell, and she shrank into her robes. "Clan Leader, we are unable to warp away. Our drive has been sabotaged. Reports are coming in from the rest of the fleet. Other warp drives have been disabled."

"Clever," Fizgig said. "They knew we'd attempt to scatter, so they've ensured we cannot leave. We fight, or die."

"Those treacherous bastards," Takkar roared. "They must have spies on my ship. Seeker sympathizers." He glanced up, his fur going ashen. "We cannot fight a battle within and a battle without at the same time."

"Which they no doubt know." Zakanna sighed wearily. "We have no choice but to retake the ship, and before that can happen, Kthul cruisers will have already boarded. That's assuming they don't just end us. Their cannons are nearly recharged."

"We have been badly outmaneuvered," Fizgig said, shaking her head. Her tail slashed behind her, lazily. "Look at those ships. They are untouched by war, every turret operational. Our own fleet is heavily damaged. Even if we retook the ship immediately, the Kthul would crush us. More, I think you will find that the warp drive is not the only thing they sabotaged."

Takkar rounded on the techsmith. "Fire the main cannon. Now! Deploy all fighters."

"Clan Leader, the main cannon is nonfunctional," the Saurian said. A series of pulses flowed to and from the arcanotome. "We are deploying fighters, but there are reports of fighting on the lower islands."

The dreadnought shuddered under another volley, this one targeting their engines exclusively. Takkar looked up at them, defeated. "I've no doubt they'll dock soon, bringing over enough troops to pacify this vessel. Our alliance is doomed, before it even really began."

Zakanna's fur shifted to a whirling pink-white as she struggled for control. They'd endured so much, yet every challenge they overcame was followed by a worse one.

11

THE MISSION IS YOURS

Khar clenched and unclenched his hands, preparing himself for combat. There was no immediate threat, but that would come soon enough. He took a protective step toward Zakanna, and she did the same toward him.

"Zakanna." Fizgig walked slowly toward the empress, removing a silvery belt from her waist. "This is a stealth belt. It will cloak you from almost all known sensors, including anything the Void Wraith have. It will be useful both here and on the strike team you will lead to Imperalis." She handed the belt to Zakanna.

"I don't understand," Zakanna said, her eyebrows knitting together in consternation. "Won't you need it?"

"I will not be leaving." Fizgig sat on the edge of the dais and began massaging her thigh. Khar had seen her perform the motion often since her final battle with Admiral Mow during the war with the Void Wraith.

"Why?" Khar demanded. "There is absolutely no reason to stay. If we flee, we flee together. Those who remain behind will die."

"Ah, I see her plan now," Takkar said. "One step ahead of me, again." He walked around the dais, kneeling respectfully before Fizgig. "I have misjudged you—assumed that you were a treacherous opponent, honorless and callow. You know honor as truly as any Ganog, and you are the worthiest foe I have ever faced."

Fizgig blinked at him, but said nothing.

"Ahh," T'kon said. "I believe I understand as well. The seekers are coming for Takkar, so he cannot leave. If he flees, they will chase him. If he stays, he occupies them long enough for the rest of us to flee."

"Indeed," Takkar said, "but what I do not understand is why Fizgig must also stay. There's no reason for anyone else to remain." He rose to his feet. "Fizgig, you are the finest commander among us. This admission pains me, but it is the truth. If we are to win this war, we will need you to lead it."

"No, you won't," Fizgig said. She nodded at Khar. "The real battle will take place on Imperalis. The real battle is taking the beacon. We have an opportunity here—a way to turn their victory into the secret dagger aimed at their heart. Let them take us both. They will believe they've decapitated the serpent, and it will make them careless." She turned to T'kon. "You should battle your way back to your vessel as quickly as possible. You will very likely be caught in the attempt, but I do not believe they will kill you."

"Why not?" T'kon asked, clearly puzzled.

His wife, Jehanna, spoke. "Because they have plans for the Azi," she said, eyes widening. Her fur brightened. "They seek to turn us back to the Nameless Ones, and T'kon's name would lend great strength to their cause. If they capture us, they will use you to get more of our people to capitulate. They will likely use a threat to me to secure your cooperation."

"You married well, T'kon." Fizgig nodded respectfully at Jehanna. "This one sees clearly. Keep her close."

"Let us depart, then. If Jehanna and I gain our freedom, we will take the fleet to a safe place to gather survivors." T'kon hurried toward a transport disk. Jehanna moved with him, and their guards followed behind.

"Khar," Fizgig said. "The mission is yours. Get to Aluki's cruiser. Go to Imperalis, and find a way to seize control of the beacon. With or without the fleet, turn the Void Wraith back on their masters."

"Mighty Fizgig," Khar lowered his cheek, brushing it against hers.

She stepped back with a look of distaste, then began cleaning the fur where he'd left his scent. Yet she didn't chastise him.

"I will lead this mission, and I will succeed. Come, Zakanna. We have a planet to win back."

They hurried to a transport disk on the opposite side from T'kon and climbed aboard. It zoomed over the edge, carrying them toward the lower section of the ship. Below, Ganog elites fought on many islands. The chaos was total, and there was no way to distinguish friend from foe. They all wore the same armor and fought with similar weapons.

"How does this stealth belt work?" Zakanna asked, buckling it around her waist. It fit her, just barely. She was larger than Fizgig.

"It generates a field that will bend light," Khar explained, "cloaking you on that spectrum. It will also dampen your thermal signature, but cannot erase it entirely." The disk zoomed a wide path around another island, no more than forty meters from the fighting. "The belts consume enormous energy, and the internal battery will only last for about two hours. We must move swiftly, and conserve power when possible."

"Reaching the cruiser will be impossible. That's where the Kthul reinforcements will be docking," Zakanna's fur had settled to an eggshell white, not as pristine as Yulo's but impressive nonetheless.

"I have an idea about that." Khar gave a toothy grin. "I know someone—you'd call them a *ka'tok*—that can get us to the docking bay without being seen. He dwells in the underbelly of the ship, along the hull. If we can reach him, we have a chance."

12

AZATOK

T akkar unlimbered his axe and took an experimental swing. It hummed through the air, drawing a grim smile from him. The techsmith had already fled, leaving him alone with Fizgig. He glanced at the Tigris and was appalled to find her licking her own fur. It was disgusting.

Was she...bathing? With saliva?

"Are you not going to ready yourself for battle?" Takkar demanded, looming over her. Despite recognizing her skill, he'd never trust or like her.

"I *am* ready for battle," Fizgig said, not looking at him. She began chewing on her shoulder, then licked the fur around it several times and looked up at him with those odd, slitted eyes. "What is it you feel I should be doing, exactly? You can hear the sounds of battle as well as I. They're growing closer, and your forces are losing. We will be overwhelmed, and in all likelihood killed."

"You face your death calmly enough," Takkar allowed, but grudgingly. "I do not know who leads them, but there is a chance that leader will accept my challenge. If I defeat them, they may cede me the ship, or at the very least grant our freedom."

Fizgig eyed Takkar critically, and he was very conscious of the fat that had accumulated around his midsection, bulging his armor outward. But he stood proudly, still a warrior. His edge had dulled, but he would turn his appearance to his advantage. Whoever he faced would underestimate him, assuming they faced a weak, aging warrior. Takkar could still fight, though—could still kill. He would teach the enemy the price of dismissing him.

"Goddess watch over you, Takkar. If you can free us, perhaps we can salvage something. If not, we will sell our lives as dearly as we are able." She returned to grooming, and Takkar fiercely envied her calm. She'd fully embraced death, the purest expression of haak he'd ever seen. She was more Ganog than anyone he'd ever met. More Ganog than Takkar.

Even if she did bathe with saliva.

A heavy transport disk approached, packed with Kthul elites in their sickly, green armor. A second and third disk followed, the figures aboard all wearing the scarlet armor of the Vkash. Traitors, every one. All three disks disgorged their charges, and dozens of elites fanned out around Takkar and the tiny Tigris.

Rifles were raised, covering them from every direction. Fizgig didn't react, and Takkar drew on her calm. He planted the head of his axe against the ground, waiting patiently for a commander to reveal himself.

"Hello, Takkar," rumbled a heavy voice. The elites parted, allowing a short, stocky warrior to approach. His fur was shorter than most, and partially shaved as only Kthul fanatics did. He wore a pair of long daggers at his side, and had a rifle strapped to his back.

Takkar's eyes widened when he recognized his opponent.

The Kthul champion's size was deceptive, but Takkar knew he was capable of blinding speed. Some believed he was really an Adept.

"Hello, Azatok," Takkar spat back. He took a step closer, holding his axe at the ready. "I see you've come to wrest *Vkash's Fist* from me. Do you have the stomachs to fight for it yourself?"

Azatok gestured expansively. "Look around, old man. Your ship is already mine, your people already pledged to my cause. They have embraced the Nameless Ones, as I have. We serve our rightful masters once more."

"Then you will not fight?" Takkar gave a derisive laugh. "Do you really fear me that much?"

"You hope to provoke me into killing you, to spare you the shame of your latest defeat. I'm unsurprised. This is three terrible losses in a row, is it not?" Looking smug, Azatok approached Takkar but made no threatening moves. "Make no mistake, Takkar. I *will* kill you, and I will do it in the arena. Your days of winning the Imperial Games are long behind you. You've let yourself go. You are fat and weak. Yet I will still grant you a warrior's death."

"Why not here and now?" Takkar asked, still hoping. He raised the axe, resting the blade casually on his shoulder.

"Because," Azatok turned to face him, smiling wickedly, "I want to broadcast your death to the whole of the Imperium. Let the Vkash see their leader fall, know that their fate is now tied to the Nameless Ones." His fur shifted to a malicious red.

Takkar's shoulders slumped. His public execution would be humiliating—not just for him, but for his clan. In his prime he might have stood a chance against Azatok, but now? He was too slow, too old. He would die fighting, but he was under no illusions that he could kill Azatok.

"Who is your companion?" Azatok asked, crouching before Fizgig. "No, no, don't tell me. I recognize her species from the visions with which the Nameless Ones have blessed me. This must be the enemy fleet leader, the Mighty Fizgig. She is not nearly so fierce as I was led to believe. Can you talk, little creature?"

Fizgig didn't respond. She continued to lick her fur, seemingly unaware of Azatok's presence.

"I could have you put to death right now," Azatok said, leaning closer to Fizgig. "Or I could kill you myself. A wise captive gives respect, if she wishes to live."

"You will kill me sooner or later," Fizgig said, continuing to groom, "so there seems little point in cooperation." She didn't look up at Azatok, or make any move to defend herself.

"I think I will enjoy breaking you, little Tigris," Azatok snapped. He gestured to his elites. "Have them taken to holding cells."

Takkar let himself be taken, and noticed that Fizgig didn't resist either. The chance to fight and die passed, leaving them to the mercy of a merciless foe.

He hoped they'd made the right decision, and that the others had managed to escape.

13

TO ME

T'kon aimed his slug thrower at the back of the elite's head, then whistled. The shrill sound caused the warrior to turn, and T'kon shot him in the eye. A heartbeat later, the explosive round detonated, and the elite crashed to the ground. Smoke rose from his eye socket.

"You do not have to woo me, husband," Jehanna said, laughing like the girl she'd been when they'd first met. It was a welcome change, stripping away all the somberness that had settled over them recently.

"A wise husband, particularly one who has just won his wife back, never stops trying to woo her," T'kon countered, laughing as well. For the first time in as long as he could remember, there was joy in his heart.

He sprinted to the transport disk, offering Jehanna a hand. She took it, though both knew she needed no assistance. She moved in close, pressed against his chest.

"You've become wiser in your time away." She smiled affectionately. "It did you good."

"It did," T'kon said, nodding. He rested his sword against

his shoulder. "Honestly? I would not change the events that led us here. The universe made me into what I need to be to oppose the Nameless Ones, and to safeguard our people."

"That—I am surprised, husband," Jehanna admitted. She eyed him curiously, but there was pride in her eyes as well. "You endured much. To shrug it off as building character is something I'd never have expected from you. I love you dearly, but you've always carried grudges further than any warrior I've ever met."

"That was the old me," T'kon said. "The prideful, surly leader, longing for past glories. Then I lost everything." He holstered his slug thrower. "I had no choice but to see reality as it is, rather than as I believe it to be. I had no allies to coddle me, no wealth to shelter me. I lived off my wits, and often went to bed with stomachs rumbling. Everything I took for granted was stripped away, scoured to the foundation. From there, I rebuilt, and I'd like to think I am better for it."

"If we die today, husband, know that I am proud of you," Jehanna said, eyes shining. She caressed his cheek.

T'kon's fur went purple-pink, and he didn't care who saw. "That feeling is mutual, wife. You've achieved much, both as an Adept and as a voice for our people. You are the truest Azi I have ever known."

The disk finally zoomed to a halt at the command island. T'kon tensed. A group of Kthul warriors was leading the attack, and they'd already shifted to great form. Some of the defenders had joined the enemy, though thankfully only a few. The Azi defenders were clustered behind pillars, struggling desperately to prevent their enemies from encircling them.

Their position wasn't tenable, not in the long term. Not unless he did something.

He met Jehanna's gaze, and she nodded fiercely.

"Rally to me," T'kon boomed, flaring his lower nostrils. He sucked in deep breaths, growing a meter with every step. By the time he joined the defenders, he'd reached his full height.

He lobbed handfuls of flash grenades into the air over the enemy, then closed his eyes tightly.

Sharp flashes detonated in rapid succession. The instant they were over, T'kon opened his eyes and sprinted forward, running a Kthul through the back with his sword. He left the blade buried in the Kthul, and picked up the dead warrior's particle rifle instead.

He turned that weapon on the enemy, catching the Kthul's right flank in a crossfire with the defenders. They dropped quickly, and the enemy fell back. T'kon sprinted to the center of the pillars, hiding behind one near the center.

Several warriors fell in around him.

"We must cut a path through the traitors before they recover." T'kon passed out more flash grenades. The warriors looked dubiously at them, but no one turned them away. "Use these."

T'kon tossed a grenade into the air, ducking back behind the pillar. As soon as it detonated he charged the closest enemy, a Kthul in sickly green armor. The Kthul brought up his sword to block, but T'kon tossed a light grenade in his face, closing his eyes. A brief flash warmed his eyelids, and he opened them to find his opponent groping blindly. T'kon smashed the Kthul's face with the butt of his particle rifle, dropping him.

"How many of those do you have, husband?" Jehanna called from a neighboring pillar.

"I have about two dozen more," T'kon called, tossing another handful at a cluster of Kthul warriors. "That was something else I learned as a clanless hunter. Use any tool to win, and honor be damned. Ruthless warriors survive to the next battle."

"Pragmatic," Jehanna called, laughing, "and clearly effective."

T'kon spun around the next combatant, ripping his slug thrower from its holster and shooting him in the back. The elite stumbled off, clutching at his terrible wound, only to have Jehanna land on his shoulder and slash his throat with a tiny dagger. He still clutched at his throat when the explosive round detonated inside his torso.

All around them the Azi rallied, pushing back the attackers. T'kon sucked in a deep breath. "They are on the defensive. Cut them down. No mercy!"

His elites roared, surging forward in a wave. T'kon joined them, weaving between opponents with little conscious thought. The battle lasted mere moments—and an eternity—the lust carrying him through his enemy with intense fervor.

Finally, the last Kthul fell with a cry, and there was blessed silence.

T'kon tossed the Kthul particle rifle to the ground, panting. "We've won. Techsmith, to me."

A robed Saurian trotted over, arcanotome clutched in a death grip. "Yes, Clan Leader?"

"Send a message to all vessels to warp away. Head for site Theta." T'kon relaxed, gradually shrinking in size.

"At once, Clan Leader." The techsmith bowed, and backed away.

"We did it," Jehanna said, striding up as he returned to his lesser form. She smiled, laughing. But the smile faded, and her fur darkened to an uncertain red. "So what now? Where do we go?"

"That question weighs heavily," T'kon said, some of the joy leaving him. He looked out of the observation dome above them. "My heart says we should assault Imperalis with what we have. My head tells me that would end in disaster. Another course is warranted, but before I implement it we must purge our ranks of those sympathetic to the seekers. Then we will prepare to strike where they do not expect us."

14

CLANLESS

Kokar joined the warriors in the lowest tier, with Hruk trailing in his wake. He shifted uncomfortably. All around him, the best of the Nyar warrior caste stared, and he felt naked, despite wearing his best armor. Their contempt was an open challenge, but Kokar had no choice but to ignore it.

Instead, he focused on the hologram that had appeared on the royal dais before his father.

"Calm yourself, Kokar," Hruk whispered. "Do not let them see you fidget." He stared at the holoscreen as well, ignoring the others.

Kokar stilled himself, watching the hologram expectantly. A sea of multicolored particles resolved into a face he knew well: the scarred, furless face he'd last seen on Imperalis. Utfa's milky eyes stared smugly out at them.

"I have come to issue challenge," Utfa said, the words dripping scorn. "Tell me, Grak, will the legendary Nyar hide inside that little ball of rocks, or will you test your might against my clan? The Kthul have come at last, to scour you away at the will of our masters. If you refuse to fight, we will destroy your other worlds, one by one, until only this hiding place remains."

Grak ignored Utfa's taunt, but bright scarlet leapt into his fur. Utfa smiled.

Grak cocked his head, as if trying to understand his opponent. "You must know that only death awaits you here. Your fleet will be torn apart if you approach. We possess every advantage."

"In the skies, perhaps, but on the surface of that little world?" Utfa taunted. "If you meet me in the field, I will slaughter your people. My planetstriders will lay waste to your cities."

Kokar knew the seeker had struck another blow.

His father clenched his fists. His fur blackened. "Prepare your armies, seeker. We will meet you on the south slope, just outside the city."

"Perhaps you are not the coward I've heard you are. I have your word, then? You will allow my ground forces to safely warp in?" Utfa fixed his milky eyes on Grak. "I know that your Nyar honor won't allow you to break that word, but I have yet to hear you swear it."

"Very well. I swear it. Your planetstriders, and any vessel that is cruiser size or smaller, will be allowed to warp safely into our system. My dreadnoughts will not engage your vessels—but make no mistake, if you attempt any tricks they will blast your ships from the sky." Grak gave a low growl. "Now, prepare yourself, Kthul scum. Come find your death on the south slope."

Kokar's fur went ashen. He slumped into his seat, only dimly aware of Hruk's arm around him.

"Are you all right, lad?" Hruk asked.

"Father," Kokar roared, shooting to his feet.

His voice cut through the cacophony, and one by one, the

other Ganog fell silent as they realized that Grak was staring at his son.

Kokar waited for total silence before speaking again. "I urge you to reconsider. Shunt their fleet into the debris field, and let us end the Kthul once and for all."

"You would have me break my word?" Grak asked, his fur plunging into deep scarlet. "How have I raised such a coward? I know it cannot be your mother's doing. If she lived, she would be deeply ashamed—as I am shamed. We are on the eve of battle with our hated foes. We have every advantage. Yet you council us to fight like they do, to think as wretched Kthul. Have you not a shred of pride remaining?"

"Father, we must be greater than our pride. They *will* betray us. You know that. You gave your word, and Utfa will use those words to hang you with. He is vile and treacherous, but most of all he is devious. He wrested Imperalis from the Yog, and has poisoned all clans, even our own." Kokar knew that last accusation would draw his father's ire, so he plunged ahead. "Unless you wish to name your own son a liar, in front of all. You know what I saw, Father. One of our clan went over to the seekers, and were so far gone they attempted to assassinate the empress. If it's possible for one, then it could certainly happen again."

Grak unlimbered his chopping sword, his gaze murderous. "No, no more of your cowardly prattling. I name you clanless, Kokar. You are cast from our ranks. You may stay upon our world until the end of this battle, and then you will depart forever. If you are still here when I return from battle, I will deal your deathblow myself. I have no son."

Grak turned away and stalked from the chamber. Sharp whispers flowed through the Ganog ranks, as they too began to disperse.

Kokar ignored them. His fur shifted to a determined brown. So be it.

He turned from his father's retreating form, walking proudly from the hall. He saw the pain and indecision in Hruk's eyes, and it meant more than he could ever express when his mentor followed him from the chamber.

15

NYAR WILL FALL

Utfa took a deep breath, flaring his lower nostrils. He stared up at the floating ball of asteroids protecting his clan's oldest enemies. Three times in the course of Ganog history the Kthul had attempted to take this world. Each time they'd failed, either because they could not breach the warp anchor or because their ground forces were simply not strong enough.

This time, Nyar would fall. Utfa closed his eyes, savoring the pulses of data from his arcanotome. Coming into contact with a Nameless One carried a heavy price, but the rewards were great. He could *feel* his fleet readying.

The entire Void Wraith fleet—all eight hundred of them— had mobilized, ready to warp at his command. A niggling whisper in the back of his mind insisted that he shouldn't commit them all, that the Nyar could prove to be more canny than they appeared.

He was entrusting a great deal to their honor, and if they reneged on their agreement it would place him in a very difficult position. Of course, if he was honest with himself...he'd almost rather be rid of the Void Wraith altogether. They were potent, but he had no illusions about who they truly served.

The day would come when they were used against him, if he weren't careful.

A robed techsmith bowed low before Utfa. "Your command, emissary?"

"Initiate." He raised his hand to punctuate the command. Green-blue rippled briefly through his fur, and his stomachs gurgled. The fear would not be banished, even though he knew this day would deliver his greatest wish.

The world lurched and folded in on itself, and then Utfa was elsewhere. His dreadnought materialized at the rear of the fleet, and several dozen Ganog cruisers moved into a protective cloud around him. They looked so small and weak; no wonder the Nyar assumed themselves superior.

Utfa smiled as his little convoy made for the surface where, at this moment, his planetstriders were warping in. Only two— just enough to show that he was committed. The real threat would materialize only once he'd arrived, and by then it would be far too late for Grak and his pitiful defenders.

The holographic display shifted, populating with all the vessels in the system. His tome fed him additional data, giving context to what he was seeing. All eight hundred Void Wraith harvesters had cloaked, and were now swarming toward the warp anchor.

The rest of his forces were inbound to the planet, and the unsuspecting Nyar fleet had moved away from the anchor to hover over the ground battle. It was unlikely they'd intervene, but only a fool would leave such a potent weapon out of the battle.

That was exactly what Utfa had been expecting, and what Oako had predicted—and Utfa was ready for this eventuality.

He was unsurprised when the techsmith stepped forward, bowing.

"Emissary, the Ganog fleet leader is hailing us."

"Open a channel," Utfa said, smiling.

A holodrone walked over, and a lifelike version of an unfamiliar Ganog appeared, snarling. "You were warned not to bring any dreadnoughts. You have broken our agreement."

"I thought you'd allow my flagship," Utfa protested with mock innocence, "since I am not participating in the battle."

"Prepare yourself for battle, Kthul scum." The hologram vanished.

Utfa roared his laughter and, still chuckling, turned to the techsmith. "Unleash the Omegas. Once they've finished the ground forces, have them focus on the Nyar fleet."

16

A FOOL I'VE BEEN

"Cut them down," Grak bellowed, pointing at the enemy with his sword. "None survive!"

Hundreds of enlarged warriors surged forward, rushing down the gentle slope toward the waiting mass of enemies. Below them stood dozens of grounded enemy vessels —sleek, blue ships with predatory wings jutting out past the body. Ramps had lowered from every harvester, and rank upon rank of spindly blue robots advanced.

Most stood no taller than a Saurian, but one in twenty stood half as tall as a Ganog great form. Those larger ones could be a threat, judging by the particle cannons they carried. The weapons were unfamiliar, but Kokar had described them.

Grak leaned toward the battle, wishing he was joining the charge. He longed for the thrill of the bloodlust, the feel of an enemy breaking under his blade. But he had a greater responsibility. He must safeguard his people, leading them to victory with as few casualties as possible. Every Nyar was needed against the Nameless Ones. That meant a leader could not fill the role of warrior, however much he wished to.

The ground rumbled, then shook violently, in the way only

a planetstrider could cause—but it wasn't the enemy planet-striders. Both of those still stood in place, well outside the combat.

Three shapes appeared in the morning mist, the thick clouds obscuring them from the waist up. The legs weren't right for planetstriders. They were blue, just like the robots his clan now battled.

"These must be the Omegas that made Kokar piss himself," Grak snarled. He stalked forward, watching as his men engaged the Void Wraith. They rushed the first wave, crushing them.

Then the fallen began to explode. The explosions damaged Void Wraith and Ganog alike, flinging them about like refuse. Yet the Void Wraith numbers seemed infinite. They still marched from the vessels, rank upon rank wading into the combat.

The next rank of Nyar warriors took greater care, kicking or hurling fallen Judicators away from themselves before they could detonate. His people learned quickly, as their training demanded. They'd been bred and steeped in war, more so than any other clan. It was all they knew, the very reason for their existence: Stop the Nameless Ones, at any cost.

The Void Wraith lines began to crumble, and the enemy survivors were forced back toward the ships. Grak found himself more suspicious than pleased. This was too easy a victory. He turned his attention to the three figures in the mist. Their upper bodies were still obscured by the clouds, but they'd turned to face the Nyar ranks.

The ground rumbled in earnest now as the Nyar planet-striders advanced toward the Omegas. He'd ordered all seven into the fray, determined to force his opponent's retreat as soon as possible. The fact that Utfa had brought only two of the Kthul planetstriders was troubling.

A Saurian techsmith, cowering in her robes, appeared at his side. "Clan Leader, apologies. I have news."

"Deliver it," Grak ordered, still staring suspiciously at the Omegas. The planetstriders were slowly encircling them, both sides at extreme range. No one had fired yet.

"The warp anchor is under attack. Hundreds of Void Wraith vessels decloaked all around it. The station...is lost." The Saurian fell to her knees, warding herself with her arms.

Grak raised his head and roared, his fur surging into red-black. His vision clouded, and his more primal nature asserted itself. He slammed his foot down on the techsmith's back, crushing her spine.

His rage sated, he turned back to the Omegas. "So that is your game, Utfa. You draw my attention here, and then assault the warp anchor. As clever as it is dishonorable. But let us see how you fare on the ground."

Grak smiled grimly as his planetstriders surged forward and rushed the Omegas. The ground quaked violently under their lumbering charge. The first Omega turned toward them, sliding an enormous foot backward to brace itself. The motion peeled away the clouds, and a furious wind knocked Grak back a step.

For the first time, he saw the Omega fully. He blinked, and his jaw went slack. "It cannot be," he whispered.

He recognized the Omega, knew it as he knew the skin of his own face. What could it possibly mean? The cannon in the chest. The sleek, deadly arms. Every detail was the same, bringing him back to the pilgrimage he'd taken as a youth, to the tomb of Nyar.

Both planetstriders unleashed a hail of missiles, the flaming projectiles swarming the Omega. They detonated in a spectacular staccato, smoke and flame ballooning outward around the humanoid figure. The smoke obscured it, briefly, then cleared to show a shimmering veil of energy around the Omega.

The volley had done nothing.

The Omega thrust both arms forward, on either side of the cannon in its chest. The cannon began to glow. Light built, then the cannon discharged a beam of pure white that washed over both planetstriders. Everything touched by the beam disintegrated, evaporating into a fine mist that dissipated instantly. The remains of both planetstriders toppled to the slope, tumbling forward to rest at the Omega's feet. Their messy remains kicked up a fierce, foul-smelling wind.

The second and third Omegas moved to form a line with the first, both extending their arms just as the first had. Twin beams boiled away the sky, the first spearing Grak's oldest Planetstrider through the midsection. The second caught Worldender, disintegrating both reptilian legs.

"Techsmith," Grak bellowed, whirling until he spotted another cringing Saurian standing as far from the body of his fallen companion as he could get without being out of earshot. "Order all planetstriders to retreat to Derleth. What news from orbit?"

"Six Kthul dreadnoughts have warped in-system, and are moving to engage our fleet." The techsmith clutched its arcanotome, trembling.

"Order the fleet to Derleth as well." Grak's shoulders slumped. His fleet couldn't stand against the full might of the Kthul, not when the Kthul were backed up by an armada of these Void Wraith. He fell to his knees, dropping his axe to ground with a clatter. "I will be remembered as the clan leader who lost Nyar. I've been such a fool. What have I done?"

He stared up at the Omegas. None had fired a second shot, but that hardly mattered. His planetstriders were in full retreat, running until they were far enough away to safely warp. The

Omegas did not pursue. Instead they began walking toward the Ganog lines.

Grak's forces had reached the harvesters, and were locked in a fierce brawl with the last of the Void Wraith defenders. By the time they saw the advancing Omegas, it was too late. Fifty of his finest died in a single footstep, crushed into atoms by the incalculable weight of the Omega.

Wind whipped at Grak, but he refused to let it move him. He stood fast, staring hatefully at the Omega until the wind faded. Then he picked up his axe, holding it aloft with both hands. The Omega's foot rose, kicking up another gust of wind, and began to fall.

Grak dropped to one knee, using all his considerable strength to prop the blade aloft. If this was his end, he would meet it defiantly.

The titanic, blue foot blotted out the sun, giving a loud, low whistle as it approached. Then it crashed down on Grak, ending his shame.

17

DON'T DO THIS

Nolan leaned through the airlock, clinging to the doorway against the fierce wind. A pair of Ganog sprinted furiously toward him, the sound of their passage drowned out by panicked screams as vessels attempted to flee.

"Get on board," Nolan roared over the wind, stepping aside to allow Kokar to squeeze past. The Ganog's ever-present mentor slid inside a moment later. Nolan slammed the airlock button, and the door hissed shut behind them, bringing relative quiet. "Let's move to the cargo bay. We need to discuss a plan of action."

"A plan of action?" Hruk snorted. "This world is lost, fallen before the treachery of the Kthul."

"It falls before the stupidity of my father," Kokar snapped, whirling to face Hruk, "not because of the Kthul." He grabbed Hruk by the straps on his armor, tugging him closer. "I know you love him, Hruk, but in this he is wrong. Our people's fate may have been sealed, dooming us on the eve of the Nameless Ones' ascendance. If this human can help us fight back, then yes...we seek a plan of action." He released Hruk, and turned back to address Nolan. "Please, lead the way, Captain."

Nolan nodded, leading the pair up the corridor and into the main hangar. Predictably, Burke and his pilots all stood in small clusters. Each group of people was conveniently located near the stall where their mech was parked.

All eyes were on a view screen mounted high on the south wall, where it met the ceiling. Outside, the Void Wraith Omegas were tearing the Nyar defenders apart. Elites died by the score, and the survivors scattered like ants fleeing the destruction of their hill.

The perspective shifted slightly as the battleship shuddered into motion. Nolan couldn't see it, but he had no doubt that Burke had engaged cloaking the instant they'd left the dock. Theoretically, they'd just bought some breathing room.

"All right, Nolan, let's put this mess to bed," Burke called, walking to meet Nolan in the middle of the hangar. Alpha Company's pilots were all staring, most of their faces still hostile. "Give the word, and I'll warp us out of here. There's nothing we can do here, Captain."

Nolan noted the use of rank. "Major, I understand your sentiment, but we still have a job to do." He turned to Kokar. "How will your father respond to this invasion?"

"I do not know precisely what is happening," Kokar ventured, "especially in orbit. That will influence his decisions." His fur went a soft teal. Behind him, Hruk scowled.

"Kay, bring up a tactical display holo," Burke ordered, folding his arms. "One to a thousand, show the battle in orbit." He wore his displeasure openly, but he hadn't contradicted Nolan. Yet.

A hologram appeared next to them, its amber glow showing a miniature version of the battle. Void Wraith vessels were tagged all throughout the system, some around the fragmented remains of the warp anchor. Others were moving toward the Nyar fleet, which seemed to be retreating.

Kokar circled the hologram, studying the battle in orbit. "My father has ordered them to warp away, most likely to Derleth. That will keep our fleet from destruction here. He will send the planetstriders as well."

Nolan was watching the view screen still, which showed an Omega finishing off the last of the Ganog defenders. Nolan winced as it stepped on one of the last groups—the command group, he was fairly certain.

"Lad," Hruk rumbled, placing a furry hand on Kokar's shoulder. "Your father is gone."

Kokar didn't look at the view screen. He focused on the hologram, as if the departing Nyar fleet was carrying him away with it. Finally he turned to Nolan. "Our forces have abandoned this world."

"How many people live here?" Nolan asked.

"Eleven billion Ganog, and probably half again as many Saurians," Kokar ventured. "This is our most populous world."

"Nolan, this is no longer our problem," Burke said. "The Ganog now lack command authority. Their leadership is gutted. If we stay, we get gutted, too. It's time to bug out. Don't make this into an issue." His voice had gone taut.

Nolan turned to Burke, folding his arms as he stared up at the taller man. "Major, you remember how you said that the president had placed me in charge? I'm exercising my rights as mission commander. I hate to pull rank, but here it is: The Nyar fleet and some of their planetstriders escaped. They are still a significant military force, and our mission stands. Get them into the war on our side."

"Nolan, don't do this." Burke tensed, his hand moving to his sidearm. "Technically you've got authority, but you know exactly how far that goes. I'm not willing to let you get my men killed—not on some fool's errand."

"I know you're just protecting your people, but hear me out, Burke. We're cloaked. Right now, they can't detect us. With the warp anchor gone, we can leave at will. Let's find a safe place to land, and see if we can help their leadership rebuild. Kokar is the son of their clan leader. Maybe he can pull them together."

Nolan turned to Kokar, raising an eyebrow. Kokar didn't exactly look like he was brimming with confidence.

"He's right," Hruk rumbled, clapping Kokar on the back. "You warned us of the Void Wraith, and were right to tell us not to meet the Kthul in open battle. Our people will remember you spoke, despite the personal cost. Many of our officers survive, and they will be gathering our elites. If we can get them word that you live, we might be able to build a resistance."

"A resistance that can deal with those?" Burke snapped, stabbing a finger at the view screen. Onscreen, a hulking Omega stepped on a fleeing Ganog unit, then looked around for another target.

"We don't get to cherry-pick missions, Burke," Nolan snapped. "This one sucks, but we've got a job to do. Now get your men in line, and get this ship into cover. You handle patrols and security however you want, but you get us away from this spire and into the ruins of that city. Now."

Burke stared hard at him, and Nolan was painfully aware of Alpha pilots beginning to move in their direction.

Finally Burke spoke, "All right, Nolan. We'll play this your way. But you'd better be right, or I'll make damned sure you're not around to crow about it."

18

HALUT

Khar grabbed Zakanna, jumping from Takkar's command island. As they tumbled out of sight, he extended his wrist and fired a monofilament cable. The barbed hook sunk into the underside of the island, slowing their fall to a more controlled drop.

"Activate your stealth belt," Khar whispered, thumbing the switch on his. Energy crackled soundlessly over his fur, mapping movements all around him. In a moment he faded from sight, only a faint shimmer betraying his location.

A moment later Zakanna did the same. "Where are you leading us?" came her disembodied voice. Her arms tightened around him, and he was impressed that she trusted him enough to offer no protest when being tackled off the side of a floating island.

"Down to the slums along the hull," Khar explained. "We'll take the lift on that island there, the one with the trees. I used it last time."

They descended rapidly, and Khar kicked hard to send them arcing toward the island.

"How long is that cable?" Zakanna asked, with just a touch of nervousness.

"Three thousand meters. We have plenty of slack," Khar said, guiding them in a controlled fall. He slowed his wrist winch, willing his nanochrons into his feet, and landed hard. The nanochrons bled away the kinetic energy, and Khar set Zakanna down. "We can use that transport there."

"The cargo lift?" Zakanna asked. "I guess they won't expect that. I should be able to hold my breath long enough, but it will be difficult."

Khar began moving toward the strange transport system. The glob of amber liquid disgorged a stick-like alien, then another pushed a cart full of fruit into the bubble. Khar made his way between strange, pink trees, creeping toward the structure. His sensors detected Zakanna's faint heat signature, putting her about three meters behind him. It spoke to her training that he didn't need to tell her to maintain a little distance.

Khar paused next to the pod as another stick-like alien exited the glob of amber, and then he dove in, feeling the familiar cool liquid envelop him. The goo pushed him toward the center of the bubble, and a moment later, a warm, furry form was pressed against him.

Zakanna wrapped her arms around his waist, so he put an arm around her shoulders. Whether she needed comfort or hoped to give it was unclear. It didn't really matter. They could be dead soon, and a warrior stole what moments he could.

The goo hardened into a thick, rubbery gel, freezing them in place. The glob descended toward the base of the ship, a maze of poorly constructed warrens crisscrossing the hull. Unlike the last time he'd come here, not a single figure moved between the hovels. Not one. Clearly, they could hear the battle raging above.

Finally, the glob stopped three meters above the ground, forcing them through the liquid, toward the ground. Khar landed in a crouch, and heard Zakanna land a moment later.

"Head down the road to our left," he said. "We'll meet at the intersection."

He trotted up the narrow alley, squeezing past refuse receptacles and the occasional vehicle. He led Zakanna down the same route he'd taken when originally fleeing Takkar, pausing at each intersection to give instructions.

"Tell me about this *ka'tok* we're going to meet," Zakanna said, from somewhere to his right. "The conversation will help us keep track of each other."

"His name is Halut," Khar explained, starting up a narrow passageway that seemed familiar. He remembered the red sign on the building they were passing. "He's a Whalorian. When I was here last, he helped me reach the docking bay. I stowed away in the cargo hold of a freighter. That's how I arrived on your world."

She was silent for a moment, though he could hear her footsteps. He suspected that was by design.

"It must have been terrifying, trapped on an enemy world surrounded by unfamiliar things." Her tone conveyed her sympathy.

"There were...uncomfortable moments of doubt," Khar admitted. They turned left onto a wider street, and in the distance Khar could see the bunker, butting up against the wall of the ship itself. "Yet is that not what we are trained to face? It cannot have been any more difficult than holding court. You were surrounded by enemies, every day. You knew they wanted you to fail, yet you persevered. You played the role they wanted you to play, but did it masterfully enough to turn their games back upon them."

"Did I?" Zakanna asked bitterly. "They hold Imperalis, and are about to take this dreadnought."

"A war is not judged by its first battle," Khar countered. "Unlike Fizgig, I *have* suffered defeat. Many times. Each time, I survived. In the end, I played an important role in destroying the Gorthian Eye. This war may appear to be going badly, but until it is over we will keep fighting to turn it in our favor."

"Thank you, Khar," Zakanna replied. "Sometimes it is difficult to keep moving under the weight of our problems, but you remind me that we do not have the luxury of despair."

The air around Khar began to ripple and fold, time stretching into infinity as the world warped around him. When the process finally stopped, he peered up at the top of the dreadnought.

Zakanna confirmed his suspicion. "We've returned to Imperalis."

"We should hurry. Eventually they'll find Aluki's cruiser."

They continued in silence after that, finally reaching the bunker. It was just as dilapidated as before, the corrugated metal rusting and dirty. The "door"—a simple hunk of bent metal wedged into the doorway—was closed.

"Halut," Khar called through a gap in the doorway. "It is Khar. I have returned, and need your assistance." He heard shuffling inside, then Halut's blue-suited head appeared at the gap.

"Mmm, Khar? I do not understand. We got you off the ship. How did you return? Why?"

"If you will let my companion and I inside, we can explain," Khar offered. He checked his power reserves. The belt was down to forty-two percent charge, but his own reserves were much higher. He could recharge both belts if necessary, though it would take time.

"Of course, of course." Halut heaved the door from the

doorway, moving the metal against the wall with surprising ease.

Khar followed him inside, deactivating his stealth belt. A moment later Zakanna appeared as well. Halut moved the door back into the frame, then waddled over to join them.

"What is all the fighting about above, and who is your friend?" Halut asked. He hopped up on the narrow bed, and gestured at his one chair.

Zakanna sat.

"This is Zakanna, of the Yog," Khar explained.

"Empress Zakanna?" Halut asked, paling under his suit. His big eyes blinked up at Khar.

"Former empress," Zakanna corrected. "The Kthul relieved me of both my world and my throne."

Halut made a series of hoots that were untranslatable. He laid down on the bed. "You've brought the empress herself into my hovel. Do you realize what you've done?"

Khar did. "I am sorry, Halut. If there were not so much at stake, I wouldn't have come."

"I'll have to flee," Halut said, hopping down from the bed. "I can't stay, not now. They'll be coming for you, and when they arrive they'll give me to the melters." He began hastily packing his few belongings into a stained, brown sack. "Please tell me you have some sort of plan."

"We do," Khar explained hastily. "There is a cruiser waiting for us in the docking bay. If we can reach it, that cruiser can cloak, just as you saw us do. We'll be able to escape down to the planet. You can come with us, Halut."

"Well, I suppose it can't be any worse than here," he muttered. His narrow shoulders slumped. "I've only stayed because I hoped I'd hear word of my wife. I suppose that's unrealistic."

Khar placed a comforting paw on Halut's back. "Again, my apologies, my friend."

"Your sacrifice will be rewarded, Whalorian," Zakanna said. "And you have my apologies for embroiling you in our conflict. I realize that is not fair. But I must ask: Do you have a way to get us to the cruiser undetected? If we travel through these warrens, we'll never make it."

"Oh, I have just the thing," Halut said, giving a wide, baleen grin. "You won't much like the smell, but I can promise we won't be seen."

19

SANITATION DUCTS

Zakanna darted a nervous glance over her shoulder, then one above. Threats could come from any direction—either the lawless slums they walked through or a Ganog patrol sent to find her.

"Mmm, this way," Halut said, waddling quickly down an alley. He paused, glancing in both directions before he moved to the wall. He removed a black, metal triangle from his suit and pressed it against the grimy hull.

Zakanna followed, resisting the urge to flip the switch on the stealth belt Fizgig had so graciously given her. There was little point in it, since they had no way to cloak Halut.

"Will we be out of sight soon?" Khar rumbled, squatting next to the Whalorian.

Khar treated the *ka'tok* with the same honor and respect he reserved for her. She found that...odd. She'd already known his culture had different customs, but this one was the most puzzling. They had no barriers between castes, yet still maintained order somehow.

"Just a moment." Halut tapped the metal hull, and a panel slid open. His stubby fingers flew across a keyboard, and a door slid open a few meters to their right. Halut typed one more sequence, then waddled toward the door. "I set it to close in a few moments. Inside, quickly."

Khar followed Halut through the doorway, so Zakanna did the same. Her lower nostrils clenched shut involuntarily as the stench hit her in a palpable wave. She stepped inside a dark corridor, suppressing a gag, and hunched her shoulders to prevent her fur from touching the glistening ceiling. The sludge coating the surface appeared to be the source of the terrible stench, which grew immeasurably worse when the door slid shut behind her.

"This is, quite literally, the worst situation I can imagine," she choked out, futilely covering her mouth and nose with a hand.

"Mmm, these are sanitation ducts. All waste flows through here, from every part of the ship. The ducts had to be made large enough for cleaning, so we will be able to follow them directly to the cargo bay," Halut explained. He began moving cheerfully up the crouched corridor. "Not even techsmiths come here—only *ka'tok*. Even my people avoid them, because of the smell."

Zakanna followed, using the considerable grace she'd learned from Yulo to avoid touching any of the walls. The stench was almost a physical thing, and she longed to flee. But she forced herself to follow Khar, who in turn followed Halut. She didn't want to appear weak in front of either. Especially Khar.

They passed through corridor after corridor, each passage emitting the same abhorrent stench.

Khar looked over his shoulder in her direction. "This is one more example of the things I find puzzling about your military. My people would never allow such a design flaw."

"It cannot be that great a flaw," Zakanna pointed out.

"These vessels have served the Ganog for over two dozen millennia—perhaps even longer—and during that time I've never heard of these ducts being exploited."

"Mmm, do you really believe such things would be recorded?" Halut asked, keeping his tone deferential. "We *ka'tok* have become very good at avoiding the notice of the leadership caste. There are all sorts of things going on right underneath your feet, but since we are beneath your notice you are unaware of them."

Zakanna found the Whalorian's words troubling, because they contained an alarming amount of sense. She'd never given *ka'tok* a second thought. She even ignored lower noble families, and certainly ignored techsmiths. How many signs had she missed? How many wayposts that could have warned her about her imminent fall?

"Perhaps that will work in our favor here," she said, lamely. What must Khar think of her, and her people?

They continued in silence, eventually reaching a metal catwalk that passed over a river of sludge. If the stench had been bad before, it was overpowering now. Zakanna's chest tightened, and spots danced across her vision as they crossed the bridge. She moved mechanically, forcing herself forward. Neither Khar nor Halut seemed to be suffering, and she fiercely envied them.

On the other side, the stench lessened and became almost bearable as they left it behind them. She paused, sucking in lungfuls of air.

"What's that?" Khar asked suddenly.

Zakanna froze, listening. She heard a faint thrumming roar in the background. "That's a transport thruster. We must be near the docking bays."

They hurried forward with renewed enthusiasm, finally entering a corridor with a metal grating above. Sludge leaked down the walls, apparently dropped from above. At least it was less foul than that in the sewer. She could hear voices now—Saurians calling out to each other in their harsh tongue.

"Mmm, we are here," Halut said. "This is the docking bay you wanted. Forgive me, but I will wait here while you ensure the way is safe."

Khar nodded, climbing up a row of rungs set into the wall. He reached the grate at the top and peered through.

Zakanna ascended after him, but couldn't make out much. "What do you see?" she called softly.

"The cruiser is there, and a group of Saurians are trying to get inside." He looked down at her with those slitted eyes, whiskers twitching. "There are six of them, but they do not know we are here. I believe we can surprise them."

"I'm ready," Zakanna said, eager for the coming conflict. "These poor Saurians are about to get all the aggression and frustration I've built up today."

Khar gave her a feral smile. "I almost pity them."

20

LIFE DEBT

Khar heaved at the metal grate, bracing his feet against the rungs set into the wall. It groaned, stuck fast from years of accumulated grime. Khar strained harder, ordering his nanochrons to increase his strength. The grate came loose with a pop, a noise which was fortunately covered by the rush of a cruiser landing in the next docking bay.

He poked his head up, holding the grate above him with both hands. The Saurians were all focused on the ship and seemed unaware of him. He grinned, slowly setting the grate down, and climbed from the sanitation ducts. As he did, he flicked the switch on his stealth belt.

Zakanna did the same, her heat signature rising behind him.

"Take the trio on the right," he whispered, picking up the grate again, "and I'll go left."

"I'll be swift," she replied. "You do the same."

Khar threw the grate with all his considerable strength. The Saurian's spine broke with a sharp crack, and the creature collapsed to the deck.

The other Saurians spun, seeking a source of the attack. Khar circled wide, padding silently behind his enemies. He waited until Zakanna, still stealthed, snapped a Saurian's neck, then glided forward. Igniting his plasma blade, he rammed it into the closest Saurian and forced it up through the surprised guard's chest.

The next Saurian spun, firing a hasty burst from his plasma pistol. The scarlet beam shot into his dying companion, finishing the work Khar's blade had started. Khar hurled the corpse at the next enemy, his enhanced strength knocking the last Saurian into the wall with enough force to knock him unconscious. Khar glided forward and made certain the Saurian would never rise again.

He rose in time to see Zakanna finish her second opponent, crushing his nose into his brain with a flat-handed strike.

"Khar," Zakanna called urgently.

He looked toward the wide corridor that led deeper into the dreadnought. Four Ganog elites were charging into the room.

"I see them," he called back. "We must eliminate them if we wish to get Halut aboard the vessel."

"I will try," she called, closer now. "One we could do, perhaps two. But four? I do not see how it can be done."

"How much energy does your belt have?" Khar asked, attempting to formulate a plan.

"About 30 percent. Plenty for an extended combat. What do you have in mind?"

"We stay cloaked, and harry them," Khar suggested. "Pick up the pistols the Saurians were using. It will take time, but we can bring them down." It wasn't a great plan, but it could be effective if they executed it well.

"All right."

One of the pistols drifted into the air. It began to fire, a trio of scarlet pulses that shot into the closest elite. The flesh cooked off his cheek, and the last bolt caught him in the eye. He staggered back with a roar, slapping one hand over the wound as he attempted to find a target.

Zakanna dropped the pistol, and her heat signature moved quickly away. Khar leapt up the wall, igniting his wrist blade and ramming it into the rusted metal. He planted his feet and waited for one of the Ganog to pass directly underneath his perch.

Khar dropped onto the unsuspecting Ganog's back, plunging his blade into the Ganog's right eye. The Ganog roared and raised a giant arm to swat him away, but Khar extinguished his blade and dove from the Ganog's shoulder. He rolled silently away, scurrying back into the shadows.

These sorts of guerrilla tactics would kill the Ganog eventually, but a single mistake would cost him or Zakanna—or both—their lives. The Ganog, on the other hand, could make many mistakes and still survive.

Khar didn't like the odds or the game, but saw no other way to get Halut onto the ship.

Zakanna cried out, her cloak failing as she was flung into a wall by a random kick. She rolled back to her feet and dodged a follow-up kick from the same elite. The other elites moved in her direction now that they had a visible target.

Khar maneuvered behind them, picking up a rifle that had belonged to one of the dead Saurians. He took careful aim, then shot the one-eyed Ganog in the shoulder. It turned to face him, and Khar gently stroked the trigger. A scarlet pulse caught the Ganog in his remaining eye, blinding him fully. He charged awkwardly in Khar's direction, roaring as he flailed about with his arms.

The other three Ganog were still focused on Zakanna, and she was out of room to run. Khar thought furiously, but there was nothing he could do directly.

He opened a comm channel to the cruiser. "Aluki, if you can hear me, this is Khar. We're trying to board, and in need of assistance."

Aluki's voice boomed from the loudspeakers. "Mmm, Khar, it is good to hear your voice. I wondered who was attacking the elites, but didn't want to intervene until I knew who I was dealing with."

Two turrets on the underside of the cruiser pivoted to take aim, then unleashed a volley of scarlet death. All three elites were riddled with plasma fire. Each tumbled to the ground, and the scent of burnt fur filled the room. Khar was thankful to be insulated from the unpleasantness.

"How many people are we extracting?" Aluki asked over the loudspeaker.

"Myself, Zakanna, and a Whalorian friend named Halut," Khar said into the comm.

"Halut?" Aluki's voice rose a half-octave, booming from the speakers.

"I'm coming, wife," Halut called, huffing his way over the last rung. He rolled to his feet, and waddled with impressive speed toward the cruiser's docking door. By the time he arrived, the door was sliding open, and Aluki rushed out to embrace him.

"You two know each other?" Khar asked, cocking his head in confusion. It seemed unlikely that the only two Whalorians he'd ever met knew each other—though he supposed stranger things had happened.

"I don't even care about the stench." Aluki seized Halut in a fierce hug, crying and giving quick, little hoots of joy. "I'd given up hope of finding you. How did you get here?"

"Mmm, Khar stumbled through my hovel and I helped him escape to the surface," Halut explained, hugging Aluki just as fiercely. "Then he brought the empress. That's who we're saving."

Aluki disengaged from Halut, blinking up at Zakanna's muck-spattered form. "Mmm, well, let's be on our way before more Ganog show up. Once we're safe, you can tell me the whole story of your escape. Khar, I owe you a life debt for reuniting me with my husband. I will never forget this."

21

REUNITED

Khar leaned against the door, staring out the viewport at the rapidly growing world below. The sun illuminated the rich purple on the daylight side of the planet. The mighty city of Imperalis was invisible from orbit.

"The last time I made the trip," he rumbled, "if you'd told me that I'd not only be returning, but that circumstances would be even more dire...I'd have named you a liar."

Zakanna sighed. "I'm happy to be returning, though I wish circumstances were better." She pressed her face against the port. Her fur was still spattered from the sanitation ducts. "I should be grateful to be alive, but I'm just so frustrated. I have no idea how we're going to secure the beacon. Our armies are gone. Our fleets have scattered."

"This mission was never going to be about armies," Khar said, resting a hand on her shoulder. "It hinges on the success of a small team—and whatever we've lost, we still possess that."

She stared up at him with those wide eyes.

Aluki's voice over the loudspeaker ended the moment.

"Mmm, come up to the cockpit, please. We are about to reach atmosphere."

Khar watched for a moment longer as the ship zoomed past the edge of the ring of ice and rock orbiting the planet.

"I suppose we'd better go," Zakanna said. She strode up the corridor leading from the cargo bay to the bridge—if it could be called that. It was a small cockpit, just big enough for the pilot and copilot. Behind that was a room with a table in the center. Benches lined the walls, allowing up to eight people to gather.

Aluki and Halut were already seated, holding hands under the table. It was nauseatingly cute; were Fizgig here, she would retch at the sight of it.

And if she didn't, the lingering stench from the sanitation ducts would certainly have the same effect.

Zakanna slid onto a bench, and Khar dropped down next to her. Aluki leaned up, peering over the table at them. "You are the empress of the mighty Ganog Imperium. Mmm, you have a plan to deal with our current situation?"

A ripple of scarlet—the first Khar had ever seen—passed briefly through Zakanna's fur. She glared hard at Aluki. "Do not speak to me that way, *ka'tok*. Or you will very quickly come to regret it."

"Do not call her that," Halut growled, rising to his feet atop the bench. "You have no idea who she is, you ignorant fool."

"Halut," Aluki snapped, eyeing him sternly. "Mmm, now is not the time."

"Now is exactly the time," he countered, eyeing her back just as sternly. He planted tiny hands on his wide hips.

Khar started to laugh, a deep booming, freeing laugh. They were all looking at him now. "Our peoples stand at the brink of eradication. We are hopelessly outmatched. We have little chance of success. Yet you are concerned about how we address each other?" He shook his head, still chuckling. "Do we not all seek the same goal? Can we not set aside this petty bickering?"

"You are right." Aluki gave a surprisingly graceful bow. "Apologies for any offense myself or my husband offered, Empress. My question was genuine. Did you have a plan to approach the world? A destination? Right now we are safely cloaked and orbiting, so there is time to decide, I think."

"What did you mean?" Zakanna demanded, directing the question at Halut. "Who is she?"

"She is one of our most renowned lore keepers. Mmm, while you Ganog have been busy beating yourselves senseless, we have quietly learned all there is to know about your history. Aluki knows more of your ancestors than you do," Halut taunted. Aluki glared at him, and he moderated his tone. "You believe yourselves so superior, but for seventeen centuries my people have maintained a government right under your nostrils."

Khar's attention was drawn briefly to the viewport. They were passing directly over the capital; its ivory towers reached for the sky. He magnified his vision and the city leapt into sharper focus. Three blue giants, each surrounded by planet-strider mounds, stood in a rough triangle around the city. Countless ranks of Judicators were arrayed at their feet.

Zakanna stared too, horror and disgust blooming on her face. He couldn't imagine what it was like for her, returning to find her home occupied by enemies.

"I..." She brushed the port with her fingers, face anguished.

Khar recognized the weight of the revelation. He'd undergone the same the first time he'd challenged Fizgig. He'd believed himself the best, and she'd rudely disabused him of the notion. His whole world had shattered, and he'd had to build a new understanding from the pieces.

"I've been so blind," she said. "To everything. Not just Utfa, but...the Whalorians maintained a government? How?"

Aluki gave a wide grin. "Mmm, we are invisible. Your leadership caste cannot even read. You've had an oral education, but I can simply pick up a chip reader, or even a scroll. The mystical skill your seekers practice—and some of your techsmiths—is something all of my people are taught from birth. We've slowly built a massive data repository, and that is copied as often as possible. It contains not just our history, but everything we've learned of you, the Saurians, and every other race we've encountered."

"When you ask if I have a plan, you already know that I do not." Zakanna's shoulders slumped, and her fur faded to a wistful blue. She looked up suddenly. "But *you* do. Don't you?"

"Of course she does," Halut muttered under his breath.

Khar fixed him with a baleful eye, casually licking his chops, and Halut scooted back in his seat.

"From our limited understanding of the beginnings of your empire," Aluki explained, "the Ganog were never literate. Initially, the seekers were your scholar caste. They carried your knowledge. However, they also directly served the Nameless Ones. Mmm, when Nyar led your people against the Nameless Ones, most of the seekers were put to death. Their libraries were destroyed—full planetary bombardment in some cases."

"This is fascinating," Khar said, "but what does it have to do with a plan?" He had no patience for this kind of prattling; he'd dealt with enough of it from Tigris scientists, like Lena.

"Mmm, I'm getting there," Aluki chastised. "Please be patient."

Khar nodded apologetically.

"The ancient seeker library was in the lava fields south of the Royal Spire. There's a reason that area is now a lava field—the seekers gathered there to discuss a final defense, and were eradicated by Yog. Not 'the' Yog, interestingly. Yog, the singular word."

"You think this library is still there?" Zakanna asked.

"It could be—and if it is, who knows what it might contain?" Aluki smiled again. "We could learn about the Void Wraith, or about the defenses of the Royal Spire. It is a place to start, to learn more than we currently do."

"It's the beginnings of a plan," Zakanna admitted, "and certainly more than I can offer. Thank you, Aluki. I apologize for denigrating you and your people."

"Mmm, we are both products of our upbringing," Aluki said. "The fact that you are willing to change your opinions bodes well for your future as a ruler." She hopped down from the bench and waddled to Zakanna, patting her knee. "If we survive this, perhaps you will be the one to build your people into something greater than they are now."

22

SPIT IN DEATH'S EYE

Fizgig stared upward through the top of the vessel, directly into space. It was a magnificent feat of technology, giving the appearance that they were floating through space with no ship. Above, a new star had appeared, and the vessel somehow polarized the light so she didn't have to squint.

A single world orbited that star, and it grew increasingly larger as they approached. Two rings of ice and rock floated around a purple world, painting a beautiful tapestry. She appreciated the beauty, even as she dreaded what would happen upon their arrival.

"Do you think there was any way to avoid our sacrifice?" Takkar asked, raising his head listlessly. He'd planted his back against a pillar, and both hands were wrapped around the haft of the axe their captors had allowed him to keep.

They'd left Fizgig's stealth belt and plasma blade as well, almost as if daring them to escape. She'd considered doing exactly that, but with Aluki's cruiser gone there'd be no easy way off the dreadnought.

"You know there wasn't," she replied, tail slashing an angry arc behind her. "Do not sink into self-pity, Ganog. We did what we must to preserve our respective peoples. T'kon escaped. And, judging by the activity below, they've not caught Khar either. Goddess willing, he's already left this vessel."

"Do not provoke me, little Tigris," Takkar said, catching her gaze. His fur darkened, but only slightly. There wasn't much heat to his words.

"You've given up. You've accepted that you are already dead." Fizgig said as she rose to her feet and stalked over to Takkar, ignoring the pain in her leg.

"You do not understand the magnitude of what we face. Azatok has been the champion of the Royal Games six out of the last seven times." Takkar rose to his feet as well, setting the blade of his axe atop a furry shoulder. "The only year he lost was to Krekon, and that was an upset. Krekon lost the very next year, and never fought in the games again."

"So you fear this warrior?" Fizgig asked. "Understandable, I suppose. You've no chance of besting him?"

"None," Takkar admitted. "During my youth I was a canny fighter, and gained admittance to the games seven times. I won once, but only by chance. I was skilled, but never the best. And that was a great many years ago."

"Then what will you do?" Fizgig asked. She knew her own answer, but Takkar must decide for himself. This was his battle, his final test, from the sound of it.

"I will battle to the best of my ability. During the fight I will seek to wound him, as badly as I can. I want him to remember me every time he takes a step, or bends to don his armor." Takkar's fur darkened to a deep scarlet. "I want him to remember me with respect."

"Then do exactly that," Fizgig offered. "No more talk of 'could we have acted differently.' We took the bold course, and now we pay a bold price. Pay it gladly. If I survive, I will carry the tale to your people. If I do not, then make your enemy do it for you. Make this Azatok respect you enough that he tells the tale of your death."

"I hate you, you know," Takkar said, inspecting the blade of his axe. "Before you, I was the foremost fleet leader in the Imperium. My star never stopped rising. I won every battle."

"It made you complacent," Fizzig said, grooming an errant patch of fur on her shoulder. "You believed yourself better than others. You rested on past victories, content that there was no one powerful enough to best you."

"Yes," Takkar admitted. "I was arrogant, and you proved it. I thought your species weak, and your tactics foolish. I charged into your trap, and I paid the price."

"There is always someone better, Takkar," Fizzig said, looking up at him. "Always. Khar was arrogant when I first met him. I taught him this critical lesson, making him a better warrior. Nolan, on the other hand, had received little combat training when we met. He had no such pride, or illusions that he was skilled. Even now he underestimates his own abilities, and that humility serves him well. He never stops learning."

"Nolan, the human who bested Krekon?" Takkar asked.

She nodded. "Krekon, like you, probably assumed Nolan was no threat. And, had he fought intelligently, perhaps Nolan wouldn't have been. I reviewed the combat footage. There were two moments where Krekon could have ended the fight, but chose not to. That allowed Nolan to surprise him—a fatal mistake."

"One I hope Azatok makes," Takkar said, sighing. "We have arrived at Imperalis. He will send for us tonight."

"Let him," Fizzig said, hackles raising. "So long as we draw breath, we are a threat. Make him underestimate you, and then go for the throat."

23

DEFIANT

Takkar rolled his shoulder, wincing at the stiffness. Azatok had allowed them a single night to rest, then summoned him to the arena. Takkar had come willingly, ready for an end to this.

He stooped to pick up a handful of dirt from the arena floor, rubbing it across both palms. It would firm his grip on the axe—and besides, the ritual calmed him.

He'd settled firmly into the haak. He knew he was going to die facing Azatok, but he didn't care about that. His nervous tension came from wondering about the manner of his death. Would he be able to injure the mighty champion, to capitalize on Azatok's arrogance as Fizgig had capitalized on his own?

A smattering of jeers came from the pleasure platforms above. Takkar had expected that, from the Kthul at least. He'd even have expected it from the Azi, as they had reason enough to hate him. But the Yog were normally too proper, and the Vkash had lauded him as a hero their whole lives. To see those two clans adding to the derision? It was maddening, as if the fabric that held the Imperium together was at last unravelling.

Much to his surprise, Takkar spotted Fizgig sitting like an

Adept atop a simple transport disk. Azatok must want her to witness Takkar's death. The brute enjoyed all forms of torment, so perhaps Takkar should not be surprised.

After Takkar fell, Fizgig would likely die soon after—as soon as Azatok bored of tormenting her.

"Azatok!" Takkar roared, spinning slowly in place as he hefted his axe. His voice echoed, stilling the whispers above. "Great champion of the arena. Come and face me."

A single disk whirred into view, pausing next to the edge of the arena. Azatok hopped off, armed with nothing but a pair of daggers. Takkar's eyes narrowed at the insult. It stoked the fires within him, and he allowed a deep, smug orange to enter his fur.

Azatok blinked at that, clearly surprised. He'd no doubt sought to infuriate Takkar, which was an expected tactic. Takkar was known for his temper. Yet Fizgig's words still rang in Takkar's ears. Death would claim him this day; nothing could change that. But at the end, could he rise above himself and become greater?

"You forgot your axe." Takkar spat in the dirt at Azatok's feet. "I will let you go back and fetch it."

Azatok's fur reddened, and his eyes narrowed. He rested his hands on the hilts of his daggers. "We both know I don't need an axe to kill you, Takkar. When you are dead I will leave your body here to rot, and I will claim your axe—but not to use. No. I will have it melted down, and all mention of your name stricken from the whispers. It will be as if you never existed."

"Will it?" Takkar asked calmly, as if such a thing were of no concern. He slowly twirled his axe. "Perhaps you'll kill me today. Perhaps not. Either way, you cannot erase my victories, Azatok. You cannot erase the fact that my clan bested yours, under my command. You cannot change the fact that I have captured more worlds than any in a generation, and that even after my losses to the Coalition my battle record still rings truer than your own."

Azatok growled, exposing his teeth as he stalked closer. His fur changed to midnight—the blackest rage. He twirled his daggers, beginning the breathing. Takkar began his breathing as well, slowly circling opposite Azatok.

Each combatant grew in size, every breath adding to their height. They continued for many heartbeats, until both topped ten meters. They maintained their relative heights, with Azatok being a meter shorter. Takkar had a slightly longer reach, normally. Using daggers added to that, increasing Takkar's advantage.

Takkar used that advantage, striking at Azatok the instant he'd finished his breathing. Takkar sprinted toward his opponent, his axe humming through the air as he lashed out at Azatok's knee. As expected, Azatok vaulted the weapon. Takkar released the haft with his right hand, completing the swing with his left. He balled his right hand into a fist, using the momentum of the swing to slam it into Azatok's face.

The Kthul's nose split; blood spurted into the air. The crack of his head snapping back echoed through the arena, triggering a deep *oooh* from the crowd.

Takkar danced backward, keeping his weapon between them, and grinned at his opponent. His fur remained a smug, infuriating orange.

"You're faster than I expected, old man," Azatok spit out. His eyes narrowed, and swirls of red swept through the black. "I'd planned to toy with you, but I think you need to learn humility before I end your life."

He leapt at Takkar, his arms windmilling. The first dagger struck, and Takkar knocked it aside with his axe. The second dagger flashed down, slipping into Takkar's thick neck just over the armor.

Takkar roared in agony as the blade pierced his flesh. He dropped his axe and seized Azatok by the shoulders. Then he lunged, slamming his forehead into Azatok's face. Once, twice, a third time.

Azatok bellowed in pain, then delivered a head butt of his own. The blow sent Takkar staggering back; he released Azatok and raised a hand briefly to the wound at his neck. Thick, black blood rushed out. The fight would be over soon.

Takkar studied Azatok. His nose had been shattered, and his left eye was already beginning to swell. Neither was a critical wound, but that could work to Takkar's favor. Azatok might think the fight was already over. Takkar sprinted forward, roaring as he leapt into the air over Azatok.

Azatok couldn't ignore the obvious opportunity; he rammed a dagger into Takkar's gut. His other dagger flashed out, aimed at Takkar's eye. Takkar ducked to the side, and the blade traced a path of pain along his cheek.

Takkar seized Azatok's wrist, wrenching with all his might. Bone cracked as they landed, and Azatok bellowed a second time. He ripped the dagger from Takkar's gut with a sickening pop. Takkar sucked in a pained breath, but twisted the already broken wrist further out of alignment.

Azatok roared, then rammed his dagger into Takkar's eye. Takkar went limp, and he was dimly aware of toppling onto his back. He stared up at the sky with his one good eye. Pieces were missing from his mind. Everything was disjointed.

Azatok glared down, cradling his hideously broken wrist. Takkar saw the bone jutting through the skin, and was pleased. His gaze slid away from Azatok, to the crowd above. He found Fizgig, met her gaze.

She nodded respectfully.

Takkar nodded back, then sighed his final breath.

24

CALLED TO ACCOUNT

Utfa stepped from the shadows shrouding the docking port and nodded at the approaching cloaked figure. Vessels hummed all around them, disgorging important fleet leaders and their retinues. No one else was allowed this high on the spire—technically, not even a seeker.

Utfa went where he pleased. He ruled this world, in the name of his masters.

"I do not appreciate being summoned like a *ka'tok*," Azatok snarled, clenching a massive fist as he stalked up to Utfa. The other was wrapped in a dark, black medicast. "I am reigning champion of the Royal Games, and the fleet leader who delivered both the Yog and the Vkash into your hands."

"You delivered some of them," Utfa said, shaking his head, schooling his expression to disappointment. "As I understand, T'kon seized back his vessel and led three other dreadnoughts to safety. Fully a third of the enemy fleet lives—out there, somewhere. They've purged our spies, or we'd have their location by now."

"Is that what you're worried about? The tattered remains of

a broken fleet? Sooner or later, one of our spies will reveal their location, and we will destroy them. They are no threat." Azatok's laugh boomed around them. "You have the heart of an old woman, Utfa. Are you so far removed from your days as a warrior?

Utfa reached up, slowly removing his cowl.

Azatok flinched at the sight of Utfa's furless head. This was a common reaction; the Nameless Ones were slowly remaking his body in their image. It didn't bother Utfa—in fact, he reveled in the horror he saw on Azatok's face.

"Yes, you see now. Don't you? I have been touched *directly* by the Nameless Ones, Azatok. I am their instrument, the emissary of their will. I believe that you sometimes forget about our masters, that you dismiss our faith as some sort of empty religion, like the *ka'tok* believe. A story we tell ourselves, but not one that we will witness in our lifetimes. Tell me, Azatok—is your faith in need of...ministration?"

Azatok dropped his gaze. "No, emissary. What is their dark will?"

Another cruiser hummed by overhead, disgorging passengers onto the ring so they could enter the spire. There weren't nearly as many as they'd find below, but it was still too many for Utfa's liking. He didn't want his words overheard, but sometimes a loud, crowded place was the best place to convey secrets.

"The empress lives," Utfa growled, narrowing his eyes. He leaned closer to Azatok. "I suspect she has gone to ground somewhere on this world, attempting to take back her spire. You will find her, Azatok, or you will find that your past glories offer little protection from the gaze of our shared masters."

"What you ask...I am not certain it can be accomplished," Azatok said, still avoiding Utfa's gaze. He licked his lips. "This world is massive. Unless she does something to reveal her presence, she could live out her entire life and we might never find her. I do not wish to disappoint the Nameless Ones, but I do not know how to do what you are asking."

"You will begin by taking your face out of a tak horn, and focusing on the war. I hear many reports that all you do is feast and watch spire fights—stories that have elements of truth, if your injury is any indication. You allowed Takkar to wound you." Utfa's tone carried his displeasure, and Azatok winced. "You may seek your pleasures, but only after tending to the needs of our masters. Be vigilant, Azatok. I warn you—the Nameless Ones are not forgiving."

Azatok nodded, his fur ashen. Utfa waved the champion away and, smiling, watched as he scurried back into the spire.

25

NO LEGEND

Nolan walked his mech down the *Demetrius*'s ramp, pausing to survey his surroundings. Ruined buildings lined what had once been a broad thoroughfare. Most had been spires, but judging from the debris, Nolan assumed that they'd toppled over time. The place reminded him a good deal of Ganog 7, though it lacked the ever-present rust storms.

Instead, large trees grew among the remains of the buildings, turning them into a sort of forest. Many of the trees rose hundreds of feet into the air, easily obscuring the squad's position from anything short of full orbital scanning.

Not that such a scan would turn up anything, either. Nolan's mech was running the new stealth drive he'd picked up during the refit. It worked exactly the same way his stealth belt did, bending light around the mech. It wasn't perfect, but it would fool most enemy sensors, and almost all visual.

Sound, however, was another matter. Each lumbering step thudded down the ramp, until Nolan finally stood on the cracked stones that marked where the road had once been. He pivoted, facing his mech toward the ramp.

"Move, people," Hannan barked over the comm.

Annie started down in her linebacker class, with Nuchik following up in the new scout class they'd been given. It was considerably lighter than a linebacker, and lacked the boosters of a full aerial mech. It was small, sleek, and much faster than a larger mech.

"I can't wait to test this thing out," Nuchik purred. It was unsettling, coming from the usually stoic sniper. "Permission to range ahead, sir?"

Nolan glanced up the ramp again. Both Kokar and Hruk had shifted to great form, and were following Hannan down the ramp. "Go ahead, Nuchik. Get up high and let us know if you spot movement. Remember, they might be friendlies."

"I can tell the difference between friend and foe," Nuchik chided.

"No, you can't," Hannan snapped over the comm. "Don't think we've forgotten Sissus. Keep it in your damned pants until the Captain gives the word, Private."

"Yes, sir," Nuchik said, with an edge of laughter in her voice.

"Ya'll best shut up and pay attention," Annie groused. "Maybe you ain't been keeping score but right now it's crazy, bad guys one, us zip." Her mech fanned out to the left, while Hannan took the right.

Nolan waited for them to proceed up the road a bit, then urged his mech into a trot, kicking up puffs of dust with every step as he followed them. "Kokar," he asked, "why was this city abandoned? Looks like it could be prime real estate."

Kokar trotted a few meters behind Nolan, with Hruk just behind him. The trees swayed around them, purple leaves wriggling like fingers.

"It is a holy place," Kokar said. "Hruk could tell you more. He practices the old ways, and knows our oldest tales."

"You are the first non-Ganog to come here in many

centuries, Captain Nolan," Hruk called. He leaned heavily on the longest spear Nolan had ever seen, a heavy pistol cradled in his other hand. "This is the city of Defiant, built by Nyar himself. It marks the place where he chose to make his stand, to fight back against the Nameless Ones. It was here that he met the terrible wyrm in battle, slaying the creature in single combat. The deed cost him his life, and his followers erected a tomb at the precise location where he'd felled the beast."

"It is because of this significance," Kokar interjected, "that survivors will gather here. There are warrens under the city, and the trees themselves screen the place quite effectively. Our people can survive here indefinitely. If we hope to restore some sort of government, it will be done here."

"Captain?" Nuchik whispered over a private channel.

"What's up, Private?" Nolan asked

"You're going to want to see this."

A video request popped up on Nolan's screen and he tapped accept.

"Holy crap," Nolan breathed. He studied the image, pinching out to enlarge the hologram. "That's an Omega, isn't it?"

"Pretty sure, sir."

The image showed an Omega almost identical to the three that had so thoroughly trashed the Nyar defenders. It was overgrown with trees; its metal was tarnished and dull. A towering redwood grew from the knee joint, made tiny next to the Omega.

But that was an *Omega*.

"Kokar, Nuchik spotted something interesting a couple blocks from our current position. Is there anything you wanted to tell me? Like, say, that your clan has an Omega stashed away?"

Kokar turned to face Nolan's mech, his fur softening to

yellow-brown. "I did not think to mention it. The Omega you speak of is the tomb of Nyar. His spirt lies within the guardian —or so the legend says."

"It is no legend," Hruk insisted. All four nostrils flared as he sucked in air. His eyes were tight with pain, but Nolan noted that the older Ganog hadn't complained about their pace. "Nyar did battle here, killing his opponent. Yet his own mighty planetstrider was badly injured during the confrontation. The leader died, and his vehicle died with him."

Nolan blinked. "You never thought to see if you could fix it?" He guided his mech into a full run, the heat in the cockpit spiking as the fusion reactor hummed to life.

"You must understand, Captain," Kokar explained. "We revere Nyar, almost as a god. He freed us from bondage to the Nameless Ones. His resting place is holy, and would never be disturbed. And even were it allowed, how would we attempt such a feat? Perhaps the techsmiths could repair it, but I seriously doubt it."

"Maybe they can't, but it's possible we could," Nolan pointed out. "Nuchik, any sign of trouble in the area?"

"Nothing yet, sir. Area's clean. No sign of anyone, friend or foe."

"That's because you're looking in the wrong direction," Annie drawled. "Look up, people."

Nolan called up an aerial feed, and felt his heart sinking. Half a dozen large, black shapes had appeared in the sky.

Ganog dreadnoughts. Now that they controlled the space around the world, the Kthul fleet had turned their attention to Nyar itself.

"They will invade in earnest now," Kokar rumbled. "They'll send their elites to take slaves, and to claim tribute. It might be wise to return to the ship."

26

EXTRACTION

Nuchik slammed back into the command couch as her mech shot into the air. Not in the way she would in a booster mech, but just due to the inertia from the mech's powerful legs. She seized the crumbling edge of a broken spire, pulling her mech atop the eroded metal.

She hadn't engaged the cloak yet; that kind of power draw would cook the inside of her cockpit. It wasn't really needed—not yet, anyway. She was perched just below the tree line, which obscured her from anyone not directly below or above, as well as affording her an excellent view of the spire where the fighting was still taking place.

The Omegas had stopped stomping on the Ganog, and had returned to a rough triangle outside the city. There was a bright flash, then one disappeared.

"Captain, looks like the Omegas are warping out."

"Noted. Thanks, Private. I'm guessing they consider the planet pacified, and are relying on conventional forces to finish the job." The captain did that a lot—musing out loud—and it was something she'd never grow used to in an officer. Her former commanding officer, Major Reval, had played his cards close to the vest, never telling the men anything he didn't have to. He'd expected his men to follow him blindly, trusting that he was right. And she had trusted him.

She still trusted him, even now that he was gone.

"Sir, there's a cloud of cruisers and destroyers entering the upper atmosphere. Looks like those dreadnoughts have gotten closer as well." Nuchik appended her video feed so the captain could see the sky above her. "Looks like we weren't the only ones to notice. There are a good three dozen ships taking off from the spire. Almost all of them are heading toward your position."

"That is expected," Kokar broke in.

It bothered Nuchik that the captain had given out the comm frequency, but she supposed he needed to give the Ganog at least that much trust.

"The Nyar survivors are going to ground," he continued, "just as we are. They know that their best chance of survival lies within those woods."

Nuchik punched up the magnification. "Sir, they're getting hit hard from above. A lot of those smaller cruisers aren't built for that kind of punishment."

As if on cue, the cruiser she'd been watching burst into flames, engines going critical a moment later. It exploded in a giant fireball, streamers of flaming debris littering the ground beneath.

"We're not going to be able to protect them all," the captain said. "Kokar, if you had to save just one ship, which would it be?"

The comm was quiet for several moments, until Kokar finally spoke. "The cruiser with the red planetstrider emblazoned on the side. I've tagged it. It belongs to Bruth, one of my father's fiercest warriors and strongest supporters. If we can get her out alive, she will be able to rally many of the others."

"Then let's do it. Hannan, Annie, move into cover near the edge of the forest."

A ping showed up on Nuchik's mini-map, indicating where the captain wanted them to go.

"Nuchik, circle wide and start picking off anyone who takes an interest in our shuttle. Kokar—you, Hruk, and I will rush their position and try to assist."

Nuchik stopped listening. She had her orders. She pushed the stirrups, guiding the mech into motion. It slipped soundlessly from its perch, landing at the base of the spire with a heavy crunch. Nuchik moved to a sprint, darting around thick trees as she guided the mech into the forest.

The ship would enter the canopy about a half-click away. She needed to find a spot where she could pick off anyone who followed the same vector into the forest.

She finally found a mass of tree trunks that had grown together, where the wood was thick enough to support the enormous weight of her mech. She climbed atop the trunks, laying her mech flat against the tree to minimize her profile. The only thing visible to the enemy was the heavy Theta cannon the mech was equipped with. Even then, only the barrel and scope could be seen; the stock was tucked back under her mech's shoulder.

A cruiser roared into view, flames pouring from rents in the the aft side of the vessel. It tilted drunkenly, the result of engines producing uneven thrust. The pilot was good, expertly dodging a mass of trees—but there was simply nowhere to go. The vessel slammed into the side of a spire wall, the corroded metal giving way to the tremendous momentum.

The ship crashed to the ground, severely damaged. Nuchik zoomed in, scanning until she found an access port. Figures were already climbing out, and a black-armored Ganog helped the others out of the hatch.

"Captain, their vessel went down, but there are definitely survivors." Nuchik swiveled her sights, scanning the forest where the vessel had entered.

Sure enough, three cruisers entered the tree line. Instead of the black paint job the Nyar preferred, these vessels were a deep, unwholesome green.

"We've got serious enemy reinforcements inbound. Three bogeys approaching from nine o'clock, and they're dumping apes all around the crash site. If you don't get there quickly, there's not going to be anybody to rescue."

"Acknowledged. Nuchik, start picking off targets, but fall back if they respond. Hannan, Annie, see if you can get into sniper positions as well. Use every missile you've got. Kokar, unless you've got a ranged weapon, hang back with Hruk." The captain's orders came clear and easy. "Yulo, are you monitoring?"

"Yes, Captain. How can I help you?"

"I'm going to try to convince Burke to do an aerial extraction. If he agrees, I'm relying on you to get the Nyar leadership aboard safely."

"Of course, Captain. I will offer them whatever aid I can."

Nuchik stopped paying attention again, sighting down the barrel. She waited until a Ganog's back filled her crosshairs, then stroked the trigger. Its chest exploded, and the corpse dropped to the ground before it even knew it was dead.

She fired again. Aim. Fire. Aim. Fire. There was a moment when she worried the Ganog might rush her position, then the captain led a charge from between two buildings.

He feathered his mech's boosters, shooting over the hail of plasma fire coming from the Ganog position. A swarm of piranha missiles erupted from his mech, breaking into many smaller swarms as they approached the Ganog. A flurry of detonations painted Nuchik's screen temporarily white, then faded to show gaps in the Ganog line. At least a third of their front rank had died.

Hannan and Annie popped out from the cover, using the trees to screen them as they picked off targets with their particle cannons. Occasionally, one of the mechs would belch a small volley of missiles, usually ending in the death of multiple elites.

Then Nolan's mech pierced the Ganog line. He was surrounded by elites, several of whom made the mistake of turning their backs.

Nuchik smiled, then began firing again. Aim. Fire. Kill. Aim. Fire. Kill.

27

FALL BACK

Nolan knocked away a vibro-axe, lunging with his mech's plasma blade. The glowing weapon pierced the Ganog's throat, and a quick knee to the groin lifted it into the air. Nolan seized the elite with both hands, dragging it into line between himself and the next pair of Ganog.

He hurled the dying elite at its companions, then brought his particle cannon to bear. He melted off the first Ganog's leg at the knee, then took a step back to aim at the second. It leapt the body of its companion, bringing a heavy chopping sword down at Nolan.

Nolan managed to block the blow with his plasma blade, but the force threw his mech to the ground in a spray of sparks. He rolled to his feet, looking around for his particle cannon. It was behind his opponent, and several more Ganog were already charging in his direction.

"Die, human!" the Ganog roared, charging again. It was nearly upon him when its head exploded. Nolan knocked the corpse aside, sprinting forward to snatch up his cannon.

"Great shot, Nuchik." He thumbed the fire button, his particle cannon coring an elite through the chest.

"Thank you, sir." Nolan could hear the smile in her voice.

A thick, black cruiser forced its way through the trees, branches snapping and raining leaves down on the combat. A pair of turrets spun in Nolan's direction, and pulses of scarlet energy stitched a line toward him.

He feathered the thrusters, hopping back several meters, managing to dodge most of the pulses. But some cratered the armor on his right side, and chunks of superheated tritainium were flung across the jungle around him. Nolan turned and ran, juking through trees. The barrage continued.

"Burke," Nolan gasped, as he pounded around another tree. The temperature spiked in the cockpit, boiling away the sweat. "If you're coming, you'd better do it soon. Our position is collapsing."

He spun around the corner of a ruined building, skidding to a halt, and extended his particle cannon through what had once been a window. Taking a moment to aim at the lead Ganog, he fired a shot that took it through the eye. The Ganog slumped to the ground.

The closest enemy cruiser had slowed, unable to pierce the dense canopy where Nolan had run—not that that bought him much time. He counted at least a dozen elites heading his way.

"Hannan, how is the package looking?"

"Your rush worked, sir. We're picking off the hostiles approaching the downed cruiser, and the Nyar are holding their own...for now at least. Looks like three more of those cruisers are coming, and one of them is the heavy kind. We need to bug out fast, sir." Her voice was tight, but she betrayed no other sign of the immense stress an officer always felt in combat.

"Noted." Nolan leaned around the corner, just long enough

to fire a small volley of missiles. The detonations caught three Ganog, all in a line. The closest was only forty meters away, and Nolan was forced to duck back into cover to avoid the explosion.

Burke's best command voice barked over the comm. "Captain Nolan, this is Major Burke. *Demetrius* is inbound, nineteen seconds. Sitrep."

It still amazed Nolan how much Burke had changed since Ganog 7.

"We've got at least thirty hostiles at the crash site, and three vessels incoming. There are half a dozen or more three minutes out. They know we're here now, and are doing their damnedest to make sure we can't leave." Nolan turned his mech, sprinting into the foliage.

Trees exploded around him as the Ganog fired a barrage of plasma in his direction. He took hits to the rear armor on his booster, but the booster itself still registered as functional.

"Sit tight. Help is on the way." Burke's words were punctuated by a familiar sound: the whine of Theta cannons. A volley of super-bright synthetic stars shot by overhead, punching into the Ganog cruisers. Three of the lighter ones simply detonated, and one of the heavy cruisers took a hard hit to the aft engine. "Alpha Company has been deployed."

Nolan spotted mechs moving through the treeline, each firing their particle cannons. The blue beams cut down the Ganog around the crash site, and the defenders used the distraction to rally. A massive female in black armor brought her axe down on the back of an attacking Kthul, then shot another Kthul in the face with a plasma pistol.

An answering volley came from the surviving Kthul cruisers, which ignored the *Demetrius*. Instead, they focused on Alpha Company. Nolan saw at least two mechs caught in a barrage of scarlet pulses. The one on the right detonated spectacularly, the explosion dooming its neighbor as well.

"They're trying to keep us from the crash site long enough to land more kill teams," Nolan cautioned over the comm. He opened up his external mic, setting the volume to max. "Ganog defenders, this is Captain Nolan of the Coalition. Your position is compromised. Leave your ship immediately, and fall back to the southeast. Our men will screen your position."

Nolan knew that giving that order undercut Burke's authority, but Burke wasn't close enough to communicate directly with the Nyar defenders. Nolan was. He charged in their direction, firing a hipshot that caught a Kthul in the arm. Nolan juked right, barely dodging the return fire from the Kthul's companions.

"Nolan speaks true," Kokar's voice boomed through the forest. "We leave now, or not at all. Come, make for the safety of the human battleship." Kokar paused only long enough to see that his people were following, then plunged into the trees.

Most of the Ganog followed, though Nolan noted that the massive female was the last to do so.

"All right, people," Nolan said, keying the squad-only frequency. "Let's fall back to the *Demetrius*. Do what you can to keep the Nyar alive."

Nolan sprinted into the forest, making for the battleship that was descending into a clearing in the distance. Its guns were chewing up any Kthul who got close, but things were going poorly for Alpha Company. Nolan counted at least four smoking wrecks, and one mech had lost a leg. It was pulling itself along the ground, trying to make it back to the docking bay.

Nolan guided his mech into a run, pausing next to the damaged mech. He heaved it over his shoulder in a fireman's carry, aware of his own mech's hydraulics straining at the weight, then ran toward the *Demetrius*.

He sprinted up the ramp and into the hangar bay as explosions lit the forest behind him and the last few surviving mechs staggered inside.

28

THE FIRST ARCANOTOME

Khar watched over Aluki's shoulder as she guided the cloaked cruiser over the magma field. Lava geysered into the air, forcing her to change course. She wove around the pillar of superheated rock, which reminded Khar of the tendrils around a sun's corona.

"There," Halut said, pointing to the west. "There's a building there, under the crust. It looks like the tip of a broken spire."

Khar peered at the area Halut had indicated, spotting a bit of white. The top of a spire had broken off, and only the jagged tip poked from the hardened, black rock.

Zakanna moved into the doorway next to Khar. She'd taken the time to bathe; her fur was now immaculate. "If that's a spire, the lava must be hundreds of meters deep."

"That isn't necessarily a bad thing," Khar mused. "It will have preserved the buildings themselves. We saw something similar on one of the Tigris worlds. Ancient Primo ruins were sealed for millennia, their inner chambers completely protected from the ravages of time."

"Mmm, I will set down on that lava shelf. It seems stable."

Aluki guided the craft smoothly down to a flat stretch of black volcanic rock. It was duller than the surrounding shelves, hinting at its age.

The cruiser rumbled to a halt. Aluki unbuckled her harness, hopping down from the pilot's chair. Khar started back up the corridor, but had only made it a few steps when the entire ship lurched. He caught himself against the wall as the ship tilted wildly.

"Mmm, not so stable!" Halut shrieked from the cockpit.

Aluki tumbled past Khar, and he shot out a paw to seize her by the scruff of her suit. He pulled her to safety.

Zakanna landed nimbly across the corridor. "We're in free fall," she yelled, seizing the bulkhead.

"Hold on!" Halut said.

Straining to hold Aluki—she was surprisingly heavy—Khar risked a glance into the cockpit.

Halut had gotten an arm onto the pilot's chair, and was struggling against inertia to pull himself up. Khar had no idea how far they could fall before reaching the bottom, but doubted they had much time.

The Whalorian gave a titanic bellow, pulling himself into the pilot's seat. He snapped the harness in place, then seized the controls. The ship continued to drop for a few moments more, then halted abruptly. Stone tumbled all around them, banging off the viewport as it rained past.

The ship righted, and the viewport turned to face a magnificent ivory spire. It was nearly identical to the one where he'd met Zakanna, and at its peak had probably been just as tall.

Halut guided the ship lower, settling near the base of the spire. Everyone held on for a good thirty seconds, waiting for the ship to lurch again. Finally, Halut turned off the engines, and everyone relaxed.

"Mmm, thank you," Aluki said, patting Khar's arm. "Our

bones are more brittle than yours. I would not have survived that fall."

"You're welcome, little one. You are a strong ally." Khar nodded respectfully to her, the nod he reserved for warriors.

"We're fortunate to have you, Aluki," Zakanna said, smiling warmly. She glanced behind her at the viewport. "Shall we see what we've found?"

"How long do we have?" Khar asked, starting for the cargo bay.

"What do you mean?" Zakanna asked.

"Won't your world's satellites pick up the tectonic disturbance?" Khar asked over his shoulder, slapping the button next to the ramp.

The door slid up, and the ramp began to extend. A wall of heat blasted into the ship, not enough to harm them but certainly uncomfortable to everyone not currently in an artificial body.

"There is no such monitoring, at least not that I'm aware of." Zakanna recoiled before the heat. "I do not believe Utfa possesses any way of detecting our arrival, but I could be wrong."

"It's possible the Void Wraith might be monitoring, but they'd be unlikely to do so unless ordered," Khar allowed. "We may be fine, but just to be safe I'd suggest we be as swift as we are able."

"Agreed," Zakanna said, nodding.

"Mmm, it is best we stay with the ship, I think," Aluki suggested. "Until you've determined it's safe."

Khar looked to Zakanna, who nodded. Aluki looked back at Halut, giving him a wicked grin.

"We will inform you of any threats, but will not disturb you otherwise," Khar said, smiling as he trotted down the ramp. He burst into a full run and sprinted across the hardened magma.

Heat shimmers twisted the air, blurring the spire even as it grew larger before him.

Zakanna glided to perch atop a narrow twist of black rock, laughing. She eyed him mischievously, then sprinted toward the spire's entrance.

A race, then? Khar poured on the speed, dipping into his power reserves. He leapt from rock to rock, narrowing the gap between him and Zakanna. He'd nearly caught her when she leaned into a sprint and zipped ahead through the entrance.

Khar grinned, slowing as he reached the entrance. "You were toying with me."

"Maybe," Zakanna said, still smiling. Her fur was a soft pink. She looked around her in wonder, eyes wide. "This place is the truest representation of our people still in existence. Our culture has changed and evolved, and everything we know about our beginnings is layered under myth now."

Khar took in the majesty of the place, the high vaulted ceiling abruptly cut off by a wall of black rock. It wasn't dissimilar to the spires currently in use, but instead of floating islands the place was more conventionally structured. Each island was connected to the outer ring by a slender bridge.

"Those bridges hardly look strong enough to hold up these islands," Khar mused. "Yet they've done so for many millennia, apparently."

"Built for form *and* function, as I'd expect," Zakanna said and started for the closest bridge. "I think that island would have been reserved for greeters. We no longer use them for an entire spire, but most families still employ one."

"Greeter?" Khar asked, following her up the bridge. It was less than a meter across, and would be even more dangerous for a Ganog.

"It was their responsibility to make sure guests were properly attended to. Greeters would wash their visitor's feet, and allow them to take their ease while waiting for an audience with the host," Zakanna explained, taking sure steps up the bridge despite the width. She reached the top and stepped off to the right to give him room to join her.

A literal labyrinth of tall shelves awaited them, covering the island in a maze of narrow walkways. Three paths led into the shelves, which were covered in strange cylindrical objects. Khar approached one and picked it up cautiously. "Are these... scroll cases?"

"They are," Zakanna said, moving to inspect one. Reverently, she ran a hand along the case. "These predate the discovery of arcanotomes, I'd imagine."

"Why are the shelves laid out like that, and what lies at the center of the maze?" Khar asked, scanning ceaselessly. He didn't trust this place.

"I don't know. My people have forgotten this place's existence. I couldn't even begin to guess why they built what they built." Zakanna took a trio of quick breaths, flaring all four nostrils. She leapt into the air and kicked off a shelf. Two more kicks took her to the top of the shelf, where she landed lightly.

Khar followed, not nearly as gracefully. He pulled himself over the top of the shelf and rose into a crouch next to Zakanna. "Clever idea. This will be much faster than navigating the maze."

Zakanna picked a path across the shelves, angling toward the center of the island. She paused at the final row and waited for Khar to catch up.

He trotted up next to her and peered down at the center of the maze. "What am I looking at?" he asked, studying the strange blocky contraption. Six black cables snaked from the box, but they weren't connected to anything.

"I believe we've discovered one of the first arcanotomes." Zakanna turned a worried gaze to Khar. "We should get Aluki."

29

INSIDE THE TOME

"Mmm, I concur," Aluki said. "This is some sort of primitive arcanotome." She peered inside the end of one of the cables that snaked from the strange contraption. "Since the device is immovable, I imagine seekers would have utilized it to learn whatever they needed, then unplugged."

"Fascinating," Zakanna said, inspecting another cable.

"Is it possible, then, that connecting to this device would allow us to see into the enemy's data stores?" Khar asked. "That kind of intelligence would be invaluable, particularly right now. We might be able to learn what defenses they've placed around the spire, and, more specifically, the beacon."

"True." Zakanna pursed her lips. "I don't like the idea of it —entering their world. We don't really understand that world, though it's something I doubt they'd expect us to attempt."

"Mmm, how would we connect though?" Aluki asked. "None of us have been outfitted to utilize a tome, unless there's a facility somewhere here to install one. Halut is still exploring. I could ask him to keep an eye out for such a device."

"I can connect," Khar volunteered. He picked up one of the

cables. Its dull surface seemed to absorb the thin light filtering from the holes in the rock above. "This is, ultimately, Void Wraith technology. My nanochrons can easily adapt to fit this. I'm not the best person to explore data archives, but I can at least perform the procedure."

Zakanna shot him a wide smile, then composed herself, looking to Aluki. "What do you think, lore keeper?"

Aluki gave a wide, baleen grin. "Mmm, that's a title I'd never expect to hear from Ganog lips, much less from an empress. I believe there is much value to be had in forging a connection. We could learn vital information, something we desperately need."

"What are the risks?" Khar asked.

"Mmm, I don't know." Aluki gave a shrug. "We have no idea how this technology works. My people have done well to preserve what knowledge we have, but have never deciphered an arcanotome. Both times our people procured one, the Ganog slaughtered millions in retaliation."

"Then I will discover them," Khar said, wrapping his paw around the end of the cable.

Nanochrons pooled in his palm and enveloped the end of the cable. He snapped erect as sudden energy flooded his nervous system, the last biological part of him. He relaxed a moment later, as the pressure eased.

"I believe I have forged a connection. The sensation is... dizzying. The data is located in a temple, and I am not alone."

Khar could see two worlds: the ancient spire library, and a dark, vaulted room. It looked much as the spire did, with shelves of scrolls piled in the cubbies on the shelves. Ganog moved between them, occasionally plucking out a scroll for examination.

There was very little light, filtering down from a high mist where the ceiling should be. It made this place shadowed and mysterious, no doubt intentionally.

A deep thrumming came from the center of the library, washing over Khar like the bass of some mighty drum. He kept his head down, hurrying through the stacks as he attempted to trace a path toward the center. There would be no vaulting to the top of the shelves, not here. He wanted to avoid notice, as much as possible.

Thankfully, if any of the Ganog had noticed him, they did not react. Each seemed fixed on their own task, to the exclusion of all else. They moved robotically, as if they had little control over their own actions. Khar circled around another, making his way up a row of shelves.

When it ended, he was suddenly spilled into a room with a wide, empty dais, like the empress used. Atop that dais floated a ball of black energy, pulsing and rippling. Streams of purple pulses flowed from the ball and zipped off in all directions. To the Ganog, he imagined.

A Ganog voice rumbled behind him. "You should not be here this fully. How is this possible?"

Khar turned slowly, tensing as he recognized those milky eyes. Utfa stared hard at him, all four nostrils flaring suddenly. He'd changed since Khar had last seen him. More of his fur had fallen out, and only a few wispy strands remained.

"You are the alien who attached himself to Zakanna. Is she with you?" Utfa gave an evil grin, his wispy fur darkening to a predatory brown-black. His robes shrouded him, completing the ghastly image.

"Perhaps. Perhaps she pillages the secrets in this place, while you waste time speaking to me," Khar taunted, giving as nonchalant a grin as he could muster. "You don't really expect me to tell you, do you?"

"No matter," Utfa said, his cruel smile broadening. "I will

carve up your mind and devour your secrets. You *will* tell me where she is. You made a mistake, entering the tome."

Khar considered his options, not liking the short list. He could fight, with no understanding of the rules of this place, or he could flee. The latter seemed the safest course. He willed the nanochrons to sever the connection, gasping reflexively as the second world vanished.

His last view was of Utfa's shocked face, reaching out to catch Khar.

"What happened?" Zakanna asked, eyes wide with concern.

"Utfa was there. He saw me. Talked to me." Khar shuddered. "I do not think he knew how I was there, or where I was coming from. I left as quickly as I could, in case he had some way to glean information from my mind."

"Mmm, a wise precaution. A frightening experience, but perhaps one that will not harm us," Aluki mused. "Utfa doesn't know which world you were on, though he may have figured out that we made it back to Imperalis. Even if he did, this is a very large world. There are many places to hide. He will never find us."

"I hope you're right," Zakanna said, staring up at the light filtering through the holes above. She looked at Khar. "At best, we're no closer to a plan. At worst, we will be forced to flee."

"Perhaps, and if it comes to that, we will run," Khar said. He rose to his feet, giving her a confident smile. "But I do not think things are so dire. We have suffered a setback, true. But we have a safe place, filled with ancient lore. Let us see what can be gleaned. If we cannot find an answer, then I will brave the tome again. One way or another, we will learn what we need to know."

30

MORE GUARDS

U tfa's eyes snapped open, and he rose slowly from his supplications. He pulled on his heavy robes, donning the hood as he stepped from his chambers. Agitation, with undertones of confusion, rippled through what remained of his fur.

What had he just witnessed? There was no doubt—that had been Khar, the Tigris from this...Coalition. Somehow they'd found a way into the arcanotome, which was most troubling. What had they learned? Would could they learn?

He examined the entire experience as he waited patiently for the transport disk to arrive, pondering what he'd seen and sifting through it as he sought some clue, some bit of data that might tell him where to find Khar—and thus the empress.

There was nothing. Not a single shred of evidence that might provide their location.

Utfa's fur drifted to red, and he paced back and forth. Finally, the transport disk arrived. He mounted it, enjoying the breeze as it carried him aloft. It brought him to the command deck, where a single techsmith stood.

The disk deposited him on the edge of the island, and Utfa

strode to the center, motioning for the techsmith to attend him. Unlike other clans, the Kthul did not trust techsmiths. They too were inducted into the seekers, and while they were not given the same standing, their minds were forced open to the Nameless Ones, ensuring their loyalty.

What could the empress be after? There was no doubt she was on Imperalis. Was she attempting to raise an army? No, such a move would have resulted in at least a few rumors. Besides, it was unlikely to be effective. Any army she raised would be swiftly destroyed by the Void Wraith. Unless she found a way to deal with *them*, there was simply no way for her to retake her world.

And there it was—the reason she'd returned to this world.

"Techsmith," Utfa snarled, staring through the observation dome at Imperalis. "Have a full detail of warriors moved to the beacon. Also include a complement of Adepts, and enough labor-slaves to build fortifications."

Zakanna was coming. They both knew she'd need the beacon if she wished to wrest her throne back. Utfa might not be able to find her, but he could be ready for her return.

That matter dealt with, he turned his attention inward, closing his eyes as the whispers provided a tantalizing tidbit. He focused on the data pulses and watched the feed coming from his scout vessel.

It had arrived at Akadia, a populous Saurian world that supplied most of the Nyar labor-slaves. Normally, Utfa would have ordered his dreadnoughts to incinerate the world from orbit. Instead, they'd merely destroyed the small Saurian fleet, leaving the world intact.

The world was no longer occupied. All nine billion Saurians were gone, as was every other biological entity. Even the trees had been devoured.

Part of Utfa wished he had footage of the Nameless One

devouring Akadia, but mostly he was glad he couldn't see it. That level of destruction was disturbing, a subtle reminder that no world was safe from his masters.

Not even Imperalis.

31

BRUTH

Nolan tapped the eject sequence, then wiped a thick sheen of sweat from his forehead. The mech's chest slid open, allowing a blast of blessedly cool air into the cockpit. He undid his harness and started down the rungs on the mech's leg. Once out, he straightened, giving the chaos in the hangar a weary once over.

Annie and Hannan were parking their mechs in the neighboring stalls, while Kokar and Hruk stood off to one side. There was no sign of Nuchik yet, but Nolan wasn't worried. She was damned good at taking care of herself, and probably just wasn't done killing Kthul yet.

Alpha Company's surviving mechs were streaming in, but Nolan only counted eight. Fortunately, there were a few more pilots being helped in, suggesting they'd survived the destruction of their mechs. Behind them came a thick cluster of armored Ganog, most still in great form.

They huddled together nervously, each clutching a rifle or a melee weapon. The cluster was centered around the massive female Nolan had seen earlier. She stood head and shoulders over the others, pointing a thickly muscled arm as she barked orders to the other Nyar. They snapped to, and Nolan couldn't blame them.

"May as well get this over with," he muttered.

Squaring his shoulders, he strode over to the Ganog. By the time he arrived, most had noticed him, including the woman he assumed to be the leader. Many had shifted back to their lesser forms, but they were still taller than he was.

He paused about three meters away, nodding respectfully. "I'm Captain Nolan. Welcome aboard the *Demetrius*. The vessel belongs to Major Burke, who is making his way over now." Nolan waved in Burke's direction.

The copper-haired soldier's eyebrows were knit together in a mixture of irritation and anger, and he stalked up to the Ganog like he wanted to do violence. "Who's in charge of this rabble?"

"I am in charge of *this rabble*," the female Ganog said. She stepped from their ranks, towering over Burke even after shifting back to her smaller form. "My name is Bruth, of the Nyar Clan. Your companion identified you as Major Burke, and claims you are the leader of this vessel."

Burke shot Nolan an annoyed glance. "It's technically true that this is my vessel, but we've been placed at Nolan's disposal. He's the one you'll want to deal with. Before we do that, though, I'm going to need your people to pile their weapons up against the wall. I'm also going to need you to have everyone get back into whatever you call your regular-sized bodies."

"We keep our weapons." It wasn't a request. Bruth leaned closer to Burke. "I will order my warriors to resume their lesser forms, but make no mistake, little human. If you seek to do us harm, to imprison us, or to remove our weapons...I will kill you."

"We just saved your asses," Burke snarled. He scowled up at Bruth. "I lost over a third of my unit out there, and, by God, you will treat me and mine with respect. Or you'll find yourself walking."

"What Major Burke is trying to say," Nolan interjected, hating that he had to be the diplomatic one, "is that we need to work together. If you want to keep your weapons, that's fine. Major, would it be acceptable for the Nyar to take the area around those berths over there?"

"Why not? The mechs we were storing there have been destroyed. There's plenty of room, with a third of my pilots dead."

Burke turned on his heel and stalked away—not that Nolan could blame him. Losing men was hard under the best of circumstances.

"It is only because you have done us a great service that I do not separate your head from your shoulders," Bruth said, matter-of-factly. She stared disdainfully down at Nolan, her fur taking on a sickening green tint. "My people have lost much this day, and we long for vengeance. Do not test our patience, for my people seek a target for their anger."

"I get that." Nolan turned to scan the hangar, noting two things. Hannan and Annie were still in their mechs, still ready to fight. Nuchik had just arrived too, and had left her mech idling. "Kokar, get over here."

The Ganog was still standing by the wall, as if trying to avoid Bruth's notice. At the sound of his name he reluctantly strode over. Hruk followed him like an ever-present shadow.

"Listen," Nolan began, once Kokar had joined them. "I don't really understand your political structure. I'm not sure who's in charge. I'll let you sort that out. When you can tell me who that is, great. I need to speak to that person about a formal alliance with the Coalition. Your people are in desperate need of allies, and I think we all know it."

Kokar's fur went a watery yellow, but he flared his nostrils and it settled into a deep brown. "Bruth, you know you are the only one left whom most will follow. You must assume command."

Bruth seemed more than a little surprised, eyeing Kokar warily. "I agree. It's that simple then? No challenge? No arguments for your cause?"

"I have no real support in either the warrior or leadership caste. Our titles aren't hereditary, and everyone knows my father hated me anyway."

Hruk started to speak, but Kokar waved him to silence.

"There's no chance I can command," he said, "so for the good of our people I will lend whatever weight my word carries to your cause."

Hruk snarled. "You gained respect when you defied your father, especially in light of the fact that you were right." He stepped up next to Kokar, glaring at Bruth. "Kokar may support you, but do not forget his lineage or his deeds this day. You owe him your life. All of you do. Kokar secured the allies that allowed you to survive the execution wrought by Grak."

"Lingering respect allows me to ignore your tone," Bruth snarled back, "but learn to curb your tongue." She flexed powerful shoulders, making it clear that she could easily snap his neck. "I will accord Kokar the honor he has earned, and it is true that he earned much of it. I am honored by his support, and will see that he serves among the leadership caste." She turned to Nolan. "Since I now speak for the Nyar, you may deal with me, Captain. You said we needed an alliance, and you are correct. What do you propose, exactly?"

Nolan had already considered how to approach this moment, so he made his argument simple. "We keep your leadership caste alive, and evacuate as many survivors as possible to the world of your choosing. As you're no doubt aware, the *Demetrius* can cloak, and we've installed a warp drive. With the warp anchor gone, we can leave whenever. If there are no additional survivors, we could depart right now. Once we're free, you send a delegation to meet with my government. The alliance can be formalized there, but the gist is this: We help you in the war against Utfa and the Kthul, and when that war is over you leave my people in peace."

"That last part is nothing. We would never leave our space to conquer inferior species. We exist to shield our kind from the Nameless Ones, and will be here until that is accomplished. However, honor dictates that we defend this world. If we abandon Nyar, we abandon our history. Our people will lose hope, and this war will be over before it has fully begun. No, we will not be leaving. If you wish to stay and help us retake our world, then so be it. We welcome the aid."

Nolan's mouth worked, and he fought for words. They weren't willing to leave, but what the hell could he do to help them retake this world? It was an impossible task.

Yet what choice did he have? His orders were clear: Secure the Nyar alliance, at any cost.

"We'll stay," he said, "as allies. Rest up. We'll need time to repair our mechs. After that, we'll see what we can do to help."

"Very well. We will mend our wounds and prepare ourselves for the next battle." Bruth turned without a word, heading for the area of the hangar that had been allocated for them.

Nolan sighed. Someday, they'd give him an easy mission.

32

LONGSHOT

Nolan ducked into the conference room, noting that he was the last to arrive. He hated that, but there'd simply been too many things to deal with before he got there.

Kokar and Hruk sat on one side of the table. Burke sat on the other, in clear opposition. Both groups eyed each other like cats dumped together in a room, and Nolan knew this would be an uphill battle. He moved to Burke's side, sliding into a chair next to the major.

"Welcome, Captain," Kokar rumbled, nodding respectfully. "We can begin, then."

"Before we begin, I wanted to apologize for earlier," Burke said, running his fingers through his hair while avoiding eye contact. He looked up suddenly, meeting Kokar's gaze. "I lost people today. It's only the second time since I took command of Alpha Company. I let it affect my professionalism, and you have my apologies."

"Too little, too late, if you ask me," Hruk said.

"I did *not* ask you," Kokar snapped. His eyes never left Burke. "I understand completely, Major. I lost people on Imperalis. Friends. Brothers. It...unhinged me for a time." His fur darkened.

"We've all been there, in this war or another," Nolan said. "It's water under the bridge, gentlemen. We're friends here. More than that, we're allies. We want the same thing. Does anyone at this table think that we're going to get it by having Bruth in charge?"

"She's going to get everyone killed," Burke said, shaking his head. "The Nyar can't stay on this world. That's suicide. Even if they muster enough of a force to take on the garrison, the Kthul will just call an Omega or two back here."

"True, but what would you suggest?" Kokar growled, his nails digging into the table. His frustration was clear, though it didn't seem to be directed at any of them.

"Hruk," Nolan said, meeting the wizened Ganog's gaze. "You're a historian of sorts, right?"

"I am." Hruk's tone was suspicious, but his eyes were curious.

"Nyar's tomb is an Omega. There's no mistaking it. That means that, at one time, your people used Omegas in war. How much do you know about that time?"

"I know the legends, but we have no way of knowing how true they are." Hruk stroked the fur on his chin, considering. "The only story that mentions the first planetstrider are those of Nyar's final battle, in this very city. We know little of use, I'm afraid."

"All right," Nolan said, more than a little frustrated at the historian's lack of...well, history. "But at the very least, Nyar's Tomb is holy, right?"

Hruk looked affronted at the question. "It is our most holy site."

"So if the son of a former clan leader showed up piloting the tomb, that would probably give him a lot of influence in the clan, right? Say...enough to be declared Clan Leader himself?"

"I see where you are going with this," Kokar said, eyeing Nolan dubiously. "Even if we could resurrect this Omega, I do not think the clan would follow me."

"You may be mistaken, lad." Hruk gave a seated, and very deferential, bow. "If you led them into battle using Nyar's war machine, they would follow you into the maw of a Nameless One. Nyar would flock to your cause—not just here, but everywhere."

Kokar looked decidedly uncomfortable at the prospect, his fur rippling between runny green and washed-out blue. Finally, he looked up. "I do not think I will make an able leader, but Bruth is blind to the danger that staying here presents. I will do whatever I must to lead my people to safety."

"Are we in agreement then?" Nolan asked, looking around the table.

"I'd much rather have Kokar in charge than that brute," Burke said. He turned to Nolan. "Do you really think you can get that Omega operational? It's been sitting out there for millennia, right? From the little I saw when we passed by, it's got trees growing out of its joints. Who knows what parts are corroded?"

"We won't know until we take a look. It's possible this is a fool's errand, and if the Omega can't be fixed, I'm willing to admit the mission is a failure and pull out," Nolan offered. He turned to Kokar. "Will anyone try to stop us from going to Nyar's Tomb? I know you said it was a holy site."

"Any warrior or leader may make pilgrimage," Hruk mused. "I doubt they will attempt to bar our passage. Is it really possible that you might be able to resurrect Nyar's war machine?"

"Possibly. I'll let the rest of the squad know we're moving

out. Annie is good with repair and improvisation. We'll have her do an assessment." Nolan rose to his feet. "How does two hours sound?"

"Works for me." Burke rose to his feet as well. "Just enough time for a shower and a meal."

"Indeed," Kokar agreed. "I will tend to my own dinner, then stand ready to lead you to Nyar's Tomb."

33

WE HAVE THE TECHNOLOGY

Nolan's mech lumbered around the corner of an overgrown building, where the stone disappeared amidst the foliage. Before him stood the Omega that Nuchik had originally spotted. Its sleek metal frame towered over most of the surrounding buildings, though one or two were taller. He guessed it stood around 6,000 meters—taller than most planetstriders.

Dense, green vines grew through its joints, overlaying the blue-and-chrome armor with a riot of green. Three concentric rings stood around the Omega, much like a scaffold would be used with an orbital launch back home. Perhaps that supplied it with power?

"Kokar," Nolan asked over the comm, "why do the Nyar wear black armor if your founder used a blue war machine?"

Kokar paused a few dozen meters away, staring up at the Omega. "An excellent question, and one I have never considered. Hruk?"

"I do not know. It is said we wear armor to hide us in the void, but I do not know when the tradition began, or why."

Nolan guided his mech closer, noting on his mini-map that

the squad was moving a little way behind. "Hannan, you and Nuchik stay out here and keep an eye on things. I'm going to go inside with Kokar. Annie, we'll bring you to assess the Omega's technical situation."

Kokar started trotting toward the Omega, moving to the structure behind it instead of the mech itself. He paused next to a shadowed doorway leading inside. Nolan ran his mech over, then triggered the eject sequence.

He dropped from the cockpit, trotting over to Kokar. The Ganog had already returned to his lesser form and was moving into the building. Nolan followed, his hand resting on his sidearm. The interior was dimly lit, and a series of wide stairs led upward.

"Is there an elevator of some sort?" Nolan asked, remembering how tall the building was.

"I'm afraid not. We run." Kokar began trotting up the stairs, and Hruk hobbled after him.

Nolan waited for Annie to finish disembarking from her mech. She trotted over, spitting a gob of black into a cluster of plants. "Hope you're okay with a bit of a climb."

"They don't have any beer on this world. Now you want me to exercise? I should've stayed with Bock." Annie laughed, then started up the stairs. "I ain't as fast as you, so you feel free to run on ahead with Kokar. I'll be along eventually."

Nolan patted her shoulder as he passed, then trotted up the stairs after Kokar. This was going to take a while. He was in good shape, but there were a *lot* of stairs. Within a few flights, he'd broken into a thin sheen of sweat; by the time he'd passed the first twenty, his breathing was ragged. By thirty there was a stitch in his side, and by fifty he knew he wasn't in as good a shape as he thought he was.

Nearly an hour passed before he finally reached the top— almost a thousand stories, if his count was accurate. Nolan grabbed the top of the stairwell, leaning hard against it as he sucked in deep breaths. Sweat poured off him, splattering the metal floor.

"It took you long enough. I've been here for ages." Kokar clapped Nolan on the shoulder. "It is a difficult climb, but worth it. Come see what I have seen."

Kokar led Nolan across a narrow U-shaped chamber filled with rows of consoles. On the far side, a two-meter-wide bridge of blue energy extended to the back of the Omega's head. The wind howled outside, rocking the Omega gently.

"I guess we may as well get on with this," Nolan prompted, giving Kokar the chance to be first.

Kokar hesitated, so Nolan plunged boldly down the glowing ramp. It felt solid under his feet, as much as any deck on any vessel. But there were no handholds, and this high up there was a stiff wind. Nolan kept his legs bent, hurrying toward the Omega. A sudden gust knocked him to the side, and his arms windmilled.

Kokar's hand seized his shoulder, steadying him. "We are nearly there."

Nolan nodded quickly, unable to speak past the sudden dryness in his mouth. He almost ran the last ten steps, finally bracing himself against the back of the Omega's head. Looking around, he saw no means of entry—no doorway or keypad.

"Any idea how we get inside?" he called over the howling wind.

"I do not know, not precisely," Kokar called back. "No one has made a pilgrimage here in generations. But the legends say that if we call out to Nyar, he will be there in our time of need."

"Worth a shot, right?" Nolan asked. He chuckled, then cupped his hands around his mouth. "Hey Nyar, we need your help."

A thin crack appeared in the back of the mech's head,

slowly widening into a narrow passage. Possibly even too narrow for a Ganog. "This can't have been designed for your people. It's almost like...they designed it for Primo. The ancient Primo."

"The who?" Kokar called over the wind.

"It's not important, not yet. Let's try to get inside." Nolan gestured at the passage. This was a holy place for Kokar's people; he should enter first.

Kokar squeezed his bulk into the narrow tunnel, his armor scraping audibly along the walls as they pushed their way inside the head. Crossing the fifty meters underscored both how thick this thing's armor was, and how large the Omegas truly were.

They finally emerged into what Nolan thought must be a nerve center for the Omega. Five sleek chairs of the same blue metal he had come to expect from the Void Wraith sat arrayed in a perfect circle. Floating in the center, bobbing up and down lazily, was a blue cube traced with glowing, white circuitry.

"I should have known." Nolan shook his head slowly, then walked to stand next to the cube.

"Clearly you recognize this place." Kokar picked a path around the chairs to approach the cube from the opposite side. "What revelation have you had?"

"This Omega was constructed by the same hands that made the Void Wraith. We already knew that, but seeing it is a whole other level of confirmation. It also raises some troubling questions about the origins of both the Void Wraith and the Ganog." Nolan turned his attention to the chairs. "The chairs face away from the cube, and each has these prongs on the back."

"What do you think they do?" Kokar mused, inspecting another chair.

Nolan bent to inspect one. "I'd guess they plug into the spinal column. Interface with the nervous system."

Annie staggered into the room, panting. She dropped her pack by the door and wiped sweat from her face. "That bridge about made me wet myself. Pity the Ganog ain't discovered railings yet. Would probably cut down on falling deaths."

"You are a techsmith, yes?" Kokar asked Annie.

Annie said, shrugged. "Uh, sure."

"Can you repair this titan?" Kokar folded his arms, looking at Annie with the kind of contempt most Ganog reserved for *ka'tok*.

"How the hell do I know?" Annie snapped. "I ain't even looked around. Tell you what, fuzzball. You give me an hour to figure out how this thing works, and I'll let you know what I think."

"Annie, would it help if I asked Burke for techs?" Nolan asked. "They'll probably speed any repairs. This thing is massive."

"I'll take all the help I can get, sir," she drawled. "Might even be worth getting Hannan up here, and whoever else you can scrounge up. I'll find a use for 'em."

34

REPAIRS

Nolan ducked past an exposed conduit, wincing as sparks shot up from the weld Annie was making. He continued into the Omega's nerve center—what he assumed must be the brain. Repairs were going well thus far, at least from what he could see.

Per his directions, Alpha Company's techs were working only on internal systems. From the outside, there was no sign that any change had been made. He'd even made sure the techs entered with stealth belts and under cloud cover to prevent orbital satellites from picking up heat signatures.

He scanned the room, trying to find the person in charge. Once, that would have been Lena, but after Imperalis she'd been transferred to intelligence. She was helping the Coalition to understand who the Nameless Ones were, something Nolan desperately wanted more data on. Unfortunately, without her, all Nolan had access to was Annie. No one in Burke's outfit was qualified either as a scientist or full engineer.

"Get that conduit down to the knee," Annie barked, with the kind of authority a drill sergeant would envy. The sharp tone was new for her. She ambled up to Nolan, giving a wide, deceptively innocent smile. "Welcome, Captain. Repairs are going smoother than a Primo's bald head."

"What are you working on there?" Nolan asked, nodding toward the conduit a tech was ripping out of the wall.

"We're cannibalizing conduits to repair damaged areas. We can't manufacture the fiber used in the Omega, so we have no other choice." Annie half-turned to face Kokar as the Ganog approached.

"Captain." Kokar said, stopping next to Nolan. "A word, please?"

"Sure, what's up?" Nolan asked, distracted by the slowly bobbing cube in the center of the room. It reminded him so much of the master core in Primo libraries. The connection was troubling.

"I begin to believe that your people may be able to repair this titanic weapon," Kokar rumbled, his fur rippling between tan and chocolate. "I still do not understand what you intend to do then. How will we pilot this?"

"Well, we didn't find any consoles," Annie interjected apologetically, "or any other obvious means for a person to interface with the Omega."

"What do you mean?" Nolan asked, pointing at the ring of chairs around the cube. "Those are how you interface with the machine. It plugs into your spine, and presumably you link up with the Omega. We're not going to find a yoke or foot pedals."

Kokar's fur drifted toward yellow. "I suppose that is the heart of the matter. Hruk warns that if I forge a connection to this machine, I will never be the same. He further warned that I could die in the attempt, though he won't say how he knows these things."

Nolan rubbed his jaw, considering his answer carefully. "If you're saying that you're unwilling to use the chair, I completely understand. I'm not in a hurry to either. We can find another volunteer."

"Not if we wish to see me become Clan Leader." Kokar shook his head, then sighed. "It is really very simple, Captain. If I am to lead, I must do it in battle. I must control this machine, and my people must know that it is I that do so. There is no other way."

"So, what is the problem, exactly?" Nolan demanded. He'd long since lost patience with the Nyar clan, and while he liked Kokar more than any of the rest, the youth's constant angst was getting really old.

"I merely seek to understand my fate." Kokar's tone was both defensive and hurt. "Why are there five chairs? Why not one?"

"I'd guess different functions are controlled by different pilots." Nolan shrugged. "The only way for us to know is to try one of the chairs. I know you have to pilot this thing in order for your people follow you, but if you'd like, we can have a volunteer test it before we plug you in."

"No," Kokar snapped, his fur dipping to a deep, envious green. "I will be the one to test it. This is my heritage, no other's."

"All right," Nolan said, raising his hands in a placating gesture. "But if you're going to be the one to do this, now might be a good time. If it doesn't work, or if there's a problem, the sooner we know about it, the more likely we'll be able to fix it."

Kokar gave a tight nod, and his fur slowly faded back to its more normal tan. "If I am to do this, I suppose there is no point in avoiding it any longer."

Kokar moved to the closest chair, running his furry hand along the metal. He looked at another chair, finally stopping next to the third. There was no difference between them that Nolan could discern, but Kokar laid down in the third chair. He pushed his back up against the prongs, and there was a sudden snap.

All four prongs shot out, silvery tendrils shooting into Kokar's neck on either side of the spine. He gave an agonized roar, thrashing violently in the chair. His arms slapped down onto the chair, pinned as if held by magnets. He gave one more spasm, then lay still.

Nolan shot to his side, feeling for a pulse. There was one, just as strong as he'd ever felt.

"He's still breathing." Nolan sighed. "I wish we had a doctor on hand. We really need to add support staff to these missions."

"You know what the admiral would say about that," Annie said, ambling over from the conduit she'd been welding. "Manpower, blah, blah. 'Sides, there ain't many doctors left after the last war. Maybe the Ganog have one."

"They'd probably use leeches," Nolan said.

Kokar was on his own, like it or not.

35

NYAR

Kokar whirled, his lower nostrils flaring as his body instinctively readied for combat. He was smothered in darkness, soundless and impenetrable. He had the sense that he was in some great cavern, though he could see no rock in the inky blackness.

"Show yourself," he boomed, thumping his chest with a fist. "I am Kokar, son of Grak. I will not be ignored." His voice echoed through the darkness for long moments, fading to silence.

A deep voice rumbled from the blackness. "Is this what my descendants have come to?"

Light sprang up near Kokar's feet, a roaring campfire of the sort he might strike while hunting. It appeared, already crackling, as if it had been there all along.

A Ganog warrior stepped from the shadows, his flat-black armor absorbing the firelight. He had intense eyes and long, tangled fur. The hilt of a two-handed sword jutted over his broad shoulders, and a heavy plasma pistol was belted to his side.

"Who are you?" Kokar demanded, wrapping his hand around the haft of his axe.

"I am called Nyar, son of Nuun." Nyar dropped into a cross-legged position on the other side of the fire. "Sit. Join me, Kokar, son of Grak."

Kokar sat, releasing his axe. He folded his hands in his lap, staring at the Ganog in wonder. "Are you really Nyar himself?"

"I am unsure how to answer that question. My name is Nyar, and I am aware of no other Ganog with the same name." Nyar shrugged, unbuckling his sword and setting it next to him.

"Did you found our clan?" Kokar asked.

"I founded a clan, and that clan chose to adopt my name as theirs," Nyar conceded. He leaned forward, his features illuminated by the firelight. "You are a member of this clan?"

"I am. We trace our lineage all the way back to you, across a thousand generations," Kokar said proudly. He sat up straighter, a million questions tumbling through his mind.

"And why have you come to me after so long, Kokar? Have the Nameless Ones returned?" Nyar's fur darkened, and he adopted a dangerous look. An urgent look.

"They have, though I have yet to see one myself. Our new allies, a race called humans, slew a giant eye. They've warned that more might be coming, and I believe them. Recently, the Kthul invaded Imperalis—"

"Kthul lives? You have seen him?" Nyar demanded, his fur shifting to match the fury of the campfire.

"I...do not believe so. I meant the Kthul clan, led by one of the treacherous seekers," Kokar struggled to hold the ancient hero's gaze. Finally he looked away.

Nyar spat into the fire, the saliva burning away with a sizzle. "And this clan serves the Nameless Ones?"

"They do. The fact that he has openly seized power

suggests that the Nameless Ones have finally returned. I've come to you to win your aid. This mighty war machine might be able to help free my people from the Kthul boot." Kokar rose to his knees, picking up his axe and holding it before him. "I will do anything you ask, great Nyar. Show me how to pilot this beast, and I will use it to slay those who serve the Nameless Ones."

"It is not so simple, son of Grak." Nyar shook his head sadly. "Controlling this war machine is no easy feat. Most who attempt to do so fail. Many die in the attempt. Even if you succeed, the price is high. You will be bonded, and when your physical body dies you will merge with me, as I merged with my predecessor. You will become this machine, a part of us."

Kokar licked his lips. Nyar's words suggested there was still time to change his mind, to go back to being a simple Ganog elite. To serve, instead of lead. To die, next to Bruth.

"I am ready." And he was. "Make me a part of you, Nyar. Give me control of this mighty beast."

"Very well. Prepare yourself," Nyar said, intoning the words with reverence that his previous words had lacked.

Fire flooded Kokar's body, his every nerve becoming a bonfire. The universe flickered around him, alternating between the strange fire and an entirely new perspective.

He was a giant machine, staring out at the forest.

Then he was Kokar again. He struggled to maintain the new perspective, briefly flexing the fingers on one hand, but the giant slipped away, and he was once again seated at the fire.

He hung his head. "I have failed."

"Indeed." Nyar rose to his feet, eyeing Kokar sadly. "You lack the will, Kokar, son of Grak. If you try again, you will not survive."

36

CATCH OUR BREATH

K har completed his circuit of the crust surrounding the ancient spire, then returned to the cable he'd set earlier. He rappelled down into the darkness, dropping silently to the island they were using as a staging camp.

Zakanna sat by herself, crosslegged in what humans called a lotus position. Khar didn't know what a lotus was, but suspected the beast was fearsome.

He landed not far from Zakanna, but she didn't react to his presence. Her eyes were closed, her breathing slow and rhythmic. Khar sat down next to his pack, leaning his back against a shelf. He didn't need sleep, and had grown used to long stretches when everyone else slumbered. He often used the time to recharge, but that merely meant he needed to be immobile. Sleep itself was denied him.

"You are a conundrum, Khar of Pride Leonis," Zakanna said, eyes still closed. Her pristine fur shone in the afternoon light filtering down from the holes in the crust above. "You are a warrior, yet embrace science. You have fierce pride, but willingly set it aside to work with former enemies. I have never met anyone like you."

"I am merely a product of my training," Khar explained, resting his paws in his lap. "Mighty Fizgig showed me how to be more than a warrior. More than a savage brute. There is more to honor than feats of valor, something I didn't understand at a younger age."

"You speak very highly of her," Zakanna said, finally opening her eyes. She turned them on Khar, and he was once again struck by their intensity. "Is she really as good as you say? The way you and Nolan speak of her, it's as if she's a deity, a goddess of combat."

"She is, and more. Fizgig terrorized the humans for many years. Only one of their commanders ever faced her and lived, and he narrowly escaped with his life," Khar explained. He smiled warmly at the memory. "The humans are allies now, but there was a not-so-distant time when we were foes. Fizgig was the first to realize the need for an alliance. She battled Admiral Mow, or rather the creature Mow had become. He'd been infected by the Gorthians, and that infection gave him great physical strength. It did not matter. Fizgig tore out his throat, freeing my people and turning the war back on the Gorthians."

"Why does Nolan speak of her with affection if she is such a bane to his people?" Zakanna asked. She rose gracefully, and moved to sit next to Khar. Her intense gaze was fixed on him.

"During the first battle for the Void Wraith, compromises were made. Nolan was placed in charge of a mission, and Fizgig agreed to serve under his command. He earned her respect, and she began to teach him to fight. Humans do not teach their officers hand-to-hand combat, believing it a waste of time."

Zakanna goggled at him.

"Lunacy, I know. Fizgig rectified that. She taught Nolan to

fight, and he's become quite deadly. She mentored him, even as she mentored me. That is why Nolan honors her, and he is right to do so. She is old but far from weak. She wears her age as a mask, and woe to anyone who underestimates her."

Shuffling footsteps echoed from the bridge, and Aluki waddled into view, panting from the exertion. The bridges were tough on the Whalorians, but neither her nor her husband had complained. They'd both been thrilled at the prospect of so much new knowledge, and were already carting piles of scrolls back to the ship.

"Mmm, a moment, please," Aluki said, resting against a shelf as her piping breaths returned to normal. "I have news. Halut has discovered a data repository. It appears much like the arcanotome, but with a more conventional interface. I believe we can use it to explore a digital repository, without fear that they will be able to see us."

37

THE VOID WRAITH

Z akanna knelt next to the terminal, sitting gently upon the chair, something she'd previously only seen aboard Saurian or Whalorian ships. She found the concept of sitting...odd.

The terminal's screen filled with purple text on a black background, the sigils maddeningly familiar. She turned to Aluki, more than a little agitated that she couldn't read the words herself. "What does it say?"

"This part talks about the war before war. The Ganog were a slave species to the Nameless Ones," Aluki explained. She tapped the screen, and the sigils changed. "It goes on to talk about the overthrow and the end of the war. Nyar killed a Nameless One, and after that the rest left. The Ganog were unsure what to do."

Aluki was silent for a while as her eyes scanned the sigils, and Zakanna tried not to fidget. She waited patiently—well, as patiently as she could.

"Mmm, it seems that in overthrowing the Nameless Ones, the Ganog cleared the path to taking this world. They seized

Imperalis, and the beacon. Once they'd done so, there was a great schism among the clans." Aluki tapped the screen again. "Some wanted to destroy something they call 'the guardians'."

"The Void Wraith," Khar supplied. He was crouched against the far wall, polishing his pistol with a rag.

"Yes, the Void Wraith. Mmm, some wanted to free them, which could apparently be accomplished by the destruction of the beacon. A third faction won out over the others." Aluki pointed at the screen. "That faction had the Void Wraith locked away, to aid the Ganog if the Nameless Ones ever returned. Yog, Vkash, and Azi were stationed here. Nyar was entombed at the site where he'd slain a Nameless One. Kthul was never found, hidden by his clan."

"What does that mean exactly?" Zakanna asked, pursing her lips. "The way they speak of the clans, it's as if they were individuals. Great warriors."

"A great warrior would not be enough to kill a Gorthian," Khar said, shaking his furry head. He licked his chops, exposing impressive fangs.

The illusion was perfect, and Zakanna once again marveled that he was synthetic.

"Gorthians—adult ones, anyway—are strong enough to survive entry into a star. A single warrior, even a Ganog elite, would be nothing more than a minor irritation."

"Then what do you think they're talking about?" Zakanna asked. "A metaphor, perhaps?"

"Mmm, possibly. But I do not think so. The context for this sigil—it suggests that they are weapons of some kind." Aluki tapped the screen again, peering at the symbols.

"There were three of these weapons left behind?" Khar asked.

"Yes," Aluki confirmed, nodding.

"The Void Wraith are still alive, in a way. Their nervous

systems are taken from living beings. What if Yog, Azi, and Vkash are Void Wraith? They could be the Omegas we saw when we last fled this world."

"Mmm, I believe you are onto something," Aluki said, still reading. "This says that the only Nameless One killed was by Nyar, and that it happened in defense of the people of all worlds. The Nameless Ones had come to devour them all."

"That matches what we know of them. They harvest all genetic material from entire planets." Khar shuddered. "Their appetite is endless, but they are often vulnerable at the moment of feeding."

"There is more," Aluki said. "The officers among the Void Wraith, and the Omegas—they all came from high-ranking leadership caste. They were Ganog. In enslaving them to the beacon, your people were forcing their own heroes into something worse than slavery."

"It seems barbaric," Zakanna said, "particularly since the tactic has ended up delivering an army to our enemies." She shook her head regretfully. "My heart goes out to those warriors. Perhaps we can finally free them."

"Doing so will be very dangerous," Khar pointed out, folding his arms. The muscles bunched, just as they would have in a Ganog male. "The Void Wraith have been in stasis for many millennia. Odds are good they remember nothing, so as far as they are concerned, they were just betrayed by the Ganog yesterday. If we free them, they may see all Ganog as enemies. Your people could be in danger."

Zakanna paused, considering the implications. "As terrible as that might be, it is still a better option than having them serve the Nameless Ones. At least it would deny Utfa a powerful weapon, and it could weaken his hold on this world. We must take this world back, no matter the cost."

"Then our course is clear," Khar rumbled, smiling grimly.

"Whether we take the beacon or destroy it, we must plan our attack on the Royal Spire. The Void Wraith will accomplish what we were unable to."

Fizgig stepped onto the transport disk, unsurprised that one had finally shown up. It zoomed into the air, carrying her away from the prison island where they'd stored her. It was both simple and effective, this isolated island. The only way off was jumping to the deck several hundred meters below.

Her passage kicked up a cooling wind, ruffling her fur as she neared Azatok's command arena—the same arena where he'd executed Takkar just a few days earlier. Fizgig had known a brief moment of regret when Takkar died. He'd had potential.

Yet his death had not been in vain. She had learned much about Azatok during that battle.

The disk paused at the arena's edge. Fizgig hopped off. She seated herself cross-legged, gritting her teeth as she tugged her bad leg into position. Its range of motion wasn't what it once was, but it still performed admirably enough. Age had dulled her, but not as much as many assumed. Much of what made a warrior deadly was mental—the ability to force your body past what you believed it capable.

Azatok's voice boomed from above. "Ahh, the little cat has

arrived. 'Cat' is the correct word, is it not?" A wave of laughter passed through the crowd she had yet to look at. The shadows of their islands passed over the arena.

She briefly weighed the advantages of silence, but decided speaking would be best. Azatok might give something away. "It is a word used in the Coalition, yes. By the humans. They had a tiny mammal on their world that they kept for a pet, and it resembles my species."

"Pet. This word is unfamiliar to me, but your translation virus gives me some idea. Yes, you are a pet."

The shadow of his disk moved to cover Fizgig. Still she did not look up.

"Today, my pet, we will see if you can fight. You face a pack of my finest Saurians. They will crush you slowly, and I will enjoy your screams."

"You are sending *ka'tok* to fight for you? An interesting choice, though I suppose you are wary of fighting after Takkar injured you." Fizgig rose to her feet. She finally looked up, unsurprised that Azatok had positioned his disk in such a way that the light from above silhouetted him.

"You misunderstand the situation," Azatok boomed. "You are beneath me. Unworthy of breathing the same air, much less sharing a battlefield. You are not even worthy of fighting Saurians, but I thought your screams might amuse me."

Fizgig's tail lashed behind her. She gauged the distance between herself and Azatok's disk. Too far to jump, but maddeningly close.

A transport disk zoomed into view, and five Saurians hopped off. Each wielded a crude club—shaped stone with a simple, iron spike driven through the end. They wore nothing but loincloths, quite unlike the Saurians she'd dealt with previously. Some sort of ancestral garb maybe?

Fizgig made no move to defend herself as the Saurians

spread out to surround her. She very slowly groomed the fur on her wrist, not looking at her opponents.

"Defend yourself, or be cut down," Azatok roared.

Fizgig chanced a glance at the Ganog, pleased to find that his fur had gone black. He was furious that she refused to present the spectacle he was after.

"If you wish a fight, come fight me," Fizgig said, calmly.

"Kill her!" Azatok roared.

The Saurians closed as one, moving as only lifelong battle brothers could. Two stayed in front of her, both launching strikes with their clubs. The weapons were heavy and slow, and no doubt devastating...if they connected with their target.

Fizgig merely stepped to the side, dodging both blows. Two of the Saurians behind her attempted to take advantage, both launching clumsy strikes. She easily evaded, rolling between the Saurians, then back to her feet. The crowd howled with laughter.

"If you wish to fight me, then come down here. Takkar was under the mistaken impression that you were honorable. I find it surprising that you employ others to battle for you." Fizgig stepped out of the path of another club, this one wielded by a tall, heavily-muscled Saurian. This last one came the closest. Fizgig elbowed the Saurian in the gut, then took two steps to put him between her and the others. "I could kill your little lizards, if I wished. I don't wish. I wish to kill you."

She had no idea if it would insult his honor, but given everything she'd seen so far, she strongly suspected it would. Azatok was a young leader at the height of his power. Anything that might detract from that power, or make him lesser, would threaten the identity he'd so carefully crafted.

Fizgig dodged several more blows, quite easily. Had the lizards dropped their weapons and moved to grapple with her she might have been in trouble, but as it was, they'd never land a blow.

More laughter came down from above, growing in strength as minutes passed without the Saurians landing a single blow.

"Enough!" Azatok roared. He zoomed down into the arena, and for a moment Fizgig thought she might have her chance. "Have the cat brought back to her cage. I will kill the Saurians myself."

Several of the guards above her fired large nets, pinning her to the arena floor. Azatok drew his daggers, and began carving up Saurians.

Fizgig smiled. A small victory, but victory nonetheless.

39

INTO THE SPIRE

Khar's nervousness began long before they reached the spire itself. He had plenty of time for that seed to take root, as he and Zakanna walked to the spire instead of taking the cruiser. They'd joined a trickle of other travelers from a dozen different races. They resembled the *ka'tok* on Ganog 7, though if anything these were even more downtrodden.

"You are certain they cannot detect the explosives?" Khar whispered. He hunched under the makeshift cloak as they stepped under a broad arch. The Kthul guards paid little attention to the throng of travelers passing into the lowest level of the spire.

"This is the *ka'tok* entrance," Zakanna explained, pulling her own cloak tighter. "It is beneath notice. The guards assigned here have all been convicted of one crime or another, and so have their superiors. I'm ashamed to admit it, but my caste is blind to this place."

"I do not understand such an obvious gap in security." Khar shook his head as they approached the domed doorway. It had the same golden sigils he'd seen on other levels, but the ones down here were faded and cracked. Some had winked out entirely and were now little more than flaking paint.

They passed safely through the doorway into the lowest level of the spire. They were on the ground, with the spire stretching miles above them. Hundreds of islands rotated slowly above them. They grew smaller as they went higher, then finally disappeared into the distance.

"How will we make it all the way up?" Khar asked, following Zakanna into a thriving market. There were dozens of species, many he was seeing for the first time. He found it interesting that those aliens weren't allowed on the upper levels, at least not that he'd seen.

More Ganog arrogance.

"Slowly." Zakanna picked a path through the market, making for a trio of thick, rusted chains that ascended up into the distance. "These chains are free for any to use, but they require both strength and endurance. Weaker *ka'tok*, or those who misjudge their strength, often fall to their death. It is a way to keep them in their place."

Zakanna picked an empty chain and began climbing. Khar waited for her to gain a little distance, then followed. The chain's links were excellent handholds, making progress very easy. They climbed for nearly a hundred meters before catching up to a yellow-scaled Saurian who'd paused to rest. He was shaking, and clearly unable to continue.

Khar watched Zakanna, uncertain how they should proceed. His eyes widened and he reached out instinctively when she leapt from the chain. She caught the neighboring chain, spinning in a tight arc as she secured her footing.

"Jump," she called, holding out a hand for Khar.

He leapt, catching her wrist and using the momentum to swing himself above her. He caught the chain, digging his claws in for purchase. "This is a most...unconventional means of travel."

"It's part of the reason there is no security below. Simply making it to the next level can be lethal," she called back.

Khar began climbing again, leaving the resting saurian as they climbed another hundred and fifty meters, then switched chains again. Another hundred meters brought them to the base of the first ring, over three hundred meters above the now-distant spire floor.

"A better security precaution than I thought," Khar said, "though obviously it doesn't stop all." His energy reserves were still hovering around ninety percent.

"This is merely the first ring. We have many more before we reach the upper spire, and there are many dangers between here and there. Most are easily bypassed with money or guile, but there are some we still need to find a way to defeat."

Zakanna made for a restaurant built on a platform. A narrow bar ringed a bartender who stood at the center of the platform. He tended a grill next to him, and was serving some sort of meat to patrons. The disk was large enough for about three dozen passengers, though only a few stood around the bar.

"Come on, it's about to depart." Zakanna hopped onto the disk.

Khar hurried to follow. The disk zoomed into the air.

Zakanna moved to the bar. She nodded respectfully to the cook, a disinterested Saurian. "Give us two steaks and some tak nectar."

The cook wordlessly provided a pair of skewers and plastic horns of nectar. Zakanna handed one of each to Khar, lowering her voice. "We can use transports such as these to continue up the levels, though it would make sense to seek lodging periodically. If we rise too fast in a day we run the risk of discovery."

"How many days will it take to reach the top?" Khar asked, more than a little horrified. He'd assumed it would take no more than one.

"Three, or perhaps four." She chewed daintily at the pink meat. "We may as well enjoy it. Our chances of discovery are remote until we pass into the Royal Span, and that won't happen for two more days."

"All right," Khar said, sampling a bit of the meat. He couldn't taste it, of course. But he could process the nutrients and pretend, for a little while, that he was still alive in the traditional sense.

40

YEAH, STILL NO

Again, Fizgig was summoned by a transport disk. She stepped atop it, enjoying the breeze as it carried her back to the arena. This time, Azatok had only waited two days to send for her. She imagined he must have other duties to attend to, though she had no idea what he did with his time. He never left the Royal Spire; if there was a war being fought in the Imperium, he wasn't a part of it.

She glanced skyward, noting the ceiling high above. The hole Nolan had made was covered now, but the coloration was all wrong. The repairs were embarrassingly bad—just a large piece of metal clumsily bolted to the stone.

The disk glided to a halt, and Fizgig hopped into the arena. She put her hands behind her back, and casually walked to the center of the ring.

Azatok's disk hovered near a cluster of female Ganog— either wives or concubines, she guessed. They all smiled at him with simpering, vacant expressions, the kind women reserved for men whose egos were easily stroked. Azatok smiled at them, basking in their adoration. Clearly, he valued them.

"Have you decided to finally face me yourself, Azatok?" Fizgig roared, drawing his irritated gaze.

Laughter came from a few disks, though it was quickly silenced when Azatok glared at the offenders. He zoomed down until his island was only three meters above her. That was within reach, if just barely.

She tensed, then forced herself to relax a moment later. No, not yet.

"You are an amusing pet, little cat," Azatok taunted. He grinned cruelly down at her, his fur a deep scarlet. "Today, you are going to fight. I assure you. You will face a champion of my choosing, and you will battle until she kills you."

"And why would I do that, Azatok?" Fizgig asked, mildly. "I told you: I will not fight. When you are ready to face yourself, *then* I will fight. Only then."

Another disk zoomed into view and a young, female Ganog hopped off. She wore an Adept's robes, and moved with impressive skill. Fizgig watched her carefully, realizing this Adept could be a true threat—far more so than the Saurians.

That was good. It meant that Azatok was taking her more seriously. If Fizgig played her role well today, she'd leave him little choice but to face her himself.

"Is that so?" Azatok boomed. He chuckled, zooming his platform over the edge of the island. "Come, look at what I have prepared for you."

Fizgig walked to the edge of the island, staring over the side. Below was another island, just large enough for about a hundred people. It was packed with Ganog, in a variety of different armor. It looked like every clan except the Kthul was represented—even a few black-armored Nyar.

"What am I looking at?" Fizgig asked, blinking up at Azatok. Her tail lashed behind her, and she longed to sink her claws into his furry throat.

"If you do not fight, everyone on that island dies. They are prisoners, your allies in this war. Do nothing and I will have them put to death." He grinned down at her, clearly savoring the moment.

"Seriously? This is your ploy to get me to fight? I don't care about those Ganog, or any other," Fizgig said. She turned from the edge and walked back to the middle of the arena, sitting down comfortably.

Azatok zoomed his disk around to hover before her. "Perhaps you underestimate my resolve, little cat. Perhaps you think I am bluffing."

"Oh no," Fizgig said, raising her paws to her face in mock alarm. "Please don't put your own people to death for no reason. How will I ever live with myself?" She calmly began grooming.

Laughter rippled through the crowd above, and Azatok's fur shifted from scarlet to a deep red-black. "Kill them! Kill them all!" he roared, zooming to the edge of the island again. From there, he studied Fizgig, gauging her reaction.

Fizgig gave him nothing, and didn't have to fake it. She really didn't care about any Ganog, especially some random warriors who'd very likely had a hand in killing her people at Ganog 7.

Plasma fire sounded from below, and Ganog bellowed in pain. A few screamed their defiance, but the sounds quickly dwindled.

When they stopped, Fizgig could smell the stench of burnt fur. She continued grooming. "I do not bluff either, Azatok. I will not fight. You can kill as many of your own people as you like. It does not matter to me."

She glanced at the Adept out of the corner of her eye. If that one came for her, she'd have no choice but to fight. She couldn't defend forever. So she needed to play this a bit differently. She stayed seated, refusing to rise as the monk approached.

She intentionally pitched her voice loud enough to carry. "If you wish to kill me, do so. But I will die knowing that the great champion, Azatok, is a coward, unwilling to face me."

The audience gasped, and there were shocked whispers.

Azatok's fur slid to full black, and he glared hatefully down at Fizgig. For an instant she was convinced that he was going to order her death, or at least have the Adept attack her.

"Have the cat brought back to her cell." He zoomed lower, within easy reach. "Make no mistake, little Tigris. I will break you. You *will* fight. I merely need to find the proper incentive."

He smiled evilly, and Fizgig knew a moment of fear. It was clear that some new idea had just occurred to Azatok, and she worried that sooner or later he'd find something she genuinely valued. This game couldn't go on for much longer.

Odds were good she'd have no choice but to attack him the next time he summoned her.

41

NAMELESS ONE

Nuchik tore open the protein pack, sucking at the almond-flavored paste inside. It wasn't half bad, as far as rations in the field went. She preferred the mess on the *Demetrius*, but the temperature there was frosty these days. The new members of Alpha Company didn't know her, but they knew she was one of the last survivors of the original unit, and that she'd chosen not to help rebuild. It made her an outsider, in more ways than one.

Hannan plopped down on the foot of Nuchik's mech and rested her rifle next to her. "You got another one of those?"

"Sure." Nuchik fished another packet from her jacket and tossed it to Hannan. "You know, for being a repair op, it sure doesn't seem like much repair is happening." She nodded toward the Omega, which looked exactly like it had yesterday. And the day before. A flock of four-winged birds burst out of the elbow, winging out into the forest, and she shook her head. "They're using it as a nest."

"It's a big machine. It will take time. The last thing they'll do is clear the debris from the outside." Hannan tore open the wrapper, and sucked on the edge. "It wouldn't do to have the

Kthul realize what we're doing. If they find us before we finish, we're basically handing them another Omega."

"I'm still not sure giving a Void Wraith super-weapon to these Nyar is much better. They've been very clear that they don't give a crap what we think. What's to stop them from turning around and using it on us?" Nuchik finished her paste, then carefully folded the wrapper and tucked it into the pouch she used to collect her garbage. Leaving anything behind meant leaving a trail an enemy could follow. Besides, she hated littering.

"Odds are good it won't survive very long, even if we can get it operational." Hannan's words were matter-of-fact, delivered between sucking bits of paste from the packet. "If we get an Omega up and running, they'll send back all three of theirs to deal with it. Three fully functional Omegas against one battered one is even worse odds than we usually have to deal with. But, if we somehow miraculously overcome the enemy, yes, there's a chance the Nyar could turn it on us. Captain's betting that their hatred of the enemy is greater than their disdain for us. I think he's right."

"Yeah, I guess—" A tremendous shadow fell over them, followed by an awful humming that rattled her teeth. Nuchik looked up, struggling to understand what she was seeing. It wasn't a dreadnought, or a vessel of any kind. It was...some sort of creature. "Is that—a giant wasp?"

"Wasps don't have teeth, and they don't have a tail that could impale a planetstrider. It looks like a scorpion stinger." Hannan stood up, tucking her paste into a pocket. She tilted her head, speaking into her comm. "Captain, we've got some crazy shit inbound. I don't have a lot of details, but I'm guessing we're looking at a Nameless One in the flesh. This thing isn't nearly as big as the eye was, but it's about ten times as ugly."

Nuchik didn't realize she was backing away until she

thumped into the side of her mech. Her mouth was dry, her stomach heaving. A stench like insects molting made her eyes burn, even though the creature was still miles away.

She shivered, longing to be anywhere but here. "When I was a kid, my brother knocked down as hive of wasps. He got stung a couple dozen times, and I had to watch." She kept her eyes fixed on the mountain-sized bug. "I've been terrified of them ever since."

Hannan picked up her rifle. "Yeah, well, I'm *not* scared of wasps, and that thing scares the piss out of me."

The Nameless One had dropped below cloud cover, and was now hovering over the Nyar city. The awful humming came from a pair of dragonfly-like wings mounted to its back. The creature gave a deafening screech, then vomited a dense cloud of black specks over the city.

Each speck moved off in a different direction, zooming unerringly toward one of the larger spires. The specks slammed into the side of the buildings, and against her better judgement Nuchik tapped magnify on her goggles.

"They're miniature versions of the big one," she muttered, watching in horror as the flying insects tore their way inside the tower. They tunneled through the metal like a beetle through sand. "My god, that thing is a living hive. There are thousands of them."

Hannan's strong voice came over the com. "Captain, we've got a bunch of little ones, and they're swarming the Ganog spires. I don't want to leap to conclusions, but they look hungry."

"Acknowledged." Nolan's voice was calm, as always. "Just monitor for now. I'm going to hightail it back to the Nyar, and see if we can come up with a plan." The captain's confidence helped a little—as much as anything could when one was faced with the kind of impossible horror she was looking at now.

"Let's get saddled up," Hannan ordered, and started climbing her mech.

Nuchik did the same. She hadn't quite reached the cockpit when she heard the first scream. It rapidly became a cacophony as hundreds cried out in terror. She risked another glance, going pale when she saw what was happening.

The smaller bugs were flying out, carrying living Ganog back up to the mother. They flew back into the mouth, disappearing inside the monstrous thing.

"Oh, my god," she said. "They're feeding it."

42

I'LL GET RIGHT ON THAT MIRACLE

Nolan strode into the hastily-erected Ganog camp just outside the *Demetrius*. As far as he could tell, Bruth had gathered every last Nyar together. They were donning armor and picking up weapons, clearly readying themselves for war.

"Bruth," Nolan yelled, stalking into camp. "What are you doing? I thought we were supposed to be allies."

"And so we are," Bruth confirmed, tightening the strap to her scabbard. She checked the action on a thick, black rifle, then slung it over her shoulder. Finally, she turned to Nolan. "We are leaving to defend our people. If you are truly allies, then you are welcome to die gloriously at our side. Let us meet death, laughing."

"Wait a minute," Nolan snapped, pointing at the Nameless One casting a shadow over the entire city. "You're just going to charge this thing and hope for the best? Do you have any idea how idiotic that sounds? That's not a plan. That's creative suicide."

"A Nameless One devours my people, Captain. If such a creature came to your world, what would you do? We cannot allow our people to die undefended. We must try to save them."

"What would I do? I'd either come up with a plan to take it down, or I'd lead my people to safety—like any responsible leader. You know you can't win that fight. You couldn't even take out the Kthul garrison." Nolan glared up at Bruth. "If you go out there, your people die. Every last one. Have you considered saving what you can? What about your other worlds? They need you, damn it."

"Clearly you understand nothing about our people, Captain. We exist to resist the Nameless Ones, even if it means the death of our entire culture. If this is the final day of the Nyar, then so be it. Our course is clear. We ride to war. You're welcome to join us, if you've the stomach for it. If not, stay out of our way." Bruth started walking toward one of the few cruisers that had survived the Nyar escape from the city.

"Wait," Nolan said. He wasn't sure if this was a good idea, but he didn't have a better choice. Not if he wanted to stop her.

Bruth turned to face him, her expression irritated.

"We've been working on a plan. My people have repaired Nyar's Omega. We believe it's possible we could get it up and running, with Kokar as the pilot. If so, it might be able to fight that thing. Why not wait to see if we can do that, then go in together?"

"You've desecrated the tomb of Nyar?" Bruth's fur darkened, and she loomed over Nolan. "I should crush your skull and devour your heart. You are lower than *ka'tok*, and your eyes are not fit to touch it. Give me a reason why I shouldn't kill you."

"I guess you could," Nolan said, offering a noncommittal shrug. "Of course, you're well within range of the *Demetrius*'s guns, so you wouldn't survive long enough to make it to the Nameless One."

"This alliance is over, human."

"Fine, but don't be an idiot. Give me just a little more time to get Nyar's tomb operational." Nolan knew he was wasting his breath, knew there was precisely zero chance of Bruth being reasonable. None of the Nyar were, and she was one of the worst.

"If you could have done such a thing, you'd already have done so. We will not stand by while our people die, hoping you can save us with some...seeker trick." Bruth turned from Nolan, striding up the ramp into the cruiser that had arrived with the last wave of refugees. Her warriors followed, packing the hold with dozens of Ganog.

Nolan gave a heavy sigh and trotted away as the thrusters kicked up gravel and dust. He waited for it to die down before speaking into the comm. "You on the line, Major?"

"Affirmative," Burke said. "And yes, I see the creature kicking the crap out of the Nyar. At least it isn't a giant eye, I guess. Please tell me you have a way to stop that thing. Is that Omega operational?"

"I'm about to find out. Guess we're out of time." Nolan sprinted to his mech, leaping up the side and climbing into the cockpit. His fingers flew across the controls, ordering the cockpit to seal. "I'll order my squad to park our mechs just outside the Omega. I know you've got pilots with no rides."

"You realize it isn't too late to pull out, Nolan." Burke's voice was thick with emotion, revealing a side Nolan had never seen. "You can't complete the mission if the Nyar leadership is dead, and from what I can see they're flying right into that mess. I know you hate losing, but be realistic. Please."

"I wish I could, man. I wish I could. If we lose here, this is bigger than the Nyar entering the war. That thing is a baby. How big is it going to be after devouring this world? And the dozens of other worlds within a few hundred light years. We stop it here, or maybe we don't stop it at all. I'm going to make one more attempt to get that Omega operational."

"And you want me to try to keep the Nyar leadership alive?" Burke asked, wearily.

"I'm sorry, Burke—I mean that. Do what you can to protect the Nyar, but fall back when you have to. I'm parking my mech now. She's all yours."

"I know you're sorry. It isn't your fault, Nolan. I get why you're doing this, and I can't say you're wrong to do it. Go get that thing operational and come save the day. Alpha Company will deploy and do what we can to slow down those things in the meantime. Just one request, Nolan."

"What's that?"

"If you're going to produce a miracle, hurry the hell up with it."

Burke actually laughed, and Nolan found himself joining in. Sometimes a situation was so impossible, you had to either laugh or go crazy.

Maybe they were all going to die here, but if they took that thing with them, it was worth it.

43

GET THEIR ATTENTION

Burke tightened his grip on the booster mech's controls, then leapt off the ramp of the *Demetrius*. The wind from the giant bug's wings caught his mech immediately, flinging him toward the ground. Burke fired his main booster, then the stabilizers on his feet.

"Watch that first step, everyone. Things are a little choppy out here." Burke tried to muster the kind of confidence Reval would have shown. He didn't feel that—quite the opposite, in fact. But Reval had told him, when he'd first promoted him to Lieutenant, that you never let the men see your fear.

Mechs dove off the ramp after him, fanning out into five-man groups. Thanks to Nolan graciously allowing Alpha to use his mechs, they were only down one. It looked like that extra strength was going to be critical.

Thousands of insectoid creatures with three-meter wingspans flitted around not just the city below but every occupied spire. They were grabbing as many people as they could, flying them back to the monster above. It was as horrifying a fate as Burke could imagine.

"Break into fire teams and fan out around that Ganog

cruiser. Do what you can to pick off any bugs that stray too close. We need to keep those idiots alive." It galled Burke that they were risking human lives to protect these prideful Nyar, but he followed orders—even the stupid ones.

And maybe this one wasn't so stupid. Nolan wasn't wrong about needing to kill the Nameless Ones, or about it being worth all their lives in trade.

Theta shots burst sporadically from Alpha Company, picking off the bugs that strayed too close to the cruiser. Finally, the cruiser landed and began disgorging Nyar elites already in their great form.

They charged at the bugs that were carrying away their people, and at first they enjoyed some success. The bugs were much smaller than the elites, and a single blow usually killed one of the bugs. But there were a lot of bugs. They soon began swarming the elites, and the first one to begin the assault disappeared under a writhing mass of legs and thoraxes.

Burke lined up a shot, then fired his Theta cannon. The instant he recovered from recoil, he added a volley of missiles. The combined assault blew the bugs apart, clearing a path to the Ganog underneath. The elite stared sightlessly above, blood flowing liberally from dozens of holes in his armor. Most of those holes were covered in a sticky, green substance.

"Looks like their stingers are poisoned. Take care, people, these things are nasty," Burke said, again with the confidence he didn't feel. Did it really matter how many hundreds of bugs they picked off? That wouldn't even put a dent in the swarm.

A larger swarm moved toward the Ganog, but the *Demetrius* finally entered the fray. Every cannon it possessed swung into alignment with the swarm, and a staccato of Theta cannons blasted huge holes in their ranks.

"That's right, you slimy bastards," Burke growled. "You

might not fear our little mechs, but you don't like dealing with a full Coalition battleship, do you? Nice work, Kay."

"Thank you, sir," Kay's voice filled the cockpit of his mech. "I seem to have gotten their attention. The swarm is moving in my direction. I will do what I can to repel them. Oh, and one other thing. I think the queen has noticed me. She seems upset."

A massive shadow passed over Burke's mech, and he didn't even need to tap the magnify button. The tail, easily a hundred meters thick, whipped past him, the stinger dripping green goo.

A gob the size of a transport plunged past Burke's mech.

"Holy mother of God," he said. "That thing is huge. Kay, turn everything you have on that monster. Fall back slowly toward the forest. See if you can lure this thing away from the city."

Burke feathered his mech's thrusters, zooming in the direction the *Demetrius* was heading. He hadn't been at the Battle of Earth. He hadn't seen the Eye, though he'd seen the aftermath of the continents it had laid to waste. They'd had the combined power of three races, and barely stopped it.

Here, they had a single battleship. He just didn't see a route to victory.

44

EVERYONE IS ONLINE

Nolan sprinted into the Omega's control room, still out of breath from the climb. Most of the techs had left, leaving only Annie, Yulo, Nuchik, and Hannan. They huddled around Kokar's body, whispering quietly.

"Any news?" Nolan asked, moving to join them.

Kokar's fur was ashen grey, and his lips worked soundlessly. His eyes twitched in classic REM sleep.

"A little," Hannan allowed. "About ten minutes ago, not long after Kokar went under, the Omega's fist clenched. Just for a second, then it stopped. Kokar hasn't moved since. We wanted to unplug him, but that thing is attached to his nervous system. I'm not sure what it would do to him."

"Crap," Nolan snarled. What the hell was he supposed to do? He needed this thing up and running, and Kokar had been given plenty of time to do that. He turned to Hannan. "I'm going in after him."

Hannan raised a blonde eyebrow. "Sir, are you sure that's a good idea?"

"It's a terrible idea, but we're out of options. I'll see if I can wake him up and get this thing moving. If not, we're all in a world of hurt," Nolan said, settling atop the chair next to Kokar.

Having seen Kokar bond with the Omega, he had some idea of what to expect. He slid his back against the prongs, then braced himself. Something slammed into his back, and he could feel worms wriggling their way inside his flesh. He gritted his teeth, squeezing the chair with both hands.

The pain faded, and blinding, white light filled his vision. When it cleared, the room had gone entirely dark.

"Hannan? Annie?"

Nothing. No response. He felt around him, but there was nothing in any direction. Just more empty darkness. Finally, in the distance, he spotted a small, flickering fire. With no other options before him, he started in that direction.

As he approached, he caught sight of two figures next to the campfire. The shadows made their features monstrous. Both were Ganog, but Nolan only recognized Kokar. The other Ganog, black-armored like all Nyar, stood across the fire with his arms folded.

The unknown Ganog called to Nolan in a clear, deep voice. "Another approaches, though I am not familiar with your species. How do you come to be here, stranger?" He studied Nolan with intense, sober eyes.

"He is a companion," Kokar said, gesturing at Nolan. "Nyar, this is Captain Nolan of the Coalition. He is a human—the race I mentioned earlier."

"Interesting, a *ka'tok* pilot. Such a thing has never been done." Nyar smiled at Nolan. "Though, in desperate times, one must take desperate measures."

"Pilot?" Nolan asked, directing the question at Kokar. "What is he talking about?"

Kokar's fur flushed pink, and he avoided Nolan's gaze. "The

chairs allow us to link with Nyar himself, and our intelligence powers this war machine."

"Okay, I get that. But aren't *you* the pilot? And, if so, why the hell aren't you rampaging all over the Kthul?" Nolan demanded. He didn't understand where he was. It felt real, but was obviously some sort of mental construct being beamed directly into his mind by the chair.

"I—" Kokar dropped to his knees, finally giving Nolan an agonized look. "I have failed, Captain. I am not strong enough to pilot Nyar."

Kokar's fur faded to muted grey, and Nolan struggled not to choke the angst out of him.

"The youth speaks truly," Nyar rumbled. "One day, he might be ready for such a feat. He could serve as an adequate co-pilot, but nothing more than that." He fixed Nolan with a granite stare. "What about you, human? Will you attempt the bonding?"

"Kokar?" Nolan asked, helping the Ganog back to his feet. "What is he asking me to do exactly?"

"You may attempt to wrest control of the Omega," Kokar explained. "If you succeed, you will be forever linked to it. Nyar claims that when a pilot dies, his consciousness is merged with the core."

Nolan considered that. It made a lot of sense. Keep adding pilots to the core running your mech, and you never stopped expanding your knowledge of tactics and strategy. Who knew just how much this Nyar had seen in his life? Or how far back that life stretched?

Hannan's voice called hesitantly from the darkness. "Hello? Captain?"

"We're over here." Nolan frowned disapprovingly at his XO as she approached. "What the hell, Hannan? You plugged into a chair, didn't you?"

"Well, you were gone for over twenty minutes, sir. I wasn't sure how long we should wait. I thought that—"

Another shape appeared in the darkness, and Nuchik popped into existence. A split second later Yulo materialized.

Nolan massaged his temples. "Are you even kidding me? All of you came?"

"Ah," Nyar rumbled, "it has been countless millennia since we've had a full set of pilots. A Ganog Adept, and more of these humans, it seems. Most of you are not Ganog, but you will have to suffice." He rose from the fire, propping his sword against a shoulder.

"You asked me if I was willing to be pilot. Before I decide, what can you tell me about the Nameless Ones?" Nolan asked, narrowing his eyes. It sounded like time passed more slowly in here, which meant they were falling behind the situation on Nyar. But he had to know.

"Much. I led the rebellion that freed the Ganog from the grip of the terrible Nameless Ones. Before that day, I spent a lifetime doing as I was bid, conquering worlds so that they might be devoured by the insatiable gods." Nyar shuddered in distaste, then slammed his blade into the ground. The tip sank into the earth.

"You oppose the Nameless Ones," Nolan said, "and you've killed one. So have I. I'm willing to bond." There was no reservation, no hesitation. If he could fight the Nameless Ones, then he was damned sure going to do it.

"Very well," Nyar said, and extended a hand toward Nolan.

Nothing visible happened, but a wave of energy enveloped him. Nolan dropped to his knees, staggering under the curtain of flame that seared his entire nervous system. It was like the million pinpricks of a limb waking up, except many times more painful and all over his body. Nolan was dimly aware of screaming himself hoarse, but he couldn't focus on anything.

Finally, the fire faded.

His perceptions changed. Instead of the darkness, he now stood in the ruined Ganog city. Combat raged all around him; Ganog and mechs engaged swarms of bugs. In the distance, the *Demetrius* fled the bugs' queen, a dreadnought-sized monstrosity.

She wasn't anything like the Eye he'd killed, proving that there were different types of Gorthians. Her wings resembled a dragonfly, but her body was more like a wasp. She cast a shadow covering most of the city, and he guessed she was many times larger than an Omega or planetstrider.

Nolan realized that he was seeing through the Omega's sensors, and that his 'body' was the Omega itself. He could feel the limbs, feel the areas that were still in need of repair. He could feel the Omega's fusion core—and as he focused on it, that core roared to life.

Power surged through the Omega, gradually bringing systems back online.

Kokar's disembodied voice sounded in his head, like a comm. "Nyar has accepted you. Well done, Captain. You have accomplished what I could not."

"A pilot is weaker alone." Nyar's voice also sounded in Nolan's head. "There is a reason the Omegas were designed as they are. Add your strength to our new pilot, Kokar, son of Grak."

Sudden warmth spread along Nolan's scalp, and he was dimly aware of another consciousness. He could *feel* Kokar's mind, see his hazy surface thoughts. It was dizzying. There was Hannan, and Nuchik. Even Yulo was there, his mind the most difficult to pierce.

"Can you all feel the same thing I can?" Nolan asked in wonder.

"I can see into your mind," Hannan said, giving a little laugh. "This is nuts."

Nuchik spoke. "Uh, I'm not sure how I feel about you seeing into my head. Keep your eyes on your own thoughts, please." She sounded immensely embarrassed, and Nolan did what he could not to look directly at her thoughts.

"Captain," Yulo whispered, "I believe you have rediscovered the secret that allowed us to win against the Nameless Ones. I am...simply awestruck. Everything Adepts are taught prepares us to do exactly what we are doing. Suddenly, I understand the origins of my order."

"You are correct," Nyar rumbled. "Pilots were drawn from the Adepts, and only the best were selected. For millennia, our finest warriors rode these machines into battle."

"Well it looks like everyone is online," Nolan said, feeling a rush of elation. "Let's find out what this thing can do."

45

UPPER SPIRE

T he last two days had passed too quickly—a blissful interlude that seemed to be exactly what Zakanna needed. It had made her feelings for Khar clear, though of course she'd not articulated them. Neither could afford the luxury of romance. Distractions could be catastrophic.

And that was assuming Khar even felt the same way.

Zakanna flared her lower nostrils, effecting the image of a haughty noblewoman with a purpose. She clutched her cloak tightly about her, stepping aboard the transport disk. The mask was easy enough to wear, and she'd been surrounded by the best and worst noblewomen from every clan.

"Those guards are eyeing us," Khar muttered, moving a little closer to her. He too clutched his cloak, his Tigris features obscured under his armor.

"They're trying to decide if we're a threat. If we pass on their watch, then cause trouble above, they'll be blamed." Zakanna glared down her nose at the guards, presenting an image they'd no doubt seen a dozen times in the past hour. "They're unlikely to do anything, since we aren't carrying obvious weapons."

Khar pointed at the bracelet housing his plasma blade, and rested his paw on the sidearm belted at his side. "I beg to differ."

"You've fought an elite in great form. Neither of those weapons is a real threat, and the guards know it. They don't care about small, personal weapons." She found it odd that the Coalition so tightly controlled who could have a weapon, and where.

The guards continued to eye them until they drifted out of sight. Only then did Zakanna close her lower nostrils, and begin to relax. The disk continued to the next level, the first part of the Royal Span. She hopped off, quickly scanning the crowd as Khar joined her.

"Even the Saurians have been replaced," she whispered, drawing herself to her full height and once again becoming the imperial noblewoman. "All the guards are new, and they haven't had time to learn names or faces."

"That might make them stressed and distracted, but also more wary," Khar cautioned. He shook his head. "That's a bad combination. Perhaps it is time for us to use the belts."

"Not yet. I want to make it as far as we can before we resort to them. As you said, the battery is limited. I have an idea—just play along."

Willing her fur not to mirror the roiling in her stomachs, she strode boldly over to the guards, pausing before them with the kind of impatience that being a ruler had perfected in her. Eventually, the bored Kthul turned his face in her direction. Brief interest flickered in his eyes when he realized she was a female, but it dulled when he saw the sour expression on her face.

"Excuse me," she said. "I need your assistance."

"Yes?" the guard said, sighing heavily. His fur was a faint, bored brown.

"I need to reach the 33rd ring," she snapped, then paused, forcing an obviously fake smile. "Apologies, I do not mean to take it out on you. Azatok took me as a consort, then I was mistakenly left behind. I'm trying to make my way back to him."

Khar stiffened beside her, but at least had enough wisdom not to say anything.

"Uh," the guard said, glancing briefly upward. His gaze came back to her, and she saw defeat enter his gaze. He knew she'd be persistent.

She tapped her foot impatiently.

That did it. "Of course. A common oversight. Please, take that disk over there." He pointed at a row of rather official-looking white disks, which were under heavy guard.

"Thank you," Zakanna said primly, and eyed Khar with mock distaste. "Come along, laborslave."

She hurried toward the disks, and one of the guards moved to stop her. He paused, looking at the guard she'd just been speaking with. The first guard nodded his permission, and the second guard stepped aside.

Zakanna and Khar stepped onto one of the disks and zoomed away from the ring. Zakanna tensed, waiting for the guards to realize they'd been duped; both went back to what they were doing, already having forgotten her.

"What just happened?" Khar asked, looking down at the guard she'd tricked.

"Champions of the arena frequent parties, and at these parties they bed noblewomen. When those noblewomen suddenly find themselves with child, they are sent to petition for marriage." Zakanna grew more relieved as they ascended into the upper third of her spire. "He had no way of knowing what family I was from, or if offending me was dangerous. Far simpler to just let me go become someone else's problem.

I'm probably the third jilted noblewoman to approach this shift."

"Clever." Khar laughed. "Make him believe he knows exactly what he is dealing with, so he does not look deep enough to see the truth."

"I wasn't positive it would work, but this will shave almost a full day off our trip. We can reach the beacon in an hour, if we are careful. When we near the top we should activate our belts. The guards may think it odd that an empty disk arrived, but they are unlikely to report it. We should be able to sneak higher without being detected." The disk continued to zoom upward, passing another cluster of islands. She could see the next ring above them. "Now."

She thumbed the switch on her belt, shivering as the cool energy tingled over her fur. The technology was wondrous, as was the casual manner with which Khar talked about it. He took never-ending technical innovation as a matter of course, never understanding how alien it was to the Ganog.

The disk rose above the first royal ring, gliding to a stop next to the edge. She hopped quickly off, hearing Khar land next to her. She leaned closer, whispering. "We'll wait for one of the larger disks to leave."

"Genius," Khar rumbled, more loudly than she'd have liked. Fortunately, it was covered by the hum of departing disks.

Zakanna hurried over to the part of the ring with the larger transport disks used by full parties. She had no idea how, but Khar never seemed to have any issue following her. That both impressed and exasperated her. No one could detect her when she didn't wish to be detected—or so she'd always prided herself. The fact that he might be using some sort of technology reduced the sting.

She paused near a group of Kthul nobles boarding a disk,

their Saurian attendants filling the space around them. Jumping off the side of the ring, she caught the transport disk with both hands and dangled beneath it, painfully aware of the endless drop below her.

A whoosh of air and a soft grunt told her Khar had landed as well, perhaps a meter away.

"Your plan begins to impress me," Khar rumbled as the transport took off.

"If this works, we can repeat the process all the way to the highest levels. There is enough traffic this early in the day to get us all the way to my former quarters. From there we can easily make it to the beacon."

She dared to hope they might actually succeed.

46

ASSAULT THE BEACON

Khar leapt from the island, catching another transport disk as it winged upward. Zakanna's faint heat signature showed directly across from him, hanging from the other side of the disk. Above them stood a Ganog elite in brown armor, which Zakanna had told him identified the Azi clan.

He'd been shocked to hear that many members of the Azi, and even the Yog, had chosen to ally with the Kthul. The Tigris considered their pride a family, and did everything to protect it. Casting it aside was almost never done, for any reason.

The disk glided higher, passing another large island with what appeared to be an arena of some sort. The elite atop their disk roared out a jeer, adding to those being called by Ganog in the cluster of small islands orbiting the arena.

Khar magnified his vision, numbing when he realized he recognized the Tigris standing in that arena. It was Fizgig, her arms casually folded, her gaze filled with distaste and focused on a black-furred Ganog standing on a golden disk.

The disk carried them aloft, finally stopping perhaps seventy meters over the arena. To their right hovered a gigantic holoscreen. That screen showed the world of New Jaguara, one of the most heavily populated Tigris worlds, post-Eradication. A fleet of Ganog dreadnoughts hovered menacingly around that world.

A sharp click came from the area occupied by Zakanna, and Khar glanced up to see a monofilament rope streak up into the darkness. The line snapped taught, but the sound alerted the Ganog on the disk Khar dangled from. The warrior eyed the cable suspiciously, then reached for a plasma pistol.

Khar activated his nanochrons, flinging himself atop the disk. He seized the Ganog's thick head with both hands, twisting violently. The Ganog's neck snapped, and he went limp in Khar's grasp. Khar struggled to keep his balance, carefully laying the body across the disk. If it fell, their presence would be revealed. He looked around at the other transport disks, but no one seemed to have noticed.

"The line is set," Zakanna whispered. "I'm beginning my ascent." A whirring sound began, and the line shook as Zakanna's heat signature passed him.

Khar clipped himself to the line, activating his own climber. The wrist strap tightened and began carrying him upward. The arena—and Fizgig—quickly receded.

"Did you see who was in the arena?" Khar whispered to Zakanna.

"Yes. I don't know how she's still alive, but there's nothing we can do to help her." Zakanna's tone held more regret than Khar would have expected.

"I know," Khar said, forcing himself to look away from the arena. They needed to focus on the mission. If they somehow succeeded, perhaps they could help Fizgig. If not—if she died —that would be the course she herself would have chosen.

The mission above all. Pride above all.

Khar clenched his free fist. If she died, he would ensure that her valor was remembered.

A shadowy island grew above Khar. The bottom was painted black, cloaking it in shadow. It was simple, effective camouflage, and explained why most Ganog nobles had no idea this island existed, despite regularly attending games just a few hundred meters beneath it.

Zakanna's shot had attached the cable at the very edge of the disk, setting it perfectly. Instead of having to crawl along the bottom of the island, they could crawl right over the side.

"How did you make that shot?" Khar asked as the island grew ever larger.

"I remembered where the island was. There'd be no reason to move it." Zakanna shrugged.

"You made the shot from memory?" Khar asked, blinking.

"I'm an Adept. We strive for perfection, both in body and mind. It's a simple enough thing to do." Zakanna gave him a smile. "No less impressive than shots I've seen you make."

Khar privately disagreed.

The line carried them to the lip of the island, and their climbers finally stopped whirring. They'd arrived. It was time to end this.

Khar leapt onto the island, rolling to his feet. His stealth belt still had twelve percent charge, and Zakanna's should be identical. Plenty of time to do what they needed to do.

He studied the island, tensing as he scanned the enemy encampment. Tall tritanium barricades ringed the cube, largely obscuring it from sight. Khar could still see the glow, though, and occasionally the cube would bob over the barricade. Slits had been cut in the walls, allowing the defenders to peer out.

No one seemed to have detected their arrival, thankfully.

"You didn't mention their fortifications," Khar whispered, taking a step closer to Zakanna.

"They didn't exist last time I was here," she whispered back. "I'd guess that Utfa is expecting us. It's no surprise really, not after he saw you in the arcanotome. He knows we have to take the beacon."

"And we will," Khar said. "They don't appear to have detected us. Let's see if we can sneak inside." He let Zakanna take the lead, since he could see her and she couldn't see him.

She started forward, moving swiftly toward the barricade. It was constructed from bent pieces of tritainium, layered roughly on top of each other. Kits in first school could do a better job of it.

Zakanna leapt suddenly, landing on the edge of the wall above. Khar followed, landing next to her. Below stood a full compliment of Ganog elites, each already shifted into their greater forms. They stood with their backs to the cube, ready to defend it with their lives—at attention, full of relaxed alertness. Clustered around them were small knots of Adepts, many seated or kneeling.

Khar leaned closer to Zakanna. "Can we sneak close enough to plant the explosives?"

"No, they will smell us before we get there. We must fight." Her voice was calm, but Khar could hear her thundering heart.

"Then let us fight," he rumbled, leaping from the wall. Khar ignited his plasma blade, ramming it into an elite's spine. He carved his way through bone and muscle, severing the spine entirely. The elite toppled, but Khar was already moving.

He kicked off the elite's gigantic body, extinguishing his dagger. Other elites were turning in confusion, and Adepts were beginning to rise. Zakanna appeared for an instant, snapping an Adept's neck, then breaking another's leg with a sharp kick. Then she was gone.

Khar landed on the next elite's shoulder, re-igniting his plasma blade and slamming it into the Ganog's ear. The blade punched through the eardrum, continuing into the brain. The Ganog roared, slapping a massive hand over its ear.

Khar ducked the blow, rolling off the shoulder. He extinguished his blade, dodging the elite as its still-dying body toppled to the ground.

47

NO, YOU ARE NOT

Fizgig eyed the transport disk, mildly surprised it had come so quickly. It had been less than a full day since the last time Azatok had summoned her. She rose slowly, arching her back as she yawned. What did he have in store for her this time? It would be her final chance to fight; of that she was certain.

She stepped on the disk, bending her knees slightly as it zoomed aloft. It traced the now-familiar route, heading unerringly back to the arena. As she approached, Fizgig realized there were dozens of islands clustered around the arena, easily triple what she'd seen last time.

"He has something special planned," she muttered, mustering a grim smile. She had gone through a long courtship with death, and she was ready for the chase to end.

The disk zoomed down to the arena, depositing her across from a single Saurian. It wore black scaled armor that perfectly blended with its own dark scales, and it rested its hands on a pair of heavy plasma pistols. The Saurian was taller than most, though not so heavily muscled as some. Lean, and likely fast.

Azatok could learn, apparently. He'd come to understand

that her speed was her chief weapon, and brought someone to counter that ability. Fizgig had no doubt the Saurian would be fast enough to get a shot off before she could close.

Fizgig began to stretch, preparing for battle. Obstinance now, before such a crowd, would warrant immediate execution. Azatok would suffer no further slights to his honor. Yet she was still curious to see what scenario he'd devised. There would be some tactic designed to get her to fight. What would he use?

Azatok zoomed out over the crowd, alone on a magnificent golden transport disk. He raised his arms expansively, gesturing at the crowd. "I am thrilled to see so many of the new Imperium's mighty gathered here to witness an historic event. Many of you recognized Siskus, the champion of the lower games. He has bested every species, even Ganog. Today, he faces the champion of the Coalition, an alien challenger."

"She won't fight," someone from the crowd yelled. It was echoed many times over.

"What's that?" Azatok cocked a hand to his ear, his fur going smug orange. "You think she will not fight? Rest easy, friends. She *will* fight. Observe."

A holoscreen floated up over the arena so that it was visible to everyone in the audience. It flared into photorealistic life, showing a planet Fizgig recognized. It was New Jaguara, the world where Carnifex and the Jaguara had chosen to resettle after the loss of their home world.

"Fizgig—or 'Mighty Fizgig' as her people call her—refuses to fight because we have been unable to threaten anything she loves," Azatok explained, grinning savagely at Fizgig. "I believe I have finally found something she cares about. This world possesses over fifty million of her species. Begin orbital bombardment. Continue that bombardment until Siskus is dead, or the surface of the planet is molten."

The single dreadnought and its fleet of supporting cruisers

unleashed a barrage, the scarlet streaks boiling away the atmosphere before continuing on to melt the surface into a sea of glass. The bombardment moved west, eradicating everything it touched.

Hundreds of thousands of Tigris died as death rained on their cities. A few vessels attempted to resist, but the largest was a single destroyer. The cruisers made short work of it, then returned to their grisly mission.

Fizgig ignited her plasma blade and charged the Saurian. She used her free hand to thumb the button on her belt twice, to set it in shield mode. The Saurian was as fast as she'd feared, yanking his plasma pistols from their holsters with astonishing speed. He aimed them unerringly at her chest, squeezing off a quartet of scarlet blasts.

The energy washed over her shield, discoloring the area around her chest as it revealed the protective barrier. The Saurian's eyes widened, and he fired frantically. One pistol aimed for her face, the other her crotch.

Fizgig vaulted into the air, spinning over the last few blasts. At the apex of her jump, she darted her plasma blade toward her target. The humming, blue energy sank right through his body armor, severing the spine in a single blow.

She landed in a crouch and darted to the Saurian's side. Fizgig ripped the pistols from his limp hands, noting the hatred in his reptilian eyes. He was paralyzed, but still very much alive. She extinguished her blades, and turned to face Azatok.

"You are right," Fizgig said, as respectfully as she could muster. "You have discovered the correct leverage. My foe is dead. Please, stop this madness."

Azatok stared down at her in consideration, tapping his jaw with his index finger.

"Had you cooperated earlier, perhaps I'd show mercy. You chose to embarrass me. Continue the bombardment," Azatok said, waving at his techsmith. The holographic screen showed the destruction, unabated. "In fact, have three planetstriders warp to the southern continent and begin laying waste to their cities. I want to watch their young run from death."

Fizgig mastered her rage, mentally calculating. She looked from platform to platform, but there was no easy way to reach Azatok. By the time she did, he'd simply have moved his platform. That left her only one option. She must get him, to come to her.

"You are a true coward, Azatok. A weak brute relying on others to support your own power. I ask you one last time: Fight me."

"And why would I do that?" Azatok said, laughing.

Fizgig scanned Azatok's harem—to which she had paid a great deal of attention during her previous times in the arena—and picked out the two females that had spent the most time simpering before Azatok. She raised the Saurian's pistols, and executed them both. Their bodies toppled from the disks, plummeting to the arena's sandy floor.

Azatok gawked, mouth working. Fizgig shot two more, smiling calmly up at Azatok. "You will fight me, because I have *also* found the correct leverage. I will kill your entire harem, unless you stop me. Where is your honor now, Ganog?"

Azatok's eyes blazed. He roared his fury, knocking a techsmith from his path as he leapt over the side of the transport disk. He landed across from Fizgig, growling. "I'm going to enjoy this, little cat."

"No. No, you are not," Fizgig answered, sliding her feet apart. She reignited her plasma blade, dropping the pistols.

48

SACRIFICE

Khar rolled away from a Ganog's kick, air whooshing past as the blow just missed his face. Behind him, an Adept was waiting. She glided forward, her fist rabbiting into the small of his back. His nanochrons dispersed some of the kinetic force, but a warning light flared.

Khar's elbow shot into the Adept's face, slamming her nose into her brain cavity. The blow knocked her away, but before Khar could follow up, another Adept had stepped into her place.

A shimmering figure landed next to the Adept, then a roundhouse kick flung her into the air. Khar lunged, punching his plasma dagger through her throat as she sailed past. He twisted, putting his back to Zakanna's heat signature.

"We've hurt them," she said, panting.

"Not enough," he said, warding off a blow from an Adept. Most of the elites were down, at least, and the last trio was circling around the beacon protectively. They weren't leaving it, but were instead allowing the Adepts to wear them down.

"We've lost the advantage of stealth. They know what to look for now."

Then there was no more time for words. Khar blocked another punch, returning one that broke his opponent's forearm. He battled furiously, watching as his power reserves dwindled. He hadn't really expected it to be easy, but this protracted combat was more than he'd bargained for.

Zakanna flipped over an Adept, and that Adept turned to face her. Khar plunged his dagger into the back of the Adept's skull, pivoting to dodge a strike from another Adept. That opened him to a kick from a third, which flung him to the ground.

A hail of punches and kicks rained down, and it was all Khar could to do protect his vital systems. Warning lights sprang up all over the place, but try as he might, he couldn't regain his feet. There were too many enemies.

"Zakanna!" he yelled.

The blows slackened, and Zakanna roared in anger. Khar lashed out with his foot, shattering a kneecap. He rose to his feet, nanochrons already repairing the worst of the damage. The Adepts were converging around Zakanna, and her belt finally failed entirely. She was fully visible, and was now the focus of their collective attention.

Khar knew there'd be no way to stop them all, no way to prevent them from killing her. He had to try anyway. Khar sprinted forward, dropping an Adept with his plasma blade, then launched his knee into another, shattering the Adept's spine. He fought like a demon, slashing and whirling and kicking.

The battle was glorious, and he lost himself in it, ignoring the bitter whisper that survival was impossible. One of the elites moved to attack Zakanna, so Khar vaulted into the air. The elite was ready, its fist blurring out.

The blow caught Khar in the chest, flinging him into the barricade wall. Yellow lights shifted to red, showing the catastrophic damage throughout his limbs and torso. Behind the elite, Zakanna battled desperately.

She blurred through combat forms, fighting off Adepts as she dodged the elite. It was as impressive a martial display as Khar had ever seen, yet he knew it must end soon.

Zakanna caught Khar's eye, and time seemed to slow. In that eternal instant, her gaze conveyed everything, her feelings for him, her hopes for the future. Her knowledge of her own imminent death. Her willing sacrifice.

A Ganog stumbled in front of Zakanna, ending the moment. Khar glanced at the beacon, realizing that all three elites were converging on Zakanna, determined to end her. They'd already dismissed him, stopped considering him a threat.

His path was clear. He must destroy the beacon.

K har hung in agonized eternity. He looked to the beacon, then back to Zakanna. He shared her feelings—not just her affection, but her willingness to sacrifice everything. She'd created an opening, and he would honor her sacrifice by taking full advantage of it. They were both probably dead anyway.

Khar triggered his stealth belt again, feeding it power from his own dwindling reserves. He sprinted toward the beacon, pulling a block of ferrogel from his pack. The Ganog explosive had proven far more effective than the Coalition equivalent, with the added benefit of being relatively stable.

Only one elite somehow detected him, and Khar ducked under a clumsy fist. He darted forward hurling the block at the beacon. Khar ripped his particle pistol from its holster, aiming at the ferrogel. His reticle lined up, and he stroked the trigger. A blast of blue shot into the ferrogel, igniting it instantly.

"Shield!" Khar roared, using the nanochrons to amplify his voice.

He thumbed the switch on his belt, turning it from stealth

to defensive field, and added a torrent of energy from his reserves to amplify the protective field.

A wave of brilliant light burst from the beacon, slamming into Khar. He was flung away from the center of the blast and sailed past the elite who'd been trying to stop him. The flames and debris shredded the elite's armor, picking him up with the same force that had flung Khar into the air.

The wave of flame blasted him into the wall of the barricade, and Khar rebounded off as the explosion burst upward out the top of the barricade.

He landed in a heap, confused and unable to rise. Red warning lights covered every system, and those few that functioned were being shut down to allow the nanochrons to effect repairs. Khar overrode that process, continuing repairs but keeping critical systems active.

The area around him was filled with smoking bodies, and the wisps rising from the elite mostly obscured his view. Khar slowly stretched out a hand, pulling himself past the elite. He allowed himself a weak smile when he was finally able to see the beacon—or its smoldering remains, anyway. A single hunk of warped, white metal lay where the cube had been, the circuitry on its blasted surface now dark.

Shards of white shrapnel were embedded in the barricade's scorched walls, and in the bodies of the fallen Ganog. A few of those bodies were still moving, writhing in blind agony and unable to rise.

Khar scanned the pile of bodies where Zakanna had been, struggling to find any sign of her. Now able to use both arms, he tugged himself across the grass. It took long moments to reach the pile of blackened and charred bodies.

He tugged an Adept off the pile, then another. The elites were too heavy to move, so he worked around them, trying to find any sign of her.

Finally, he heard a weak cough.

"Zakanna?" he called, clawing his way over to the area the sound had come from. It was under one of the elites.

"I—I'm here," came a weak reply. "I activated the belt just in time I think. This body covering mine probably also helped, though the smell is abominable."

"Can you move?" he asked, rising to one knee. His reserves dipped below ten percent, but some basic function was returning.

"Hold on," she said, through gritted teeth.

A series of deep, booming breaths came from underneath the elite. The elite was flung upward, crashing to the ground several meters away. Zakanna flipped to her feet, moving to Khar's side. Her chest heaved as if she'd run a marathon, and her gaze was thick with weariness.

"Oh, Khar," she said, kneeling next to him. "Your fur—"

Khar looked down at himself and began to laugh. His fur had been cooked away from his face and shoulders. "It will grow back by this time tomorrow, I'm sure. Come, let's see if our actions have had any affect."

Khar opened a communications channel to Aluki. "Aluki, the beacon is destroyed. Can you give us an update?"

"Mmm, it's a full-on war out here. The Void Wraith have begun attacking Ganog. All Ganog, everywhere. They're slaughtering them, both down here and up in orbit." Aluki sounded thrilled. "Are you ready for extraction? We're in position, just outside the spire."

"Yes," Khar said, accepting Zakanna's hand as she pulled him to his feet. "But we have one more errand to attend to before we escape."

"Mmm, it had better be quick," Aluki cautioned.

Above, the spire shuddered, then stone rained down. Aluki's cruiser shimmered into view as it dipped through the very same hole they'd left when they fled this world before. It descended toward their island, a ramp already extending as they landed.

Zakanna helped Khar up the ramp, and he was embarrassed to admit he needed that help.

"Mmm, what's so important that we need to risk the Void Wraith?" Halut demanded, slapping the red button to close the ramp behind them. "We should leave. Now."

"No," Khar growled, glaring at the little Whalorian. "We must save Fizgig. Then we can be away from this place."

AZATOK

Azatok had rarely been this furious, and had never been so humiliated. The crowd's cruel laughter prodded him forward, toward the little Tigris that had caused such catastrophic damage to his reputation. The alien had even goaded him into sending part of the fleet to destroy a Coalition world. Utfa would be furious, if he learned of it.

All because he wanted to break an aging enemy commander. He'd blundered, and he knew it. But there was still some satisfaction yet to be gleaned. He would enjoy watching the life fade from Fizgig's eyes.

Azatok withdrew the same daggers he'd used to kill Takkar. He began his breathing, circling Fizgig. The Tigris was already smaller than him, but soon he'd dwarf her. There was no way she could stand against him in great form.

Fizgig shimmered out of sight. Azatok's eyes widened as he frantically scanned for any sign of his opponent. He sucked in a breath to comment on her cowardice when a humming, blue blade came at his face. He staggered backward, desperately struggling to get one of his daggers up in time to block.

Unfortunately, the attack came toward his wounded side. His arm was still healing, and was slower than it should have been. The blue dagger scored his cheek, nearly taking his eye before he was able to disengage.

"Coward! You began a duel before I completed the change. Have you no honor?" he roared, slashing at the air in front of him with one of his daggers. "Show yourself."

He continued his breathing, growing a full meter as he took a step. A humming came from behind, and he spun. Too late. The blade punched into his back, through the armor and deep into his flesh. He roared, swiping behind him in a wild slash.

Azatok whipped his foot around in a roundhouse kick, but found only air. He spotted a shimmer in the air, like heat. "Ah, there you are. Your little trick won't work any more. I can see you now."

Fizgig reappeared, standing where he'd seen the shimmer. "It won't save you." She charged, launching a slash at his face, toward the other eye.

Azatok knocked the blade away, backpedaling to gain room. He tried to focus on the change, seeking the great form that he knew would end this fight. She gave him no opportunity, coming at him relentlessly. Again and again she struck, and each time he was barely able to parry. He flared his lower nostrils, needing the extra oxygen they could provide. His fur was a mass of red and yellow and black, broadcasting his emotions for all to see.

Azatok lunged, suddenly on the offensive. His first dagger shot toward Fizgig's face, but she dodged the blow. His second would have disemboweled her, but she knocked it to the side with her plasma blade. He began a third strike, but she was faster.

Fizgig slashed at his wrist—the uninjured one. Her blade bit deeply, nearly severing his hand. Azatok's dagger clattered to the ground, and Fizgig scooped it up as she continued to press her attack.

He staggered back, keeping her briefly at bay with wild slashes from his remaining dagger. She switched fighting styles, coming at him with both daggers. Azatok tried to adjust his defenses, but his wounds were mounting, and he knew he was slowing.

He breathed frantically, continuing the change, and gained another meter in height. He towered over her now, but she darted in again, scoring his side with his own dagger. It carved a line of pain, adding to the chorus.

He swiped half-heartedly at her retreating form, but focused on his breathing. He gained another meter.

She never let up, stabbing and slashing. Somehow, he survived the onslaught. He grew taller, his reach greater. It became easier to keep her away, and he gained a brief respite to think. He needed to regain the offense, but it was unclear how he could do that, even now that he was in his greater form.

Blood poured from his wrist, and the hand had gone numb. His back throbbed, and a thick flow of blood stained his fur all the way down his leg. Dozens of small cuts scored his hide—none fatal, but their accumulated damage a drain on his strength.

"You're larger now," Fizgig taunted from just out of reach. "But you are injured and slow. Time is on my side. Surrender, and I will allow you to live."

Azatok saw red. He charged, bellowing his rage as he brought his now much larger dagger down toward Fizgig. She stood placidly until the very last instant, then leapt over his blow, digging her blade into his knuckle. She flipped onto his wrist, bringing the plasma blade down in a tight arc. The weapon sliced bone and flesh, completing the destruction

Takkar had begun. His hand, still holding his dagger, crashed to the deck.

Fizgig sprinted up his arm, but Azatok knocked her away with his forearm. Blood pumped from his severed stump, and from his many other wounds. Black spots danced in his vision, but he refused to be beaten. He struggled to keep Fizgig in sight, but she'd engaged her stealth belt, and he'd lost the shimmer.

She appeared suddenly, at the edge of his blind spot. Her dagger lashed out, sinking into his calf. He roared, swiping at her with his stump. Fizgig rolled away, coming to her feet on the other side of the area.

Azatok limped toward her, forcing her toward the edge of the island. He launched a low kick, capitalizing on his greater reach. Fizgig effortlessly rolled under his foot, stabbing her dagger into the same calf. She tore a ragged meter-long gash in his leg, and he collapsed to the island, unable to support himself on the injured limb.

"I will give you one last chance at the mercy you denied my people," the Tigris said. "Surrender, and I will let you live." There was no emotion in her voice, no hatred or anger. No need for revenge. This was simply business to her.

"Never," Azatok roared. He forced himself to one knee, scanning for her. There was no sign of her, either because she was in his blind spot or because she was using the belt.

Above him, the crowd had gone still. None uttered a word. Only the artificial wind broke the silence.

"Very well," Fizgig whispered into his ear. She was perched there, right on his shoulder. He had no idea how she'd gotten there undetected, and no time to wonder about it. Her dagger tore into his throat, ending his ability to speak even as his lifeblood fountained onto the hot sand.

Azatok collapsed onto his back, staring up in the direction of the apex island, a place few knew existed.

Flashes of plasma came from atop it. Someone was fighting. No! Someone was assaulting the beacon. He had to do something, had to get word to Utfa.

Azatok struggled onto his stomach, crawling toward the edge of the island. They must be warned.

A soft hum heralded the plasma blade that brought blissful oblivion.

51

RESPECT THE TIGRIS

Fizgig extinguished her blade, struggling to catch her breath. A stitch of fire lived in her side, one of the worst cramps she'd ever suffered. Her leg ached abominably. Worse, she was covered in sticky, black Ganog blood. It would take many baths to remove all of it.

"Which of you wishes to be next?" she roared, looking up at the assembled audience. They stared at her, a hundred different versions of the same horrified expression. She'd killed their champion, and she'd made it appear easy, though it had been anything but. She sucked in a deep breath, booming her next words. "*No one?*"

As if to punctuate her sentence, a deep *whoomp* came from above. She recognized the sound. It was the Ganog explosive, ferrogel. The crowd began peering uneasily upward, still uncertain what to do.

A larger explosion sounded, and stone tumbled down from above as a part of the ceiling collapsed. Disks zoomed away as the crowd finally broke and ran. Boulders crushed several disks, only adding to the crowd's panic.

Aluki's familiar cruiser descended through the hole in the

spire, disappearing above the Apex island. She realized her companions didn't know she was here, and they were too far away for her to reach. Nor could she communicate directly with them.

That meant they could not rescue her, but it didn't matter. She would finally meet death.

She walked away from Azatok's corpse, sitting heavily in the dirt. Purring, she began to groom. At least she would die clean.

Somehow, Khar had succeeded in reaching the beacon. Goddess willing, he'd be able to seize control of it. More explosions came from above, and the whine of engines grew louder. Fizgig looked up, her tongue still sticking out. Aluki's cruiser was approaching the arena.

The external speakers crackled with static, then Aluki's voice echoed through the spire. "Mmm, hello there, Admiral. Would you like a ride to safety?"

The ramp at the base of the ship extended, and Fizgig rose with a painful pop in her hip. She limped over to the ramp, where Khar and Zakanna were waiting for her.

"Quickly," Khar called, sprinting down the ramp. He wrapped an arm around her waist, helping her up the ramp. She longed to push him away, but wasn't positive she could make it up the ramp unaided. Emotional and physical exhaustion were threatening to pull her under.

"Release me," she snapped the instant she was across the threshold. Khar did as she asked, and Fizgig limped to the wall. She slid to the ground, her back against the blessedly cool metal. The ramp slid shut, and her stomach lurched as the ship began to ascend. "How did you know I was here?"

"I spotted you when Zakanna and I were infiltrating the spire. Your fight with Azatok was broadcast to the whole Imperium, and it made an excellent distraction." Khar gave her a toothy smile. "After we destroyed the beacon—"

"You destroyed the beacon?" Fizgig said, blinking.

"It was the only way," Khar said. "The defensive force guarding it was too great to overcome."

"We did all we could." Zakanna rested a hand on Fizgig's shoulder.

Fizgig glared at her until she removed it.

"You've done well," Fizgig said. "At the very least, the Void Wraith are free. Let us be away from this world." She leaned her head back against the wall. Once again, she'd cheated death. Perhaps she was destined to die in her bed, after all.

She smiled, reveling in the fact that not only had she slain the man who'd burnt New Jaguara to ash, but that his humiliating death had been broadcast to the entire Imperium.

Perhaps now these Ganog would learn to respect the Tigris.

52

NOT GOOD

Burke leaned into the harness, triggering the mech's main booster. It soared into the air, vaulting the bug attempting to grapple him. Another rushed forward, but Burke sliced it in half with his mech's plasma blade. He slammed into his command couch as his mech was knocked forward from behind.

The ground rushed up at the cockpit, then metal shrieked as forty-five tons of tritanium pulverized stone. A klaxon sounded, and warning lights appeared in the mech's right arm and shoulder.

"There sure are a lot of these things," Burke muttered, flipping his mech over onto its back. A bug landed on his chest, thrusting its stinger into his mech's leg. It slid easily into the tritanium, and Burke realized that if he were a person, whatever poison this thing was using would have instantly entered his bloodstream. These things would be hideously effective against Ganog.

Good thing he wasn't a Ganog. Burke seized the bug by its head and squeezed. The resulting pop triggered a gag reflex. Damn, these things were disgusting.

At least he couldn't smell them.

High above, the queen slowly approached the *Demetrius*, her long tail circling behind her, coiling for a strike. The *Demetrius*, as he'd ordered, fell back. A flurry of Theta cannon shots rippled from her aft guns, tearing into the queen, who shrieked as chunks of flesh and chitin were blown free.

The queen spat a mass of gelatinous yellow goo that covered three of the Theta cannons on the aft side. She angled her flight to take advantage of the blind spot, dodging another volley as she moved out of the firing arc of the remaining cannons.

She spat another gob of goo, covering more cannons. The goo began to spread across the hull, moving to engulf the next cannon. This only enlarged the blind spot, allowing the queen to fly closer. She was narrowing the gap with alarming speed.

Burke had a choice: Try to save the doomed Nyar leadership who didn't want to be saved, or try to save his ship. He wasn't likely to succeed at either.

"Alpha Company, disengage and return to the *Demetrius*. Looks like the queen is taking the guns out with some sort of adhesive goo. Let's see if we can burn that crap off."

Burke leapt into the air, pouring thrust into all boosters. His mech rocketed toward the *Demetrius*, gliding around swarms of bugs as he rapidly approached. The queen grew larger and larger on his view screen. Swarms of insects—hundreds upon hundreds—flowed out from holes in her carapace.

Behind him, the survivors of Alpha Company leapt into the air and followed into combat. They were economical in both their flight path and their use of ordnance, firing only when picking off a bug would shorten their route.

"The swarm is aware of us," Burke said, dropping into a quick dive as a cloud of bugs moved in his direction. "We've got more speed, but they've got the edge in maneuverability. Full thrust. Let's outrun these bastards."

Burke shot back up toward the *Demetrius* in a steep climb. He passed one of the bugs and the flame from his boosters roasted its wings. The creature fluttered to the ground, receding almost instantly as Burke continued to climb.

He reached an even altitude with the *Demetrius* and tapped the *magnify* button on his console. The screen zoomed in on the cannons, showing the goo flowing over them. It moved like a self-aware creature, skipping the hull and focusing solely on the cannons.

Burke blasted over to the closest cannon, whipping his mech's legs around so the thrusters faced the goo. He fired a low level burst, whooping as the goo boiled away. "Use your thrusters, boys. We can burn this crap right off."

A deafening shriek drowned out all communications, then the queen slammed into the side of the *Demetrius*. Burke was blasted violently away, his mech spinning uncontrollably as he plummeted toward the ground.

He took deep breaths, focusing on his training. "C'mon, man. You've got this."

Burke righted his trajectory, feathering his thrusters to gain more control. Above, the queen's stinger had punctured the ship's stern and now lay embedded in the metal. Her six legs had enfolded the *Demetrius*, crushing it against her thorax. Smaller bugs swarmed the vessel, searching for any way inside the vessel.

"Kay, can you give me a status report?" Burke asked, voice cracking.

"Not good, sir," Kay replied, forlornly. "The Theta cannons cannot be fired at close range without inflicting significant damage to the *Demetrius*. Even if they could, preliminary data suggests that the damage would be insufficient to cause this creature to disengage. I'd recommend fleeing, sir. This battle is over."

Dense, black smoke poured from one of the *Demetrius*'s engines, and the battleship slowly plummeted toward the jungle. She was going down, and there wasn't a damned thing he could do about it.

53

ONLINE

The alien scaffolding supporting the Omega retracted, and Nolan took an experimental step. It wasn't at all like piloting a mech. Piloting this thing was as simple as walking, a beautiful interface that explained why these things had been so deadly. He *was* the Omega.

He turned to face the battle raging over the south side of the city, where the buildings were swallowed by the forest. Hunks of debris rained from the *Demetrius*, as the queen sank her legs deeper into the ship. Her tail coiled more tightly around the stern, crushing several Theta cannons.

"Major Burke, we're finally inbound," Nolan offered, starting the Omega into a trot. Every step pulverized a city block, sending a tremor through the forest.

"If you're in a position to help, now's the time," Burke said, panting into the comm. "Is that thing operational?"

"We're about to find out," Nolan muttered, moving into a sprint. The Omega shot forward, knocking buildings and trees aside as it closed with the queen. Thus far, she hadn't reacted to their presence, though swarms of smaller bugs were already moving in their direction. "Burke, what's the status of the Nyar leadership?"

"They stayed behind for a heroic last stand," Burke said. "We disengaged to help the *Demetrius*. It wasn't my first choice, but seemed like the best option."

"I'd have done the same. We can't save people who don't want saving. Let's see if we can give you some support. Nolan out." He turned the comm off, and focused on the battle.

He was perhaps a thousand meters below the queen, but she was getting closer as the *Demetrius* descended toward the trees. Smoke billowed from both engines, and only the secondary thrusters prevented the battleship from going into free fall.

"Nyar, this thing has a cannon in the chest, but I can't find any way to fire it," Nolan said, glancing down at the Omega's chest. "Any suggestions?"

"You are not meant to," Nyar rumbled. The voice sounded like it was coming from directly behind Nolan's ear. "One of your co-pilots will fuel the weapon with their own essence."

"Allow me to tend to this," Kokar growled.

Energy surged in the Omega's reactor, pooling in a brilliant mass at the cannon's heart. It built for a precise three seconds, then a cerulean beam cut through the swarms and into the queen. Two of her legs were sheered off, and she released the *Demetrius* with a ground-shaking shriek.

Her multifaceted eyes fixed on the Omega, and she glided in their direction.

"Looks like you got her attention, sir," Hannan said, tension thickening her voice. "This thing have any defenses?"

The queen spat a gob of yellowish ichor in their direction, enough of it to cover even the Omega. Nolan tried to guide Nyar out of the way, taking a big step backward. The goo adjusted its flight, like a living thing.

"Allow me, Captain," Yulo said.

Nolan relaxed, allowing the master to assume control. The Omega flipped backward, kicking off a building, then landing behind another. It was the most impressive display of acrobatics Nolan had ever seen.

He didn't have long to enjoy it. "Crap! Brace yourselves, it's still coming." Nolan shifted the Omega into a defensive stance as the goo whipped around the building they were sheltering behind. Nolan raised Nyar's arm to keep the goo from covering their face.

The goo stopped a mere fifty meters from them, slamming into a glittering, blue shield—the kind of shield that protected a Void Wraith harvester.

"Sir, I think I did that," Hannan said. It sounded like she was gritting her teeth. "It's like holding a couple hundred pounds over my head. Can't do this for much longer."

The goo flowed around the impact point, trying to find a way inside the barrier. Nolan swept the Omega's plasma blade in a tight arc, burning away a section of goo. Several more strikes took care of most of it.

"Barrier down," Hannan gasped, as the shimmering field disappeared. The last few wisps of greenish goo fell lifelessly to the ground.

"Incoming," Nuchik called frantically.

The smaller swarms had finally reached them, covering the head as they began gouging armor with their stingers. One slammed into the eye, piercing it with a stinger. That sensor went dark, adding a blind spot to Nolan's vision.

He reached down and ripped a lingering redwood from the knee joint, to us as a club. Every swat knocked dozens of bugs from the air, clearing a spot around the face.

"Nyar, give us something to work with," Nolan roared,

lurching away from the swarm. He batted another dozen bugs from the Omega's face, but dozens more filled the gap.

"Hang on," Hannan yelled. "I've got something."

The Omega began to vibrate and the air around them blurred like a heat mirage. A pulse of subsonic energy exploded outward, knocking away the bugs. Every bug affected by the wave fell from the sky and crashed to the city below. The wave rippled outward for several kilometers, dropping tens of thousands to the ground.

"Nice work, Hannan. Burke, any chance Alpha can take advantage of this? Those bugs are dazed, but they're going to get back up."

"Affirmative." Theta cannon shots whined in the background. "I think we can reach the spire where the Ganog survivors are holed up. If you can deal with her royal sliminess, I think we can carve up the little ones. We'll establish a perimeter around the Nyar leadership."

"Sounds like a plan." Nolan looked upward with the Omega's one remaining eye, just in time to see the queen kick off the *Demetrius*. The battleship's ragged form crept away, smoke pouring from dozens of structural fires. Both main engines were still dark, and he only spotted a few functional cannons.

She'd been through the wringer, but she was still flying.

"Kokar, can you fire that cannon again?"

"In a moment, Captain," Kokar rumbled. A quaver ran through his voice. "Both it, and I, need to recharge."

"That might explain why the Omegas only fired once each when they took this planet. Maybe it takes a pilot," Nolan mused, still focused on the queen. "All right, let's see if we can get her to come to us."

He sprinted forward, charging down a wide street, then leapt into the air and wrapped a metal hand around the midsection of one of the largest spires. He used it to increase his momentum, flinging himself even higher in the air.

He arced his plasma blade around in a brutal slash, but the queen twisted out of the way. Her tail darted forward, snaking around the Omega's right leg. She flew upward, beating her wings furiously as she carried them ever higher.

The ground receded at an alarming rate, and try as he might, Nolan was unable to connect with the giant bug. She kept twisting at the last second, jerking them with her tail so the blows missed. Nolan finally got a hand around the tail, pinning it in place. He rammed the plasma blade into the thick, chitinous hide.

The queen shrieked, kicking them away from her with her remaining legs. Nolan held on. He ripped his plasma blade from the tail and brought it up in a wide slash, severing the tail in a spray of brown-yellow ichor. The queen shrieked again, struggling to gain altitude. She receded above them as they fell, unable to stop the Omega's fall.

"Hannan, any chance you can get that shield back online?" Nolan asked, praying silently.

"On it, sir," Hannan replied, tense but confident.

They plummeted toward the ground, and Nolan shifted Nyar so they could see it rushing up at them. They only had a few seconds. He winced, resisting the urge to tell Hannan to hurry.

A moment before impact, the energy barrier swung back into place. They slammed into the ground with the force of a meteor, blasting a wave of stone, metal, and earth in all directions. The blast leveled a quarter of the city, though thankfully not an occupied quarter.

"Nyar, is there any way to know what systems have been damaged?" Nolan asked. He guided the Omega back to its feet, crushing several large trees as he stood.

"The Omega will repair itself, as able. Like the cannon, it will draw on a pilot to fuel repairs."

Yulo spoke, his voice thick with concentration. "I believe I can accelerate those repairs, Captain."

"Do that." Nolan took a wobbly step around a stand of trees to get a better look at the Nameless One's retreating form. The queen was still gaining altitude, and in a few more minutes would break orbit. "If she makes it to the Kthul fleet we'll never stop her. Kokar, I need that cannon, and I need it now."

"I believe I can fire the cannon, Captain, but it's an impossible shot. She's nearly broken orbit. Even if I hit her, the blow will not be fatal."

"We have to try," Nolan thought aloud. Then he laughed. "Wait a minute, we've got the best sniper in the fleet. Nuchik, can you make that shot?"

"Second or third best," Nuchik replied, "but I think I can probably hit that bitch."

Nolan ceded control, and the Omega dropped to one knee. It aimed the cannon skyward, tracking the queen's flight. Kokar and Nuchik both screamed, their combined voices growing louder as the cannon charged. A beam of brilliant, blue energy shot into the sky, aimed unerringly at the tiny speck the queen had become.

Nolan willed the Omega's remaining eye to magnify, zooming in to see the queen. She was hideous—and then she was dead. The beam punched through the rear of her thorax, exiting through her mouth. Waves of energy pulsed outward, and she exploded into yellow-brown mist.

"Just like a bug hitting a windshield," Hannan said, a little awe in her voice. "I think I kind of like this mech, sir. Hope we get to keep it."

"Congratulations, Pilot," Nyar interrupted. "You have slain a

Nameless One. A young one, but an impressive feat nonetheless. You have saved countless worlds from being devoured."

"It isn't the first Nameless One I've killed, and I promise it won't be the last." Nolan grinned, thrusting the Omega's fist into the air. "So, Nuchik, Kokar, how do you feel about delivering me some dead Kthul dreadnoughts? I count four."

"Just let me catch my breath," Nuchik panted. "Kokar, you ready for this?"

"A moment, and then we shall end our hated foes once and for all," Kokar roared.

54

T'KON'S DECISION

T'kon stared out the observation dome, taking in the nebula staining the stars a bright green. He'd been staring at the same nebula for a week, and the view had lost its majesty. He itched to act. The waiting was excruciating.

"You sent word that you have finally chosen a course," Jehanna said, her robes swishing as she pressed up against his back. "Where will you take the fleet?"

"I will tend to the survival of our race," T'kon said, turning to face her. He wrapped an arm around her and pulled her closer. "The needs of our clan must come second. If the day comes when the Azi are no more, than so be it."

"I do not envy you the choice," she whispered, resting her head against his shoulder. "Were it me, I would be weak. I would return to reclaim our home world. Especially knowing that Oako has but a single dreadnought guarding it. If not there, then where have you chosen?"

"I've chosen the place where we can make the most difference. Only one clan is still strong enough to resist the Nameless Ones." T'kon turned to the techsmith.

"Order the fleet to warp to Nyar. Tell them to ready for combat."

"Yes, Clan Leader," the Saurian said, giving a respectful bow. He turned with dignity, closing his eyes. Pulses of data flowed to and from his arcanotome.

"Thank you," T'kon said, drawing a surprised glance from his wife. He smiled down at her. "I learned many things during my time as clanless, wife. The *ka'tok* are not less than us. They are worthy of respect, even if they fill a different role in our society. Treating them as allies, instead of as slaves, ensures that they are invested in our joint future."

"I do not know how I feel about this change to our customs," Jehanna said, blinking. She disengaged from him, peering up at the observation dome as the warp began.

T'kon waited for his innards to stop twisting, then immediately scanned the system they'd arrived in. He'd heard of the legendary world, but had never been to Nyar. The first thing he noticed was the sea of asteroids. No doubt they'd been clustered densely around the planet, but with no warp anchor to hold them in position, they'd begun to drift. Most had drifted outward, but the defense satellites were busily destroying those that strayed too close to the planet.

The enemy fleet lay beyond a field of rock—four dreadnoughts and a host of cruisers. That would make this a roughly equal fight.

"Cut a path through the asteroids," T'kon ordered, "and concentrate all fire on the closest dreadnought. Deploy fighters, with orders to harass the smaller ships." He paced back and forth as he stared at the enemy fleet.

His own fleet began to move, swarming toward the enemy. That enemy was probably just becoming aware of their presence. If he was fortunate, it was possible their commanding officer wasn't even on the command island.

The dreadnought rumbled as the main cannon built energy. A beam of scarlet shot into the black, disintegrating asteroids before slamming into the side of the enemy dreadnought. Ripples of scarlet passed through the shield, but it held. Until the other three cannons fired.

Armor fountained from the wounds, followed by puffs of blue-white atmosphere flooding into space. The enemy shields quickly patched the holes, but that only stripped them of their ability to protect the rest of the vessel.

Fighters winged toward the enemy, clusters swarming around cruisers and frigates. The Kthul ships fought back, destroying a smattering of fighters even as their own vessels were cut down. The first wave was a dramatic success, simply because the enemy wasn't prepared.

"Have the fighters penetrate deeper into the enemy fleet. Keep them on the defensive," T'kon ordered, clasping his hands behind his back.

"Command suits you," Jehanna said, smiling.

"I've missed it," T'kon said, his gaze never leaving the battle. He turned to the techsmith. "How long until the next cannon volley?"

"We are nearly ready," the Saurian said, running a forked tongue along its scaly lips. "Firing, Clan Leader."

The dreadnought rumbled again, as it and its sisters fired again at the wounded dreadnought. This time, the shields did little. The volley tore mortal wounds, and the enemy ship broke at the keel. Two pieces began drifting toward the atmosphere. It looked like they'd come down over the southern ocean, on the least populated part of the planet.

The enemy was coming about now, their three remaining dreadnoughts pivoting to deal with T'kon's forces. He smiled grimly as his fighters savaged their smaller ships. Enemy fighters were no doubt scrambling, but every moment they were absent meant the destruction of more support ships.

This, too, was something T'kon had learned as a hunter. The dreadnoughts were impressive, but the smaller ships were necessary to administer a realm. Destroy them, and you had nothing to protect your worlds. Removing them here wouldn't decide the battle, but it would cripple the Kthul in the days to come.

"Enemy dreadnoughts are firing, Clan Leader," the techsmith said, with a slight bow.

Four rivers of scarlet energy converged on T'kon's vessel, and the shield rippled red as it struggled to protect them. It failed. High above, armor screamed as superheated chunks exploded into space. T'kon spun to face the techsmith. "Order our dreadnought to retreat behind the others. The *Yog's Blessing* and the *Void Hunter* are to protect our flanks."

"Husband?" Jehanna asked, clearly confused.

"Personal glory is worthless if we are dead, my wife," T'kon explained, grinning at her. "Honor dictates that I keep our vessel in the fight until the end—but that's madness. Another volley will destroy us."

"Cannons ready, Clan Leader," the techsmith informed him.

"Have all vessels fire on the closest dreadnought," T'kon ordered, folding his arms. These next few moments would be critical.

The volley savaged the enemy's shield, and tore significant rents in the hull. A few moments later, the enemy fired as well, focusing on the *Kavast*. The dreadnought weathered the storm, barely.

"Order the *Kavast* to the rear of our ranks, and move into position to fire on the wounded enemy dreadnought." T'kon began pacing again, praying this strategy would work.

His flagship came around, its cannon charging. It fired, the scarlet beam punching through the wounded dreadnought and emerging from the other side. Structural fires blossomed throughout, and the doomed vessel began tumbling toward the atmosphere.

"Have our wounded vessels fall back. The fresh dreadnoughts will screen us." T'kon smiled triumphantly as the second enemy dreadnought plummeted toward the world below.

The first part of the battle had gone well. This next part would be more costly, and he was resigned to losing at least one dreadnought—most probably his own.

If so, they would go down fighting.

Fighters were now streaming from the two surviving dreadnoughts, but it was far too little, far too late. The Azi fighters converged on them even as they launched, cutting them down before they could establish any sort of lines.

But that did nothing to stop the enemy cannons. The familiar scarlet glow built around their weapons, both aimed in T'kon's direction.

A beam of pure white boiled up through the atmosphere, slamming into the closer of the two dreadnoughts. The vessel was vaporized instantly.

The second dreadnought's cannon fired and the shot slammed into T'kon's flagship. Huge chunks of molten metal were flung into space, but the hull held.

There was a sharp flash as the last enemy vessel disappeared.

The techsmith stated the obvious: "The last enemy dreadnought has warped away. The enemy lines are buckling."

"They've abandoned their support ships," T'kon said, laughing. "Order the fighters to finish them off, then contact

Captain Nolan to inform him that we've secured the space around Nyar. The Kthul will never recover from this loss."

55

DIRE CONSEQUENCES

Utfa glanced up curiously, his eye drawn by flashes of light and plasma fire. Clusters of sleek, blue harvesters were decloaking around every Kthul vessel orbiting Imperalis, balls of blue plasma streaking into their shields.

A beam of pure white shot from the planet, then another. The third came straight for his vessel, slamming into the dreadnought.

Utfa fell heavily, sliding across the command disk as it crashed into a neighboring island. He clutched at the edge, just barely halting his slide. The Saurian techsmith wasn't so lucky, tumbling silently past him, into the abyss.

The disk righted, and Utfa climbed back to his feet. The instant it was close enough, he leaped from the disk onto the much larger command island and rolled back to his feet. He stared through the observation dome in horror, watching as the Void Wraith swarmed the Kthul fleet.

Another beam of pure white boiled up from the planet, ripping into his fleet. Two more shots quickly followed, and the *Unending Faith* came apart at the seams, detonating into a blinding supernova. The Void Wraith Omegas were using the planetary cannons, the very same he'd used to secure this planet in the first place.

Another techsmith zoomed over, hopping from the transport disk. He dropped to one knee and properly averted his gaze. "Orders, Clan Leader?"

"Warp us to Kthul, immediately," Utfa snapped, thankful to have something to vent his rage upon. There was no salvaging the situation. The best he could hope for was survival, though surviving also meant facing the Nameless Ones.

The techsmith closed his eyes, and an instant later Utfa's insides twisted. They appeared in a clear patch of space above a green world. His world. Utfa took a calming breath, then looked for other vessels. There were none.

"Status of the rest of the fleet?" Utfa demanded.

"They are unable to warp, Clan Leader. Something the Void Wraith have done prevents them from fleeing." The techsmith remained kneeling, but looked ready to bolt.

"Then we are alone," Utfa muttered, shoulders slumping. He didn't know how, but Zakanna had overwhelmed the beacon. Its destruction meant that the Void Wraith might very well kill them all.

"Clan Leader?" the techsmith asked, hesitantly.

"What?" he roared, turning his ire on the unfortunate Saurian.

"We've just received word from Nyar. I...recommend you review the battle record."

Utfa closed his eyes, focusing on the pulses of data flowing from his arcanotome. They resolved into a holographic insect larger than a planetstrider. The Nameless One—it could only be that—flew frantically upward, beating titanic wings as it sought to escape the planet's atmosphere.

Beneath, a battered Omega took aim, carefully lining up a shot.

"No. *No.*" Utfa's eyes snapped open, and he reached for the Saurian. The techsmith wasn't there. It had wisely fled the rage it knew Utfa to be feeling. "How can this be? How did they kill a Nameless One? How did we lose our entire fleet?"

Utfa fell to his knees. His fleet had been divided, two thirds at Imperalis and one third at Nyar. He'd thought doing so would prevent it from being obliterated. Even if one fleet was lost, he'd still have the other, or so he'd thought. Now, he had nothing.

The Kthul had lost everything.

No. Not everything, boomed a terrible voice, deep in the recesses of his mind.

A vessel warped into orbit around the planet Kthul, then another, and a third. But...they weren't vessels. They were... monstrous, living things. Writhing their way toward Kthul.

Utfa's eyes widened as he beheld the spawn of the Nameless Ones. Each was horrifyingly different, alike only in their sheer size and the terror they invoked.

"What have you done?" he whispered, knowing the voice would hear.

You were warned that the consequences of failure would be dire. One of our progeny is dead, because of your incompetence. You were asked to deliver a conquered world, with no forces to defend it. And you have done so, if not in the manner of your choosing.

The Nameless Ones swarmed Kthul's cities, each belching clouds of smaller creatures. A few vessels attempted to break atmosphere, but they were quickly overwhelmed. Only a full dreadnought—something the Kthul no longer possessed— would have a prayer of fighting one of the Nameless Ones.

Ufta realized how he had been duped. His forces were spent, leaving his people naked before the storm. He closed his eyes, overwhelmed by a sudden flood of data, streaming into his mind from every world in the Kthul's control. He fought to make sense of the data, recoiling when he finally understood. "No, it cannot be."

It is, the voice boomed. *My children arrive on a dozen worlds. They devour your clan, wiping you clean from the universe. And when they are finished, they will retreat back into the Void, to digest and grow stronger. There they will slumber, until they hunger again.*

"No," Utfa snapped, rising to his full height. "The Kthul still possess one dreadnought, and I will use it to fight you."

Try.

Utfa whirled to face the techsmith. "Ready the main cannon. Fire at the closest Nameless One."

"I cannot, Clan Leader." The Saurian looked up, gaze calculating. "It is heresy to fire upon a Nameless One."

At first, he could only stare, uncomprehending. Then he realized the full scale of what the Nameless Ones had achieved, of how fully they'd enslaved his people.

Utfa began to laugh, rolling waves of it until tears streamed down his disfigured cheeks. He'd been beaten, on every level. The Nameless Ones would devour his clan, and likely all Ganog. Serving them had been a terrible, tragic mistake. The power he'd been granted was hollow. Worthless.

He turned to the edge of the island, and dove off. Utfa stared up at the observation dome, watching it grow further away as he fell. There was a split second of pain as his body impacted, and then blissful oblivion.

56

SPEECH

From Nyar's perspective, Nolan gazed down at the ruined city. Streamers of smoke rose from almost every building, and the streets were littered with the bodies of the fallen, both Ganog and insect. This place had been torn apart, but other than a few small swarms of bugs, every enemy was dead. Alpha Company was still picking those bugs off, herding them toward the Ganog defenders.

"Looks like the mop-up is well underway," Hannan said, her tone satisfied.

"That it does," Nolan agreed, finally relaxing for the first time in days. Nyar's posture relaxed as well, mimicking Nolan.

Thousands of Ganog were emerging from the spires, joining an ever-growing crowd. That crowd was staring and pointing at the Omega.

"Looks like you're about to be a hero, Kokar," Nolan said, laughing.

"I do not believe so, Captain. I am not the pilot; you are." His tone was carefully neutral, and Nolan wondered what color his fur would be if he could see it.

"That's nonsense. You're one of the pilots, and it was your

cannon shot that killed the Nameless One," Nolan pointed out. "You played an integral role in the battle that freed this world, at a time when your father, and then Bruth, failed." .

"He's got a point," Hannan agreed.

"They speak with wisdom, young warrior," Yulo said. "Your deeds today will live alongside those of your ancestor. Rejoice."

"Come on, Kokar," Nuchik said. "Revel in it a little. We all killed that thing, and you're a part of that." Nolan could hear the smile in her voice.

"Very well," Kokar said, hesitantly.

"I imagine those people would love a speech," Nolan said. "You should talk to them. Nyar, does this thing have external speakers?"

"Indeed," Nyar rumbled. "All can hear you now."

"You're on, Kokar," Nolan said.

"Nyar Clan, hear me. I am Kokar, son of Grak. Today we have returned the spirit of Nyar to guide our path. Using his mighty war machine, we have slain the Nameless One. Even now, the Kthul fleet retreats, ceding the battle for our world." Kokar's voice echoed to every corner of the city. "Tomorrow, we will mourn our dead. Today, we celebrate our survival. "

The audience erupted in cheers, and those cheers gradually gave way to cries of "Ko-kar! Ko-kar!"

Nolan's perspective shifted violently, and the next thing he knew he was waking up in the chair. The others were sitting up too, each rubbing their head. He had a splitting headache, but even that couldn't dampen his enthusiasm. They'd won. Barely, but wasn't that the way it always was?

"Well said, Kokar." Annie smacked Kokar on the back, then helped him from his chair. "Y'all did good with the piloting. I think we've given those slimy bastards something to think about."

"That we have." Nolan laughed. He clapped Nuchik on the shoulder. "That was a great shot at the end. Nice work."

"I wouldn't have been able to make it if Hannan hadn't saved our collective asses from that fall," Nuchik pointed out, nodding to Hannan.

"Indeed," Yulo said, clasping his hands before his chest and bowing. "We make an impressive team."

"Major Burke, are you on the line?" Nolan asked into his comm.

"I sure am. That was a hell of a stunt, but I'm only giving you an eight out of ten because of the face plant thing. And besides, this wasn't as inventive as warping a planetstrider into orbit." Over the comm, Nolan heard the whole company burst into laughter. "So now what?"

"We've secured the Nyar alliance. We help Kokar consolidate power, and then we head back to Admiral Fizgig for new orders. I think your babysitting days are over, Major."

"I hope so. You make a terrible baby." Burke laughed. "I'll get my people on repairing the *Demetrius*. Kay says she'll fly, but we're down seventy percent of her cannons. She needs time in dock."

"I'm sure Fizgig can arrange that. You did a hell of a job today, Major. It's been a pleasure working with you."

"You too, Captain. I never thought I'd say this, but I think we might end up friends."

Nolan laughed. "Don't get soft on me, Major."

"Never. Burke out."

Nolan turned back to the blue core floating in the center of the room. Speaking with Nyar would answer a lot of questions. They could finally learn more about who created the Omegas, and why. About the Nameless Ones, and their goals.

But all that could come later. For now, it was time to celebrate their shared survival.

57

TRANSFORM

Khar watched through the viewport as Aluki's cruiser blasted out through the hole in the top of the Royal Spire, hopefully for the last time. Sporadic fighting had enveloped the entire capital, with Void Wraith harvesters making attack runs at Ganog cruisers.

Thousands of Judicators roamed every ring, cutting down anyone who attempted to make it to their vessels. It was a slaughter, one the Ganog had no prayer of evading. They were both outnumbered and outgunned, their planetstriders cut down by the superior Omegas.

"This is an extermination," Khar said, horrified. "They are not just killing Ganog, but all races."

"Perhaps it is just as well that our fleet isn't here," Fizgig said, her tail swishing over her shoulder. "I've a feeling that the Void Wraith would welcome more targets."

"We failed," Zakanna said, hanging her head. Her fur rippled to a muted blue. Khar put a comforting arm around her.

"Did we?" Fizgig asked. Zakanna looked up, and Fizgig smiled. "It is true that you were unable to retake your world, but that was never the ultimate goal. You wanted to deny it to your enemy, and you have done that."

"I've lost our world to...to I don't even know to what," Zakanna said, beginning to pace. "No emperor or empress has ever lost Imperalis, and they certainly haven't given it to another species."

"Ultimately, I do not think they are another species," Aluki corrected gently, waddling into the hold. Khar didn't see Halut, so he assumed the Whalorian must be piloting the ship. "Mmm, remember these Void Wraith were all created from the warriors and leaders among your own species. These Void Wraith are, ultimately, your ancestors."

"What will they do now, do you think?" Khar rumbled, thankful that the Void Wraith had no way of detecting their superior cloaking. If they had, odds were good they'd already be dead.

All three Omegas were firing torrents of white plasma into orbit, detonating dreadnoughts as harvesters swarmed around them like piranha. For some reason, the Kthul fleet was unable to warp. That meant their utter destruction. If not for the cruiser's cloaking, they'd likely be meeting the same fate.

The cruiser rose above the city, rattling as it fought against the world's gravity. Finally, they punched through the atmosphere and into orbit. Below, the signs of battle were now difficult to see. But they were still there. Flashes from the Omegas occasionally shot skyward, and large explosions came from the city as vessels were shot down trying to flee the world.

The explosions below gradually died down, as did those in orbit. Within a few more minutes the Kthul fleet had been destroyed, and the city presumably pacified.

"Wait, what's happening down there?" Zakanna asked, peering through the viewport.

Khar didn't know, but something strange was happening. The world was beginning to crack apart, deep fissures running across every visible continent. Oceans drained away, though Khar had no idea where they were draining to. The spires of Imperalis disappeared under a tide of lava, swept away as if they'd never been.

A cloud of earth, stone, and dust burst from the world. When that cloud began to clear, Khar could only stare.

A smooth, blue sphere sat where Imperalis had been; as they watched, it began to reconfigure itself. It elongated, metal rippling as its form shifted.

Khar rested a paw against the viewport, in awe. "By the goddess, that's a ship."

"Indeed," Fizgig said, showing little emotion. She stared impassively at the planet-sized vessel. "I'd wondered who constructed the cities here. Now we know. Imperalis must have been built by the first Void Wraith, at the direction of the Nameless Ones."

"The entire world was a weapon," Zakanna whispered. "A weapon we just gave to the Void Wraith."

The ship's moon-sized engines flared to life, and it began moving toward the sun. At first, Khar believed that it must be a Helios-capable vessel. But the ship stopped, going into stationary orbit just a few AU from the star.

"What are they doing?" he asked.

"Mmm, charging perhaps?" Aluki suggested.

They all watched, speechless. After a few more minutes the ship winked out of existence. The cloud of Void Wraith harvesters winked out as well.

"Where did they go?" Khar wondered.

"We may never know," Fizgig said. She began to purr. "I suspect that, wherever it is, the Nameless Ones will not be happy about it."

"Mmm, Admiral, we're receiving a communication from Nyar," Aluki said, tapping a sequence on the pilot's console.

Nolan's face sprang up on the holographic projector. "Admiral! Great news. We've brought the Nyar into the war, and have successfully liberated the planet. We managed to kill a Nameless One, too."

"Well done, Nolan. I have news as well," Fizgig said. Even from several feet away, Khar could hear her purring. "The Kthul fleet over Imperalis was destroyed, along with every Ganog loyal to the Nameless Ones. The Kthul have few military forces remaining."

"T'kon warped in to help mop up the last Kthul here, so I think you're right about that," Nolan said. He took a drink from a tak horn, and Khar realized Nolan was smiling a great deal more than usual. "T'kon's got four dreadnoughts remaining, plus three more that have rallied behind Kokar. The *Demetrius* can fly, but she's going to need time in dry dock."

"Izzat the Admiral?" came a male voice from off screen. Burke came into the picture, wearing an even bigger grin than Nolan. "We frakking did it, Admiral. If you were here, I'd raise a glass to you." He drank deeply from the horn.

"Are the two of you drunk?" Fizgig asked, her tail swishing with disapproval.

"Not as drunk as we're going to be," Nolan said, grinning at the camera one last time. "Nolan out."

Khar boomed with laughter. Somehow, they'd won. A Nameless One killed. The Kthul military wiped out. There were battles yet to come, but for the time being, they could finally rest.

Planetstrider

If you haven't had a chance to read the prequel novella, **Planet-strider**, please sign up to the mailing list.

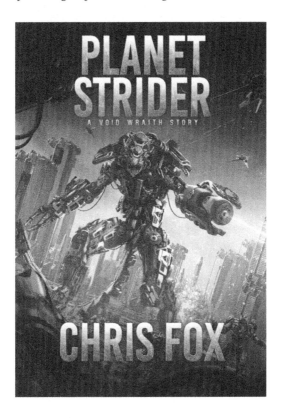

TECH MAGE

This installation of the Void Wraith Saga has come to a close, but clearly there's more story to tell. What happens with the Nameless Ones? And, oh yeah, Nolan now pilots an Omega. I will be doing a follow up trilogy, but in the meantime I've been working on something new.

I've included an excerpt from my next novel, Tech Mage. If you enjoy it, or don't, please let me know. You can reach me at chris@chrisfoxwrites.com. I'm always looking for beta readers.

TECH MAGE

PROLOGUE

Voria hopped from the ramp before the transport had completed its landing. She clung tightly to her jacket as the sudden wind buffeted her. Voria didn't let it deter her, leaning into the gale as she crossed the landing pad. Like everything in the Tender's palace, the landing pad was cut from shayawood, taken from the corpse of the goddess herself.

That wood shone in the sun, whorls of brown and red, drinking in the sunlight. Voria had never been this close to the palace, and had never seen so much shayawood. It had been designed to awe, and it succeeded.

The view only reinforced that awe. The palace floated in the sky over the world of Shaya and afforded a magnificent view of the goddess herself. Her body stabbed into the sky, the immense redwood branches scraping the upper atmosphere. A multitude of tiny starships flitted back and forth between them like flocks of tiny birds.

Were a single limb to break, it would doom the cities clustered at the base of the mighty tree. That was the dilemma of Shaya. The goddess's lingering energies created a breathable atmosphere around her body, but if you left that radius the rest of the moon was barren and inhospitable. They needed her body to survive, but that body could also destroy them.

Voria wove a path through the wind, snaking her way to a pair of wide palace doors. They were flanked by a pair of war mages, each encased in golden Mark VIII spellarmor. They cradled menacing black spellrifles, the barrels lined with spell amplification sigils. Voria could make out nothing of their faces behind the mirrored faceplates.

To her surprise, both war mages snapped to attention when she approached.

"Major," boomed a male voice from the mage on the right. "The Tender is expecting you. She's made the...unusual request that you be allowed to carry your weapons, and that you not be searched."

"What is it you think I'd be hiding, exactly? All I'm carrying is a spellpistol. If the Tender wants to wipe me from existence, no spell I'm going to cast will make any difference," Voria countered. She waved at the doors. "Let's get this over with. I have a war to fight, and I don't have time for politics."

The guards stepped aside, snapping back to attention. Voria eyed them suspiciously as she passed, trying to understand the reason for their respectful behavior. The Confederate Military was a joke to Shayan nobility. War mages did not salute officers, rank non-withstanding. Even her training as a true mage wouldn't warrant that kind of respect.

She entered a spacious greeting room lined with hover-couches. A blue one floated in her direction, nudging her hip in invitation. Voria shoved it away, and continued toward the room's only occupant. The Tender stood next to a golden railing, shayawood vines snaking around it. Shaya's branches were visible behind her, though the woman herself commanded attention.

Her hair shone in the sun, capturing all the colors of autumn. Reds and yellows and golds all danced through her hair, changing as the light shifted. It poured down her back in a molten river, contrasting beautifully with the Tender's golden ceremonial armor.

Voria had often been called pretty, but she knew she was a frumpy matron next to the Tender. Though, in Voria's defense, she didn't have the blood of a goddess to magically enhance her beauty.

"Welcome, daughter," the Tender said, beaming a smile as she strode gracefully from the railing. "Thank you for coming so quickly."

"Just because you slept with my father doesn't make you my mother," Voria countered flatly. She schooled her features, attempting to hide the pleasure she took from needling this woman.

The Tender raised a delicate eyebrow, stopping a meter away. She frowned disapprovingly, and even that was done beautifully. "I meant figuratively, daughter."

"Why did you call me here?" Voria demanded. She'd fluster this woman if it killed her.

"Because this, all of this, will be wiped away unless you prevent it." The Tender stretched an arm to indicate Shaya and the cities below her. She smiled warmly, as if she'd just related a bit of political gossip. "Would you like some lifewine? Or an infused apple?"

The Tender crooked a finger, and a crystal ewer floated over to Voria. Golden liquid swirled within, and Voria could feel the power pulsing from it. It was, for her people at least, literal life. But drinking it would cause her eyes to glow, revealing her true nature for hours.

"No, thank you." Voria stepped away from the ewer and frowned at the Tender. "Certainly your time must be valuable.

You've dropped a melodramatic statement about Shaya being destroyed. Please tell me that's just hyperbole."

"I am being quite literal, I'm afraid. If you do not fulfill your role in the struggle against Krox, then all of this will be wiped away," the Tender explained. She sighed...prettily. "Please, come with me."

"Fine." Voria crossed her arms, eyeing the Tender as the woman led her from the railing.

The chamber curved around the outside of the palace for nearly a hundred meters, finally ending at a pair of tall double doors. Unlike most of the palace, these were not shayawood. They were covered in a multicolored mural depicting Shaya herself.

Voria leaned closer, realizing that the door was covered in thousands of tiny scales. Dragon scales, each of incalculable worth. They glowed with their own inner fire and their combined magic brought the mural to life. Branches swayed as an invisible wind rippled over the doors.

The Tender placed a palm on each door, then pushed gently inward. The doors opened of their own accord, sliding away to reveal a dark chamber. Voria followed the Tender inside and waited impatiently for her eyes to adjust.

The doors slammed shut behind them, and a bonfire sprang into existence near the center of the room. The flames were pure blue, edged in white. Their sudden light illuminated sigils emblazoned on the floor in a circle around the flame. A ritual circle, possibly the most powerful that Voria had ever witnessed.

"What am I seeing?" Voria asked, abandoning all attempts to fluster the Tender. She'd fought in the Confederate Marines for four decades, and had never seen magic on this scale before. The immensity of the power humbled her.

"This is the Mirror of Shaya. It is an eldimagus for finding and interpreting auguries. You are familiar with auguries?" the Tender asked, walking gracefully to stand just outside the magical circle. The flame brightened at her approach, like a pet preening for an owner.

"Conceptually. They're visions of a possible future, dreamed by a dead god," Voria ventured. Divination wasn't one of her strong suits, though she was proficient enough with the basics.

"Some auguries are," the Tender corrected gently. "Some were created by living gods, before the moment of their death. These auguries are of immense power, designed to shape the future for hundreds or even thousands of millennia. I've spent the last several years studying just such an augury."

"And you feel that has something to do with me?" Voria raised an eyebrow.

"I'll allow you to judge for yourself." The Tender smiled mischievously, then turned to the ritual circle. She sketched the scarlet sigil for *fire*, and a pinkish one for *dream*.

The mirror flared and immense magical strength gathered within the light. It resolved into an image, so lifelike that Voria recoiled. A vast force hovered in the void, its body comprised of stars, its eyes supernovas. The creature was a living galaxy, a god that made every god or goddess Voria had encountered seem a tiny speck.

"What is that thing?" she whispered, unable to drag her gaze from the vision.

"That is Krox," the Tender answered. She rested a hand on Voria's arm, and warmth pulsed into her. It eased the fear the image had evoked, though not the horror that something so alien could exist. "The forces you fight, what you call 'the Krox', are his children. And they are united in a singular purpose, the resurrection of their dark father. This augury is a desperate cry from the past. It's meant to give us the tools necessary to stop his return. If we fail in this, the cost is incalculable."

Voria studied the flames, silently digesting what the Tender had just said. After several moments another image flickered into view. An enormous skull floated in orbit over a barren world. Long, dark horns spiraled from the temples, and purplish flames danced in the eye sockets and mouth.

"That's the Skull of Xal," Voria ventured, recognizing the Catalyst.

The face of a young man superimposed itself over the flames, covering the image of the skull. The hard eyes and strong jaw made him look older than he probably was. He held a sword loosely in one hand and dark lightning crackled from his hand into the blade.

"What am I seeing?" Voria asked. She recognized the spell, basic void lightning. But she had no idea why she was seeing it.

"This man will be instrumental in helping you triumph in your impending struggle," the Tender offered. The light of the flames reflected off her eyes as she studied the images still appearing. "He can be found at the Skull of Xal, along with something else vital to the coming battle."

"You mentioned a coming battle twice. That makes me think you've got the wrong person." Voria eyed the double doors, but didn't attempt to leave. "The *Wyrm Hunter* is low on munitions. We're down to a handful of tech mages, and no other true mage besides myself. We have no potions, and the Marines sent from Ternus have no battle experience. The worst part? We're down to six support crew. Six people, to keep an entire battleship flying. Trust me. Whatever battle this augury thinks I'm a part of, it's got the wrong person. *Hunter* should be in space dock, not leading a charge."

"I understand your reluctance, but I assure you that you are the person this augury is meant for." The Tender's rebuke was gentle, but still a rebuke.

Voria licked her lips, forcing herself to be silent as she watched the augury. It now showed a familiar man, one of her tech mages. "That's Specialist Bord."

The Tender said nothing, watching intently as the images continued. The view zoomed out to show Bord's surroundings. He stood next to a golden urn the size of a tank. The surface was covered in sigils, and a sickly grey glow came from the top.

"I do not know how, but this 'Bord' will be instrumental as well, in a different way. You will need both the men displayed in order to stop her," the Tender's voice whispered.

"Her?" Voria asked, blinking.

The augury shifted again. This time the flames showed a gargantuan dragon, floating in orbit over a blue-white world. Its leathery wings stretched out to either side and its head reared back. The dragon breathed a cone of white mist that billowed out around a Ternus space station.

"Nebiat," Voria snarled. Her eyes narrowed as she studied the ancient dragon, a full Void Wyrm. The dark scales and spiked tail were unmistakable. She ground her teeth, acid rising in her stomach. She'd do anything to kill that Wyrm. Anything.

"I thought you'd recognize her. Whoever created this augury believes you are the one person strong enough to stop her." The Tender stretched out a hand and rested it on Voria's jacket. Pleasant warmth flowed into her. Voria wished she'd stop doing that. "I know that you lack the resources you need. But I also know that you are needed. If you will not do this, then the Krox will burn another world. You can stop that, Voria, though the personal cost will be high."

"Isn't it always?" Voria straightened her jacket, already turning to the door. "I'll find a way to stop Nebiat, but that will be a whole lot easier with Inuran weaponry. They're hunting for Kazon. If I can find him before anyone else, the Consortium will provide me with enough material to pursue your augury. Help me find him, and I'll help you fulfill it."

"I already have." The Tender turned back to the flames as the augury began to repeat. "Study the augury carefully, Major. There are many layers to be delved, including Kazon's whereabouts. Pursuing the augury will lead you to him."

1

TECH DEMONS

Aran lurched awake as the transport entered free fall. Gravity pulled him upward, jerking him to the limits allowed by his restraints. The ship shook violently, the thin lights flickering for several moments before returning to a steady illumination.

"Wake up," a female voice bellowed. The speaker moved to stand in front of Aran, and he realized groggily that he was surrounded by other men and women in restraints.

The chrome harnesses pinned their wrists between their legs, preventing them from standing or defending themselves. Glowing blue manacles attached his wrists to the harness, and he could feel their heat even through the armored gauntlets. He wore some sort of environmental armor, the metal scarred and pitted from long use.

"Good, the sleep spell is wearing off." The speaker wore a suit of form-fitting body armor, much higher quality than Aran's. Her helmet was tucked under one arm and the other hand wrested on a pistol belted at her side. A river of dark hair spilled down both shoulders. "You're probably feeling some grogginess. That's the after effects of the mind-wipe. Each of you have been imprinted with a name. That will be the *only* thing you can remember. We've given it to you, because otherwise slaves tend to have psychotic breaks."

Aran probed mentally, reaching for anything. He couldn't remember how he'd gotten here, or what he'd had for breakfast. Or where he'd been born. There was a...haze over the part of his mind where those things should be. His name was, quite literally, the only thing he could remember.

A beefy man on Aran's right struggled violently against his bonds. "Listen little girl, you'd better let me out of this chair, or I'll fu—."

The woman withdrew her pistol and aimed it at the beefy man. White sigils flared to life up and down the barrel, and dark energy built inside the weapon.

The weapon hummed, discharging a bolt of white-hot flame toward his chest. It cored him through the heart, filling the chamber with the scent of cooked meat. His body twitched once and then he died silently.

"Nara, you began the demonstration without me," called an amused male voice. It came from out of Aran's field of view, but the booted footsteps approached until Aran got a glimpse of the speaker. "You know how much I hate missing it. This is my favorite part."

A tall, slender man walked over to the woman who'd executed the beefy man. He wore jet-black environmental armor, and had a stylized dragon helm clutched under his arm. One of his eyes had been replaced with a glittering ruby, and his bald skull was oiled to a mirrored sheen. His right gauntlet was larger than his left, and studded with glowing rubies and sapphires.

Aran could sense...something coming from the gauntlet. A familiar resonance that danced elusively out of reach.

A cluster of armored figures entered the room behind the

one-eyed man. They fanned out, taking up relaxed positions along the far wall. Each guard carried a rifle similar to the pistol the woman had fired. Blue-white sigils lined the barrels, though they appeared inactive at the moment.

"I'm sorry, Master Yorrak," the woman he'd called Nara finally replied. She gave a deep bow, which she held for several seconds. Finally she straightened. "This prisoner...volunteered. And I know that we are pressed for time. I thought it prudent to educate this batch quickly."

"Efficient as always. I'll handle the rest of the orientation." Yorrak patted her cheek patronizingly, then turned toward the slaves. Nara shot him a hateful glare, but he seemed oblivious. "Good morning, slaves. My name is Yorrak, true mage and pilot of this vessel. I'm going to make this very simple. In a moment we'll be landing. When we do, your restraints will be removed. There is a rack of rifles near the door. Take one, and step outside. Nara and her squad will lead you beyond that. Obey her orders without question, or meet the same fate as our late friend here." Yorrak moved to the corpse, prodding it with a finger.

"Are there any questions?" he asked, rounding on them.

"Where are we?" Aran rasped. His throat burned, and he blinked sweat from his eyes.

"The Skull of Xal, one of the more remote, and most powerful, Catalysts in this sector," Yorrak proclaimed, thrusting his arms dramatically into the air. "You're about to be granted a wonderful opportunity. If you survive, you will become a tech mage. Those of you who apply yourselves might even rise to the rank of true mage, one day. That will increase your relative value, and I treat my mages very well. Now, I'll leave you in Nara's capable hands. I'll pick up any survivors in the second ocular cavity. You have two hours. Oh and one more thing. If

Nara isn't with you when you exit the Catalyst, I'll disintegrate the lot of you."

Yorrak strode past Aran, eyeing the slaves gleefully as he exited. What a sadistic bastard. Aran caught a brief glimpse of the hallway before the door hissed shut behind him, but saw nothing that helped his current situation. The transport, if it was a transport, shuddered violently for several moments, then finally stabilized.

"If you listen to me, you have a very high chance of survival," Nara said, drawing their collective attention. She stepped into the light, affording his first real look at her. She had liquid brown eyes, and a light dusting of freckles across her entire face. She was pretty enough that Aran understood why she'd been picked to lead them. The whole girl next door thing made them that much more likely to trust her. "In a moment I'm going to release your restraints. You'll arm yourself from the rack, and then move outside. Some of you might be tempted to attack us. Before you do, consider your options. It's in both our best interests for you to survive. If you die, Yorrak has less slaves. You don't want to die, and we don't want you dead."

Her argument made sense, though Aran detested the idea of working with his captors. He didn't know anything about them, or about himself really. Was he a hardened criminal? Or just some idiot in the wrong place, at the wrong time? It was just...gone. All of it. Only his name remained, and even that might not be real.

The restraints whirred, and the harness released him. The manacles were still around his wrists, but the chain linking them together had disappeared. Aran rose to his feet and the other prisoners did the same, each looking warily at the others. It seemed an effective tactic on the part of their captors. Since none of them knew each other, they weren't likely to cooperate. That made mutiny a much lower risk.

Aran moved to the rack along the side of the wall, picking up the first rifle. It had a heavy stock, and a long, ugly barrel. The metal was scored and scratched, though the action worked smoothly. He scanned the base of the rack, bending to scoop up two more magazines. He had no idea what he'd need the weapon for, but more rounds was rarely a bad thing.

Other slaves moved to take weapons, the closest a tall man with a thick, black beard. He eyed Aran warily, moving to the wall two meters away.

Nara walked to the rear of the room and slapped a large red button. A klaxon sounded, and a ramp slowly lowered. A chill wind howled up the ramp, dropping the temperature instantly.

"Outside, all of you. Now!" Nara's words stirred the slaves into action, and they began filing down the ramp. Aran moved in the middle of the pack, and found himself next to the bearded man.

"Watch my back?" he asked, eyeing the bearded man side-long. His arms were corded with muscle, and his eyes glittered with intelligence.

"Do the same for me?" the man answered, eyeing Aran in a similar way.

"Done." Aran pivoted slightly as he walked down the ramp, angling his firing arc to slightly overlap with the bearded man. The man echoed the motion. "What name did they give you?"

"Kaz. How about you?"

"Aran." The ramp deposited them onto a bleached white hill. A hellish purple glow came from somewhere beyond the ridge ahead of them, as bright as any sun. Aran's teeth began to chatter, and his breath misted heavily in the air.

"The cold isn't life threatening, if you keep moving," Nara called. Her guards fanned out around her, covering the slaves with their strange rifles. Something about the weapons tickled at the back of his mind, but the haze muddied the sense of familiarity. "Form two groups, one on either side of the ramp."

The guards broke into groups, pushing slaves into two lines. Aran moved quickly to the one on the right, and the bearded man followed.

"Do you have any idea where we are?" Kaz asked. Aran followed his gaze, taking in their surroundings.

A high ridge prevented him from seeing beyond the closest hills. The rock reminded him uncomfortably of bone, its porous surface just the right shade of pale white.

The purplish glow flared suddenly and Aran raised a hand to shield his eyes. Harsh, guttural voices boomed in the distance, and he heard the rhythmic pounding of metal on stone.

"Those," Nara began with a yell, "are tech demons. This is their territory, and they will defend it with their lives. Your job is to kill them, without dying yourself. Follow my orders, and we'll all get out of this safely."

A brutish creature leapt into view at the top of the ridge. Twin horns spiraled out from a thick forehead and it clenched and unclenched wickedly curved claws. It stared down at them with flaming eyes, the same hue as the glow behind it. The creature wore dark armor, not unlike the armor Nara and her guards had.

"Fire!" Nara roared.

2

USED

Aran reacted to Nara's command, snapping the rifle to his shoulder and sighting down the barrel. He'd guess the demon to be about seventy-five meters away, but it was hard to judge distance without knowing how large the thing was.

The rifle kicked into his shoulder, firing a three round burst that echoed off the rocks around them. The rounds peppered the demon's left side but only pinged off armor. Kaz snapped up his rifle as well, but the shots went wide. Other slaves fired, the chattering of weapons fire lighting up the area around them as they added to the thick stench of gunpowder.

All their collective fury accomplished nothing. The rounds, even those that hit the demon directly, simply ricocheted off. The demon's face split into a wide grin, revealing a sea of narrow fangs. It leapt from its perch, bat-like wings flaring behind it as it sailed in their direction.

Only then did Aran realize the creature carried a rifle too. The weapon was heavier than their own rifles, and the fat barrel was ringed with red sigils, like the rifles their captors used.

"That thing is packing a spellcannon. Tech mages, end him!" Nara barked, stabbing a finger at the descending demon.

Too late. The creature raised the cannon, and the sigils along the barrel flared to brilliant life. The cannon kicked back, and fired a blob of darkness. The blob expanded outwards, bursting into thousands of fragments. The fragments rained down on the other group of slaves, and their armor began to smoke and hiss.

They frantically tore at the armor, but within moments the hungry magic had eaten through...first metal and then flesh. One by one they slumped to the bleached stone, groaning out their last.

The guards around Nara, the ones she'd called tech mages, opened up with their spellrifles. Blue and white sigils flared, and bolts of superheated flame peppered the demon. The bolts superheated the armor wherever they hit, painting it an angry red. The fire bolts met with more success against the demon itself, and it shrieked as a large chunk of its neck burned away.

"This way," Aran roared, sprinting low to the left, into the demon's blind spot. He dropped to one knee behind a fold of rock and sighted down the barrel at the demon. He kept his finger off the trigger, though.

Kaz slid down next to him. "You have a plan?"

"Yeah, let those bastards deal with it. They're using us as fodder. There's no way we can hurt that thing with the crap rifles they gave us." Aran plastered himself against the rock, its craggy surface bitterly cold even through his armor.

Nara strode from her ranks raising two fingers. She began sketching in the air, and wherever her finger passed, a residue of multicolored light was left behind. The light formed sigils, which swam in and out of Aran's vision. The more he focused on any particular one, the more blurry it became.

The sigils began to swirl in interlocking patterns of pale

grey, and a dark, ocean blue. They were drawn together with a sudden thunderclap, then exploded outward in a wide fan. Fist sized balls of swirling energy shot toward several of the surviving slaves, each ball slamming into their backs. The energy passed through the armor, disappearing.

Each person hit by a ball began to grow, their armor growing with them. Over the next few heartbeats they doubled in size, and now stood shoulder to shoulder with the demon.

It did not seem impressed.

The demon leapt forward and wrapped its tail around one of the giant slaves. It tugged her from her feet, dragging her across the rough stone. The demon yanked the slave into the air, just in time to use her as a shield against another volley of fire bolts from Nara's tech mages. They slammed into the poor woman, who screeched in shock and pain, until the final fire bolt ended her cries.

"Those things they're firing, spells I guess," Aran yelled over his shoulder to Kaz. "They're the only thing that's hurt that demon so far." He cradled his rifle, trying to decide what to do.

"Then unless you've got a way to cast a spell we have to sit this out and hope," Kaz called back. "We can't do anything to that thing."

One of the tech mages slung his rifle over his shoulder and drew a slender sword. He sprinted wide around the demon, clearly hunting for an opening. White flame boiled up out of his palm and quickly coated the entire blade.

The tech mage darted forward and lunged upward at the much larger demon. The blade slid between two armored plates, biting deep into the small of the demon's back. The flames swept up the blade and into the wound, which drew a roar from the demon.

The creature rounded on the tech mage and backhanded

him with an enormous fist. The blow knocked the tech mage into the air, and his blade spun away across the stone. Before the tech mage could recover, the demon fired his spellcannon and a bolt of blackness took the mage in the chest. There was no scream. No final death throes. The body fell limply to the ground and did not rise.

"I'm going to try for the blade," Aran called to Kaz. The bearded man shot him an incredulous look. "Hey, after it kills them, it's going to kill us."

Aran sprinted fast and low across the stone, the sudden movement removing the edge of the numbing chill. He bent low and scooped up the sword the tech mage had dropped and then dove behind another outcrop.

The hilt was warm to the touch and fit his hand perfectly. The blade shone an unremarkable silver, and the weapon was heavier than he was used to. Used to? He couldn't summon a specific memory, but felt certain he'd held a weapon like this, and recently.

The weapon called to something inside Aran, the same thing that had resonated with Yorrak's gauntlet back on the ship. Magic, he realized. He didn't understand how, but there was a power inside him, calling out to be channeled through the spellblade. That's what the weapon was.

"Are you mad?" Kaz roared, skidding into cover next to him.

"Maybe." Aran poked his head out of cover and assessed the situation. The remaining tech mages had scattered, and were harrying the demon from different angles. One narrowly dodged another black bolt, but was too slow to dodge the next. His right leg ceased to exist, all the way up to the thigh.

The surviving slaves had all sought cover, except for the giant ones who had nowhere to hide. Only three remained, and they made a concentrated push at the demon. It spun at the last second, balling its clawed hand into a fist and slamming it into the closest slave. That slave's jaw exploded, and he toppled to the stone with a muffled cry.

The next slave got his arms around the demon, briefly pinning it. The last giant slave jammed his rifle into the demon's mouth and pulled the trigger. The demon twitched violently, its head jerking back and forth as the slave emptied the magazine.

Aran lurched into a run, his gaze fixed on the demon. The energy in his chest surged outward, down his arm and into his hand. Electricity poured into the weapon, snapping and crackling around the blade as he made his approach.

The demon broke free from the slave's grasp and plunged two claws through the man's eye socket. It hurled the dying slave into its companion, knocking the last giant slave to the stone.

Aran circled behind the rampaging demon, keeping within its blind spot. He waited for it to pass his position, then sprinted the last few meters, ramming his sword into the wound the tech mage had already created. The armor was scored and blackened, offering little protection. The spellblade easily pierced the demon's flesh and plunged deep into the wound.

Electricity discharged, and the demon went rigid for several seconds. A trio of fire bolts shot into the demon's head, the scent of burned flesh billowing outward as life left the demon's smoldering gaze. Finally, the body toppled.

"Well done," Nara called as she rose from cover. She gestured at her three surviving tech mages. "Get the surviving slaves moving. That thing was a scout, and its death will alert the others. We need to reach the Catalyst before they mobilize."

3

ALLIES

"You there. Aran. Come here." Nara's voice held a definite edge of command, and Aran knew there was no way out of answering.

He trotted over, the spellblade still clutched in his left hand. He raised the other in a tight salute. Now where the depths had that come from? He had no memory of saluting anyone, much less this woman.

"You did excellent work with that spellblade. Clearly you are already a tech mage. Can you handle a spellrifle?" She studied him with those intense brown eyes, and he very much believed that his fate depended on the answer.

He briefly considered lying and accepting a rifle, but figured that having her find out he'd lied would be even worse than admitting the truth. "I don't know, sir. The thing I did with the spellblade was...well instinctual, I guess."

"I want you to take charge of the rest of the slaves," she commanded, pointing at the rest of the slaves with her spellpistol. "Move ahead of us, up that ridge. If we get attacked, get your people into cover. Try to distract them while my people deal with them."

"Sir, we just lost two tech mages and a half dozen slaves to a single one of those things," Aran pointed out. "If we get attacked by a group—."

"Don't mistake your position here, slave." Nara's eyes went cold. "Is this going to be dangerous? Absolutely. But keep your wits about you, and some of these people at least, will survive. How many really depends on how smart you are about deploying them. You want to save some lives? Step up."

Aran stifled the urge to take a swing at her with the spell-blade. He was fast, but there was no way he could close the gap before she got a spell off. Besides, she was right. He could hate her as much as he liked, but if he wanted to live, if he wanted any of these people to live, then they needed to get through here as quickly as possible.

"Yes, sir." Aran turned on his heel and trotted back over to the other slaves. "Kaz, you're on point. Double time it up that ridge and let us know what you see at the top."

The bearded man nodded, then sprinted up the ridge. The other slaves followed and Aran brought up the rear. He glanced over his shoulder, unsurprised to see Nara and her surviving tech mages hanging a good fifty meters back. No sense being too close to the cannon fodder.

He trotted up the ridge line, surprised by how easy it was. This place had lighter gravity than he was used to, a small blessing at least. Aran paused at the top of the ridge, looking back at the ship they'd emerged from. He was far enough away now to get a good look at her.

The starship was about a hundred meters long, a boomerang shaped cruiser. Blue spell sigils lined the hull, but many were cracked, and more than a few had sputtered out entirely. The ship itself seemed to be in good repair, though off-color metal patches dotted different parts of the hull.

The ship lifted off and zoomed slowly out of sight, leaving

an unbroken starfield in its wake. Wherever he was, it appeared they were directly exposed to space. So how was he breathing?

Yorrak had said 'other ocular cavity'. Was this the eye socket of some sort of moon-sized skull? That would mean this wasn't bleached stone. It was bone.

"Keep moving!" one of the tech mages boomed as he trotted up the ridge toward Aran.

Aran did as ordered, turning back toward the rest of the slaves. Kaz was still in the lead, picking a path across the bone field, painted violet by the smoldering orb in the distance. He raised a hand to shield his eyes from the painful brilliance. It was like staring directly into a sun, but somehow made worse because of the violent cold.

"Order your men to take up defensive positions along those outcrops," Nara ordered, pointing at a series of bone spurs that jutted out of field.

Aran trotted forward, dropping into cover behind the closest outcrop. It only came to his shoulder. "You heard the lady. Get into position behind this terrible cover, with weapons that won't do shit to an enemy that we can barely see."

Nara stalked several meters closer. "I could execute you right now, if you prefer." Her tone suggested it wasn't a bluff, and he found confirmation when he turned in her direction. Her spellpistol was aimed directly at him, her face hidden behind her helmet.

"Uh, I'm good. Bad cover is better than no cover." Aran raised his hands and offered an apologetic smile.

Nara turned coldly away, and began leading her tech mages along a ridge that sloped up into the darkness. Their path took them toward the light, but in a more winding route. It also took them away from the defensive position she'd asked him to establish. Aran shaded his eyes, but couldn't make out much as their forms became nothing more than silhouettes.

"What are they after, do you think?" Kaz asked from the next outcrop.

"I don't know, but whatever it is I'm betting it's a whole lot safer than sticking around here." Aran rolled to his feet, but stayed low. The rhythmic pounding was getting closer, and he could make out shapes now, against the blinding purple sun.

Their silhouettes were monstrous, approaching with alarming speed. He judged their approach, coming to the only possible conclusion. "They're going to overrun our position almost instantly. If we stay, we die."

"What are you proposing?" Kaz asked as he rose slowly to his feet.

"Run!" Aran turned and ran full tilt after Nara and her tech mages. He felt a moment's pity for the rest of the slaves, but staying here and dying wouldn't save them.

Kaz panted a few meters behind him, keeping pace as Aran picked a path through the bony ridges. In the distance he caught the flash of a fire bolt, but by the time they made it around the corner there was no sign of whoever had fired it.

Before them lay an unbroken wall of purple flame, the blinding sun that they'd glimpsed from the first ridge. Intense cold radiated from the flames, but there was more to it than that. There was a power there, a sense of infinite age, and time-less wisdom. He had no idea what he was looking at, but what-ever it was— it was greater than any human mind.

Something scrabbled across the bone behind him, and Aran spun to see a demon charging. Instead of a spellcannon, this demon carried a truly massive hammer, clutched effort-lessly in one clawed hand. The creature roared and charged Kaz.

The bearded man roared back, charging to meet his much larger foe. The demon brought the hammer down, but Kaz dodged out of the way at the very last moment. The hammer impacted and shards of bone shot out in all directions, pinging off their armor.

Aran glanced at the blinding purple light where Nara and her friends had disappeared, realizing he could make it in before the demon could deal with him. For a moment he was frozen. Was he the kind of person that would abandon the closest thing he had to a friend?

Screw that. He circled around the demon, waiting for an opening. "I'm going to paralyze it, like I did the last one. See if you can get that hammer away from it."

Aran reached tentatively for the power he'd felt before. The magic rose easily at his call, as if it wanted to be used. There was a separateness to it. The magic was inside him, but it was not him. It responded to his command though, and right now that mattered a lot more than figuring out where it came from.

The lightning leapt down his arm and into the blade, reaching the tip as Aran began his charge. He sprinted fast and low, leaning into the blow as he planted his blade into the back of the demon's knee. The enchanted steel failed to pierce the demon's armor, but that had never been the intent. Electricity crackled through the metal, and the demon twitched silently, struggling to regain control of its body.

Kaz stepped forward and yanked the hammer from the creature's grasp. He took a deep breath, then brought the weapon down in a tremendous blow. It crushed the creature's skull, splattering them with black ichor.

Behind them, the final screams faded to silence. Aran turned to see a half dozen demons moving past the corpses of the slaves— in their direction.

"Looks like we've got no choice but to brave the light." Kaz offered a hand. Aran shook it. "Good luck, brother."

"Good luck, brother." Aran turned, took a deep breath, then leapt into the light.

4

ENLIGHTENMENT

Aran had no words to describe what came next. A vast, unknowable consciousness lay before him—an ocean of power and memory, compared to his single drop. He fell into the ocean, became that consciousness. The universe stretched out before him, vast yet somehow perceivable with thousands of senses, all at once.

He understood how the worlds had been created, how the stars were given form. He watched the making of all things, from the perspective of a god who'd not only witnessed but participated. Xal was not the eldest of gods, but he was among them.

Understanding stretched beyond the comprehension of time. Aran saw the strands of the universe, how they were woven into existence using magic. He understood the eight Aspects, and the Greater Paths that could be accessed by combining them. The complexities of true magic, as Nara had used, became simple.

This power suffused him, endless, like space itself. If he wished, he could create a new species, or snuff one out with equal ease. Dimly, he was aware he had a body, aware of his petty temporal problems. They were inconsequential when compared with the vast infinity of Xal.

Yet, in his sudden understanding, he also saw Xal's undoing: a ghostly memory of many younger gods, all united in their purpose. They flooded the system, using their magic to prevent Xal from escaping into the Umbral Depths.

The memory seized Aran. He was there. He *was* Xal.

"You have come to destroy me," Xal said, turning sadly to face the assembled host.

"Your children are evil," called a goddess surrounded by armor of primal ice. "They have laid waste to many worlds, and Krox has warned us they will come for us next. We will not allow it. You might be stronger than any of us individually, but together we will destroy you."

"And who spun you this tale? Krox?" Xal shook his mighty head sadly. "Do you know nothing of his ways? Krox, the first manipulator? He is using you to attack me, so you will weaken yourselves. If we battle today, many of us will fall. The survivors will be weaker for it, and easier for Krox to pick off one by one. After today, there will be none strong enough to oppose him."

Xal examined all possibilities, trillions upon trillions. There was no possibility of his own survival. But the war between him and Krox would not end with their deaths. It would outlive them, unfolding until the last sun went cold.

And there was something he could do to ensure he won that war.

The smaller gods surrounded Xal, who made no move to defend himself. Instead, he allowed his foes to tear him apart, knowing that one day those same gods would dismember Krox. If he killed any of them, that possibility diminished greatly.

Aran watched Xal die. No, *die* was not the right word. A god could not be killed, not truly. They could only be shattered, with the pieces of their bodies forever seeking to reunite. Aran understood why the head of Xal had been severed.

The younger gods scattered the other pieces across the galaxy, ensuring it would be nearly impossible for Xal to resurrect. This filled Aran with rage, and loss, and pain—Xal's emotions, still echoing through Aran's dreaming mind.

Aran focused on the secrets of the universe, struggling to hold onto them. Briefly, he understood the illusion of time. He lingered with the knower of secrets, listening to his endless whispers. He peered into the Umbral Depths, and saw the things that dwelt there.

He noticed the great, and the small. Something tiny drew his attention—a speck of light he'd only just noticed. It lay in his hand, so small he'd missed it in the blinding brightness of Xal's majesty. Dimly, Aran realized it was the spellblade he'd picked up.

That spellblade was a living thing, waiting to be shaped. So he shaped it. It came instinctively, power and knowledge borrowed somehow from the god's mind.

He poured Xal's power into the blade, altering its shape to be more pleasing. Aran infused it with *void*, and the blade darkened even as it grew lighter in his hand. The intelligence within the blade grew more aware, more capable of complex thought. Aran forged a bond between them, connecting him to the new intelligence as a child is connected to parent. The weapon couldn't yet think, but there was a dim awareness there, watching.

The need to create did not diminish, and he burned to use the understanding Xal shared with him. He realized that the spell that had wiped his mind could be removed, and his identity restored. Such a thing was possible, though not trivial. Yet Aran couldn't quite grasp the spell. To do that, he needed more of Xal.

He plunged deeper into the god's mind, seeking the power that would allow him to become whole. It must be here, somewhere. An urgent buzzing began in the distance, but he ignored it, swimming toward the wonderful power.

The pain grew blinding, yet it brought with it knowledge. The pain was worth the price, if it would restore his mind.

The buzzing grew more intense, and a sharp prick shot through his palm. Aran looked down and realized that he was holding the spellblade. It was the source of the buzzing, and as he studied it Aran understood.

"You're warning me." Pain built behind Aran's temples as he stared deeper into Xal's mind. The sword vibrated in his hand, breaking the siren call.

Icy fear brought clarity. Xal's vastness was tempting, but Aran needed to flee before it reduced his mind to cosmic dust. Thrashing frantically, struggling away from the power, Aran forced himself to look away from the universe, snapped his eyes shut and tried to focus. Relief pulsed from the spellblade.

Then, as suddenly as the experience had begun, it was over. Aran tumbled away from the majesty and power, secrets slipping from his mind like oxygen from a hull breach. He shivered, cold and barren in the wake of all that power. Only a tiny ember remained, smoldering coldly in his chest. That piece was woven into him, a part of him even as he was now a part of Xal.

Aran caught himself against a bony ridge, trembling and weak, and rose back to his feet. He glanced back the way he'd come—at the purple sun—still as brilliant as ever, but he no longer squinted. He no longer felt the chill. This place was home now; it was part of him, as he was part of it.

The blade clutched in his right hand had changed. Instead of the slender short-sword, Aran now held an officer's saber, sleek and deadly. The weapon fit his hand as if molded to it, like an extension of his body. It waited, ready to be used.

"I told you," Nara's voice said, sounding muffled and far away. "He made it through, and he made it through first."

Aran turned toward her, blinking. She stood with a cluster of people, the three tech mages, and four more people in conventional body armor. All had weapons, either spellpistols or spellblades. Their posture wasn't threatening, but neither was it friendly.

Behind them sat the boomerang shaped starship, its ramp already extending.

He glanced at Nara and her companions, then at the ship. Even if he could reach it, what then? There was no obvious means of escape. That didn't mean he was giving up, though. Sooner or later these people were going to let their guard down, and when they did he'd be ready.

Made in the USA
Coppell, TX
05 December 2022